The Greatest Enemy of Rain

Also by Manu Bhattathiri

The Oracle of Karuthupuzha: A Novel
The Town that Laughed: A Novel
Savithri's Special Room and Other Stories

The Greatest Enemy of Rain

Stories

MANU BHATTATHIRI

ALEPH

ALEPH BOOK COMPANY
An independent publishing firm
promoted by *Rupa Publications India*

First published in India in 2022
by Aleph Book Company
7/16 Ansari Road, Daryaganj
New Delhi 110 002

Copyright © Manu Bhattathiri 2022

The Acknowledgements on p. 261 constitute an
extension of the copyright page.

The author has asserted his moral rights.

All rights reserved.

This is a work of fiction. Names, characters, places, and incidents are either the product of the author's imagination or are used fictitiously and any resemblance to any actual persons, living or dead, events, or locales is entirely coincidental.

No part of this publication may be reproduced, transmitted, or stored in a retrieval system, in any form or by any means, without permission in writing from Aleph Book Company.

ISBN: 978-93-91047-88-7

1 3 5 7 9 10 8 6 4 2

Printed in India

This book is sold subject to the condition that it shall not, by way of trade or otherwise, be lent, resold, hired out, or otherwise circulated without the publisher's prior consent in any form of binding or cover other than that in which it is published.

*For Mani Appan,
my conscience
and my rhythm.*

CONTENTS

1. The Greatest Enemy of Rain — 1
2. These New-Fangled Ways — 21
3. Days Without Teacher — 27
4. Shravan Kumar's Last Day — 71
5. The Sound — 92
6. The Answer — 97
7. The Singing Butterflies of Duabaag — 122
8. Uncle — 143
9. Shabari and Anita — 172
10. Mr and Mrs Pariera — 179
11. The Shit of the Seraph — 187
12. A Difficult Customer — 202
13. The Woman Who Loved to be Right — 221
14. Mani and the Ghost — 252

Acknowledgements — 261

1

THE GREATEST ENEMY OF RAIN

Contrary to popular belief, rain's greatest enemy is not the rapid felling of trees. Nor is it rising global temperatures, industrialization, the burning of fossil fuels, or even that telltale hole in the air up there. The single biggest enemy of rain is a person by the name of Gopi. He still lives in our little town and he still hates the rain.

We would sit on a parapet by a small creek, a group of us younger old men and Gopi, who was old enough to be reborn a toddler in the next life. Many a times Gopi would go into the tale of his lifelong grudge against the rain and, in spite of the fact that he was repeating it for the umpteenth time, word for word, we would listen eagerly. For he narrated with such earnestness, with so much devotion to facts, that it seemed fresh each time. In fact, Sridharan Vakkeel, who had been a bad lawyer in his ripest years, once observed that Gopi's stories touched your heart.

This much I can vouch for—on the days Gopi forgot his big black umbrella with its smooth ivory handle, it would start to drizzle slowly, irrespective of the season, proving Gopi's point with a calm indifference that comes from a lifetime of winning easily. I have myself noticed that the rain would giggle softly all around us just until Gopi hurried inside his home, muttering obscenities under his breath. For three days after the day he forgot his umbrella, Gopi wouldn't come to our parapet as he would be down with a cold. Usually when he reappeared on the fourth day, still sneezing some, the sky would be bright with a made-up innocence, as if keeping a straight face. And invariably, the old man would begin his tale the way he always did with the words, 'Bastard rain, it has bugged me all my life.'

Gopi's hatred for the rain began when he was seven years old. It was the first day of his holidays, he said, his old eyes shining through their cataracts with the strain of looking so far back in time. Always given to playing alone (his playthings were stones, used cans, plastic threads, and safety pins), Gopi was all set and running along the paddy fields that skirt our little town when the sky darkened slightly. Though he didn't yet hate rain, he did find it absurd; a sort of aberration in the natural scheme of things that came and wet everyone and created ugly puddles everywhere. In his mind he had likened rain to a black kitten that he had got home one day and that his mother had made him get rid of, because it urinated throughout the house at unseemly times. He was certain that one day when the world became more perfect, and God repaired his silly mistakes, rain would stop. The water in wells and oceans and the small stream bordering our town was enough to drink and wash in, without it having to shower down moronically from above.

But he hadn't thought too much about it until then, till that morning in the fields, when he looked up at the sky with some irritation. Why, it wasn't even the rainy season. Gopi stopped running, stood in the middle of the paddy field, and looked up: 'The only special occasion now is that you wish to spoil my play, no? My first day of holidays, too!'

As if in answer the sky ripped apart like a flimsy cloth, unable to contain the weight of some needless malignancy that

The Greatest Enemy of Rain

was waiting to be born. Unbearably cold needles poked Gopi's every pore. The expanse of the field around him turned into a soggy, foggy white and the crop bowed in submission. Water flew everywhere like shards of glass. Worse, the skies lit up here and there with lightning, followed shortly by thunder that sounded louder than his thudding heart. Scared and angry, little Gopi let go of the plastic thread he was holding, at the other end of which was a toy train he had manufactured out of cans filled with stones, and ran with all his might. A couple of times he slipped and fell into the slush on either side of the narrow ridge, resulting in small cuts on the elbow and putting permanent stains on the new red T-shirt his uncle had gifted him for the holidays.

Gopi reached home panting and crying as his mother came out of the kitchen with a towel to dry his head. But before she could, he stood on their porch, looked up at the sky, and sent up such a pungent volley of abuse that his mother recalculated his age on her fingers.

Gopi could officially put that incident down as the start of his lifelong rift with rain.

While a little later into the evening that day Gopi did think of apologizing to the rain ('No one can take kindly to such stinking abuse, I know'), he postponed it because he still was angry. His uncle had told him that if you apologized before the anger had run its course, your apology tended to be empty; not meant, not felt. So he waited, and though he later almost forgot about it, things weren't going to end smoothly. During those holidays he realized that whenever he wished to go to Ambalakkavu, the sacred forest of our small town, to meet with the snakes and scorpions that he had played with the last time, rain would wreck his plans. At such times it did not burst down like before. Instead, it drizzled the entire day, cold and nagging like some wives who wished not to fight but merely to make a point. Once, it poured through his window to mush up his textbooks for the coming year. It made a spongy mess of his new leather shoes only because he had forgotten to bring them indoors. It completely destroyed a tree house he was building, and it even cracked some tiles on the roof of his home so that his father was in a very bad mood for days.

Apologizing was out of the question.

'And that year when it was finally the rainy season! Oh, don't ask!' Gopi said, settling down more comfortably on the parapet, his thin dry legs dangling. 'I lost three umbrellas to the wind, until Father threatened that I would have to go to school with a cellophane cover on my head.' Next came the point he made every time, when we would all look at each other and smile: 'I realized it wasn't only me that hated the rain. Have you seen how, when it rains so continuously that the world is under water, all the poor ants cling on to one big leaf and drift about? Do you think they like that? Have you seen the dogs, sad creatures, all wet with their tails between their legs, looking for some roof to save them? The fallen branches of trees, broken nests, drowned kittens…I tell you, rain is a mistake.'

'But Gopi, without any rain wouldn't it be drought here?' Always asked Neelu, the retired income tax clerk whose bad breath made him stand a little away. 'No crops would grow, animals would die, and eventually we would, too!'

'Pthooo!' Gopi spat behind him into the creek. 'It's just that we are used to this particular mechanism. Before automobiles were invented, we thought we would be rendered immobile without horses. What happened then? We just invented something smarter. Then the horses were out but we only moved around faster. Don't tell me God is less smart than us, incapable of improvising.'

The Greatest Enemy of Rain

We would all nod in agreement because we knew that Gopi was too old to hold an argument if you took it any further. In any case, he would only continue with his tale, not seeing the need to justify what he had learned over such a long time.

When he was nine, Gopi decided that something needed to be done about this silly and vindictive force of nature. To test its vindictiveness, he sometimes went nonchalantly out on the backyard on sunny afternoons to throw stones at the mating dogs across the compound—a favourite pastime he reserved for hot weather—and sure enough, as soon as he had reached the back gates it would begin to drizzle. He made enquiries and found out that there was a rain god who wasn't even a full-fledged god but more a kind of an angel. His name was Indra, and he was the one in control of this stupid phenomenon.

Gopi spoke for hours to the ants in his backyard, telling them to pray to the real gods, the ones not just in charge of the rain but the entire universe, so that in the hierarchy of things up in the heavens, this so-called 'rain god' (really only an angel) could be shown his place. Besides, maybe the gods had created us humans, with our superior thinking, to take our feedback once in a while about creation. Which artist, which great performer, did not benefit from honest feedback? Gopi was sure the real gods would take a fair view of things if he, along with all the other animals that suffered, sent a petition up complaining against the rain god Indra.

So, one night when he was nine, Gopi picked himself off his bed and jumped out of the window. In the backyard he picked up a bottle he had carefully hidden in the nook of a tree's roots and looked inside. It was crawling with hundreds of black ants that he had gathered over the day using a chipping of jaggery. He checked that the bottled was corked tight, pushed it into his armpit, picked up a basket he had also hidden, and began walking barefoot under a moon that seemed big enough to burst. 'This has to be done in the night,' he told the ants. 'We don't want to have to explain to people. They'll say rain has been there forever and will be there forever. Worse, they'll laugh at us. I'm sorry if I have disturbed your sleep.'

When he was nearing Ambalakkavu, it began drizzling. He turned his face up to the cold needles and bared his teeth. 'Yes, do it now. One last time. You're going to be banished forever.'

Ambalakkavu, literally the Temple Forest, is a sacred thicket that some said grew on the faith of the creatures in it and the people around it. It is a sudden burst of busy green in the midst of our little town, full of the strangest flowers, snakes, spiders, squirrels, scorpions, and birds. Though he was barefoot, not a thorn hurt young Gopi's feet as he walked down the narrow, barely perceptible path. The stones were without harsh edges, having been rounded by the feet of centuries of worshippers who visited the three idols at the centre. Gopi looked happily at the giant creepers that seemed to glow with a light of their own. He knew that some of them were actually snakes with their skins bathed in moonlight. He was continuously talking to the ants in the bottle that he had brought along to pray with him. He needed these fellow-sufferers so that the all-powerful gods would know that he wasn't being selfish and that he was representing all creatures in his petition against the rain.

Soon, Gopi stood in the dead centre of the forest where three black stone idols stood on an altar. The drizzle had stopped but the world was still wet. This place seemed to hold its breath; yet, the leaves moved in a perpetual breeze. Under the watchful eyes of the owls and upside-down bats, Gopi set the bottle on the ground and opened it. The ants flowed out in a dark stream,

The Greatest Enemy of Rain

crawling about his feet and munching at the yellowed leaves strewn around. He then opened the little basket and took out his prayer kit. He set the camphor upon the altar and lit it, the way he had watched his father do in their puja room every evening. The aroma added to the sweetness of the night. He took out a small brass bell and rang it quite loudly as he prayed. The night swayed with him. His cheeks, wet with rain, gave him the impression of one in deep sorrow. Some birds cackled outright at the sounds he made but soon all creatures joined in the prayer against the rain.

'O supreme lords, masters of all creation,' he said, and it poured out like an established chant. It flows out of him even now and then and never, even through the forgetfulness of his old age, does he stumble in a single place. 'O vanquishers of evil, controllers of the destinies of everything that exists. Accept our homage and consider our prayer against a vile and vengeful force of nature that calls itself rain. Scarcely worthy of your creation, definitely deficient in stature to hold a position in the heavens alongside the real gods such as yourselves, this dark angel—known to mortals by the name of Indra—is torturous towards your dutiful servants. Banish Indra, banish his rain, o lords, that it might never again have us cry out loud while we're at play, nor have us crowd precariously upon one floating leaf, nor push our tails between our legs....'

In the moonlight he saw the snakes slither less and less until they had stopped moving completely, in total submission to the intensity of the moment. Two large chameleons stood motionless just outside a crevice in a black rock. Even the restless ants were now looking at the idols, their tiny antennae held stiff in attention. Gopi sneaked a peek at the sky overhead. Directly above, the trees formed a dark ring through which he saw that the rain did not dare commit sacrilege at this moment. The clear sky, with its bright and smiling stars, gave him a rush of emotion, and tears mixed with the water on his cheeks.

It was a long time before Gopi made his way back. The next morning, his mother scowled at the mud on his knees and sent him to his bath earlier than usual.

But something happened in the following days that really flummoxed little Gopi. It did not rain at all, but that was not what surprised him. At times, there was some thunder and lightning, and nature felt like a barrel of gunpowder about to burst. It smelled as if it might rain, and the frogs croaked in anticipation, but something seemed to hold the clouds back.

He was in the market one morning with his mother. While she was busy choosing vegetables and fish, he heard a farmer tell the grocer: 'It is very worrying, my friend. A week and not a drop from the skies! I hope we are not going to have a dry spell.'

'A dry spell? Here? Impossible, brother,' the grocer answered. 'It's the monsoons, after all. The last drought was in my childhood, about thirty years ago. Don't worry.'

'Hmm, we farmers will always have nightmares about drought,' the old farmer said, his forehead lined with worry. Gopi felt that the man's skin was turning into soil before his very eyes. He smelled of crop. 'My wife is praying regularly to Indra. We have six little mouths to feed, you see.'

What flummoxed Gopi was that there were people who prayed for rain! He stood stunned for a while, and then he grew very confused.

Sure enough, by the end of that week the sky opened up again. In spite of himself, Gopi noticed that the trees and the birds seemed glad. The leaves shook and danced to the tune of rain, like a harlot trying to please a vainly drunk customer. He found it very grotesque. His confusion turned to anger. He felt

The Greatest Enemy of Rain

that his prayer had been countered with an opposite prayer, and he had lost. His petition to the real gods had been superseded by another, stronger one in favour of the rain god. In an explosion of anger, he looked up at the clouds and yelled to them that they had the shape of an unmentionable body part. He told the big droplets that they were the offspring of a very disreputable animal. When it thundered, he held his chest out and dared it to strike him down. He spat up at the rain only to soil his own face.

We all smiled each time old Gopi reached this part. He often got off the parapet to pluck a blade of grass to chew toothlessly on. He said: 'I was so disgusted that my prayer was overruled, I decided to become an atheist. I secretly blasphemed by thinking ugly, perverted thoughts while looking at the pictures of gods. I told myself that if God existed, I would now be struck down by lightning. Since I wasn't, it proved my point. God couldn't stop rain, nor my blasphemy.

'In a few days, I was missing at the evening prayer sessions at home. I refused to sit down and chant mantras before the deities. I would either sneak out the kitchen door and not come in until dinner or disappear altogether to wander in the fields. Sometimes it would drizzle to spite me further, but I ignored it. Then one evening, Father pulled me by the ear and made me sit down in the prayer room. He held on to my ear and even pinched it hard until I began loudly chanting the thousand names of Lord Vishnu, hot tears streaming down my cheeks. And that was how I became a theist again.'

'But did the rain god take it out on you for praying against him?' I asked, looking at the others in mirth.

'Not immediately, no,' Gopi said. 'Rain wanted me to forget this whole thing so that I would be off my guard. You see, at this point I was always carrying an umbrella to be safe. My caution was a dampener for the rain. Besides, I don't suppose Indra wanted me to herd up all the dogs this time and march to Ambalakkavu.'

Adolescence brought about a brief turnaround in his thinking. At about fourteen, Gopi became very proud of his logical side. He was beginning to study a bit of science in school, and he started telling some close friends: 'You know, when I was little, I thought there was a rain god. I even thought he was my enemy.' At this time, mythology was reduced to funny tales meant for children. For more serious people there were phenomena like the water cycle, the science behind the seasons, and the slightly titled rotation of the earth. He explained these to his mother in the kitchen as she was cutting vegetables. 'You know, Mother, we speak as if rain has a life of its own. We do pujas and rituals to please it! Actually, it is all explained by science.' His mother would feign interest and wonder if this boy hadn't spent enough time on education and if he shouldn't now be helping his father in business.

But during one of those logical days, it was sports day at school. This was the time all the boys wished to show off to the girls what athletes they were. Gopi set out for school dressed in all white, hair plastered to his pate with extra coconut oil so that it wouldn't fly when he ran, shirt sleeves slightly folded to exhibit some muscle, a tune on his lips, a sparkle in his eyes, and no thought of an umbrella in his mind.

Smirk all you like, but it is when I consider such instances that I begin to wonder if there isn't some truth to Gopi's tale. After listening to the old man, I sometimes look up at the sky. You must, too. Especially when it begins to thunder and drizzle down unreasonably, at odd hours, spoiling your plans, catching you unawares. That's when you see cynical faces, jeering lips, and uncanny frowns up there in the clouds. Tell me if there is

The Greatest Enemy of Rain

no persistence in that patter on the windowpanes at times, that there's nothing deliberate, cynical about the drumming on the roof just when you are trying to sleep. Tell me there is nothing to the belief that lightning strikes down liars and crooks who are past redemption.

Well, so that day the rain timed itself perfectly, holding back until young Gopi was too far from home to go back for his umbrella but not too near his school to be saved. Then, with a sudden burst of thunder and flashes of lightning, it began to pour, bringing all the coconut oil on Gopi's hair to his face, soaking the folds in his shirt sleeves, even sticking his shirt to his chest so disgracefully that he might have cried had he been a trifle younger. For good measure, a rusty old car spedpast just then, splashing a quickly formed and cleverly located puddle up to his nose. Rain washed away all science and logic. Gopi looked up and observed under his breath how a particular cloud resembled a piece of something we all throw out every day but do not talk about in polite society.

It was surprising, because that day he suddenly remembered his old prayer in Ambalakkavu, beginning with: 'O supreme lords, masters of all creation.' He remembered it in its entirety and chanted it continuously like a madman.

A few days later, Gopi's father planted a few vegetable seeds in their backyard, and when it was evening, he looked up at the skies, his hands cupped at his brow. 'Damned rain,' he said. 'Won't come when you need it. It would be so great if it rained now. These seeds will simply sprout out like magic.' His mother reminded him that it was better to water the plants as usual because it wasn't the season for rains. That cloudburst a few days earlier was only accidental.

Hearing this, Gopi came out on to the backyard and said,

'Father, you want it to rain? Observe.' He went in and picked the umbrella, hid it behind an old cupboard, came out again to the backyard, and began to act as if he was playing a role in a skit. 'Oh, oh my God, no! I have forgotten my umbrella again. Please God, let it not rain now.'

His father looked at him, stunned, and then at his mother to seek an explanation. The sky remained stony and bright, looking as surprised as his parents.

'My umbrella, oh no! What an ass I am,' Gopi tried provoking the sky again, waving his arms about, looking as if with fear at a lone cloud. Two birds flitted across.

'What are…' his father began, but Gopi discreetly gestured for him to stay quiet.

'Just for today, o rain god, you real, real god, you awesome Lord Indra, spare me, spare me,' Gopi wailed. 'Let me not get drenched, great god, hold back your wrath. Give us not your rain today of all days!' But when he looked up, the cloud above was drifting away incredulously.

After five minutes Gopi walked indoors, angrily muttering: 'Won't work. Of course, what was I thinking? Rain is cleverer after so many years.'

Behind him he heard his father tell his mother, 'Your son, he is growing stupider by the day. Unnaturally stupid.'

In Gopi's tales, rain built on its ire as time passed, getting progressively more vindictive, sly, and unpredictable. If you ever met Gopi, you will know he is not a dreamer, not particularly a sceptic and far from being nutty or imaginative. Yet, his feud with the rain has lasted him a lifetime. I sometimes catch myself thinking that no one should hold a grudge for so long. At some point he ought to have made up with the rain, replaced all those expletives with a simple statement that there was intolerance and

The Greatest Enemy of Rain

stubbornness on both sides, that perhaps they should let bygones be bygones and become friends. I once even spoke this out loud near the parapet, and Jaleel Ikka, the youngest old man among us, looked at me in full amusement, observing that in old age madness became contagious.

There are plenty more instances that Gopi indulges us with: from the time rain washed down the new concrete when he was building his own house, to when it gave him a fever just before a vital ceremony after his father's death, to the time it made him slip and fall off his scooter to fracture an arm. I can someday turn this into a novel, but for this story I must come to the last anecdote with which he always ended his recollections. This was when he was a young man and had started to go to the city every day for work as a cashier in a small restaurant. He would take the morning bus to work but during those days there was no vehicle when it was time for him to return. You could take a taxi-van for most of the distance and then wait at an abandoned shed by the roadside for some tractor to come by and give you a ride for a small fee.

It was in this abandoned shed that Gopi discovered love.

She appeared in it suddenly one day like a peacock in a dull landscape. He was taken aback by such beauty in the midst of such abandon, and he later regretted that he must have stared tactlessly on that first meeting. When a tractor came, he tried to help her up but she refused his extended arm.

From then she was there every evening when he returned from the city, and he soon realized that she came there usually in the same taxi-van in which he did. He made it a practice to extend his arm in the tractor every single day, because if all this were a movie she would one day take his arm without preamble and that would mean they had become lovers. She had lovely hair that flew to her lips at times, and the days she forgot to apply her kajal she was even more beautiful. He struggled to find out where in our town she lived, but he always lost her in the marketplace where the tractors dropped them.

After many days of standing together in the shed he quietly ventured to ask her, 'What's your name?'

She said quietly: 'Watermelon.'

'Oh. And in the city, you work? Or study?'

'I sit on eggs in the central square so that they can become chicks.'

The next day he did not try to help her up on the tractor. But the day after that he told himself she was fun-loving and jocular, a quality that went alluringly well with her looks. He once again began extending his arm down for her, with her again refusing it every evening. By now he was beginning to dream about her while he sat behind his desk in the restaurant. In the van he often saw her sitting in front and imagined that he caught the aroma of her hair drifting back to him in the wind. In his mind he called her watermelon, and smiled fondly.

Then one evening when they were waiting in the shed it began to rain, predictably when he had forgotten his umbrella. His heart racing, he saw that she had no umbrella either. Now, this shed we are talking about had, by way of roof, only a thin strip of asbestos in a corner. They both stood under it and, though not exactly crowded, her awkwardness at having to share a corner gave him immense pleasure.

But rapidly, her awkwardness gave way to nervousness, then fear. The trouble was that the sun would go down in some time and no tractor seemed to be coming. Neither was the rain showing any signs of letting up.

'My name is Kavitha,' she said, her voice pitched up in a girly manner to be heard over the downpour.

'What?' he said, pretending not to hear.

'Kavitha!' she squealed again, realizing at the same time that he was teasing her.

'I work in a garment factory,' she shouted through the downpour which seemed to be helping Gopi that day. 'I live by the old cinema theatre. Now, how do we go from here?'

'No vehicle will come now, not in this rain, I think,' Gopi yelled back with some seriousness, because he thought she might start to cry. The thick clouds had hidden the sun already, in a threatening parody of nightfall. He fought the incredible urge to hug her close and tell her she was safe with him. 'We could walk the rest of the way if we had an umbrella…' then, as her eyes narrowed brightly, he added, 'Two umbrellas.'

She smiled in spite of her nervousness.

Then he had an idea. 'There is no point in waiting any longer. It'll be dark soon.' He reached up and touched the single asbestos sheet, which easily came loose. He caught himself wishing it was just above reach so that he could lift her up like in the movies.

So that evening they walked all the way home carrying the asbestos sheet over their heads between them like construction workers, she in front and him at the back because he told her he needed to watch her for her own safety. 'There are rabid dogs in these parts,' he threw in for effect. For the entire two kilometres, he did watch her back, falling more and more in love as the rain helped by maintaining its tempo. In the violent downpour, the road seemed to be engulfed in mist, so that it seemed as if they were walking on clouds.

It was a long time since his childhood enmity with the rain had started and he smiled when he thought about it. He could remember every word of the chant he had invented at Ambalakkavu that night when he was nine. He thought in amusement that perhaps, after all these years, the rain was taking the initiative of patching things up! Making the first move of reconciliation. 'Ha,' he said, marvelling at how fantastical and vain his imagination had been when he was small. Well, he said to himself, if there is a Lord Indra up there after all, he seems to be on my side now.

From the next day they spoke to each other in the shed and he said her name as often as he could with a new-found familiarity that bordered on possessiveness. She even took his hand initially to climb up on to the tractor, but then one day she told him that people would see it and make stories about them. When he asked if there wouldn't be some truth to such stories, she smiled and his heart tried to flutter out of his ribs.

They got married a year later. Though initially her father proved an obstacle, it was clear that his family was the wealthier one. His own father was secretly relieved because he hadn't thought his boy would ever find a girl. 'What misfortune could befall a girl for her to settle for Gopi?' he had asked Gopi's mother sometimes. When Gopi got himself a better job as a manager in a bigger hotel in the city, the families came together and finalized things. All through the wedding it rained.

At this point, again, most of us begin to snigger, though I always try to maintain an equanimous expression out of fear that Gopi might be offended. I know I needn't fear, though. Gopi himself sports a twinkle in his watery eyes when he comes to this part. Why, just yesterday he had told us all this again and laughed loudly when the postmaster, Mathai, had begun to smile.

'Not just the wedding, it rained throughout what you might call our honeymoon,' Gopi said, pulling a beedi out of his shirt pocket.

'She'll smell it on you,' I warned.

'Hah!' he said all warrior-like, but he didn't light the beedi. He only sniffed at it.

Gopi often tells us that he did experience true happiness during his newly married days. He remembers telling Kavitha about his obsession with the rain all through boyhood and her saying in her songlike voice that he was mad when he told her that in the end it seemed rain had turned out to be his friend, after all, gifting him his beautiful wife. They loved to laugh at the evening they had used an asbestos sheet as an umbrella.

But there is one curious thing, and I have seen this in many of our families. Kavitha had a mother who had always taught her, right from when she was young, that the whole point of a girl's life was to get married. You need to work towards it, she said. You need to abide by certain rules. Eat less so that you don't put on weight, talk softly as becomes a girl of good upbringing, do not show your teeth while laughing, never stare at people however curious they make you, avoid talking or laughing loudly especially in the presence of young men, always show an interest in womanly duties like washing vessels and cleaning tables, never come out of your room in the morning without taking a bath first, and more such. Her mother told her that it was tough observing all these, yes, but the reward was that you needed to observe them only until you were married. The effort was all towards getting a good husband. Once you tied the knot—provided you tied it with the right man—you had a lifetime of relaxation as your reward.

Well, to tell the story with the solemnity it deserves, Gopi's wife strongly adhered to this teaching of her mother's. Three days after their wedding he took her to the city, to the same hotel where he worked, to give her a sample of how rich folk dined. He had kept some money aside for this. But the romance in his head vaporized somewhat when, exercising her new-found freedom, Kavitha polished off a shocking amount of rice, more pieces of fried chicken than a man could eat and three different flavours of ice-cream. He could see the waiters, who were his subordinates, nudge each other and giggle, building a story for later.

During the months following the wedding Gopi saw that his wife was rapidly shedding the image of the beautiful, nubile girl he had fallen for. She was like a person who had smiled throughout a public function for appearance's sake, though in a very uncomfortable outfit, and now, back home, was taking great pleasure in taking off that uncomfortable dress, revelling in the very gracelessness with which she did it. She was turning into a loud, argumentative woman who very frequently exhibited needless scorn, regularly overate, hated the very idea of romance, and deliberately tried to be brash. She slept until late into the day, so that she was often asleep when he left for work. She spoke boldly to his father, answered back to his mother, and finally forced Gopi to leave his parents' place for a rented house in the city. She was too forward and patronizing with his friends, so that he eventually stopped bringing them home. She sang tunelessly even in the presence of others, and at the cinema she clapped her hands and sat at the edge of her seat.

'This isn't to say she did not love me,' Gopi says sometimes. 'She had her crude, unfeminine way of loving me. Or rather, she cared for me often in a smothering sort of way, as if it was for her own sake that she cared, and not mine.'

In less than two years Kavitha had grown fat and the young, irresistibly beautiful girl whose neck and waist he had observed under the asbestos sheet on a rainy evening lived only in an aching corner in his mind. At times, she even appeared repulsive to him, especially when she burped in loud satisfaction after a meal or

The Greatest Enemy of Rain

appeared unwashed in the mornings on holidays.

Since the risk of Gopi himself reading this someday is negligible, I might as well tell you that his wife was the ultimate blow that the rain has dealt him. I know enough of their history to know that about five years after their wedding Gopi briefly tried to become an alcoholic. He drank more than he could take, vomited in public, lost his job, and generally wrecked their finances until they almost went bankrupt. Kavitha calmly called her father, had him pick her up from the city, and went to her home, where she stayed for over a year. Gopi gradually discovered that he wasn't the type to turn to alcohol completely ('You need to be born an alcoholic,' he often said darkly). Neither was he the type to visit the brothels in the city or begin gambling or even simply commit suicide. He was a man with soft, romantic notions, who had landed a wife who was just the opposite. Coming to terms with this central paradox of his life, Gopi then came back to our little town, begged Kavitha's and her parents' forgiveness, even cried some, and was reunited with her. But her father imposed the condition that they mustn't leave for the city again. He needed Gopi where he could keep an eye on him. And that was how Gopi became our librarian, a position Kavitha's father had fetched for him in return for his unconditional and long-standing loyalty to him and his daughter. He had been a librarian at the Town Hall Library for countless years, until he finally retired some years ago. If you were heartless enough to ask if they never thought of having any children, Gopi only smiles wanly: 'Children? They never happened at all. And we pretended we didn't know why.' At times he lights a beedi after this, damning the consequences, and sucks on a mint later to hide the smell.

Only last week we sat on Gopi's porch and Kavitha brought us all coffee in little tumblers. She has grown thinner now, her fair skin hanging off her like a melting candle. After we were all served, Gopi reached the tray she held for his tumbler, but it wasn't there. When he asked her, she turned sharply and spoke with the sound of a sword drawn up in the air:

'No coffee for you after seven! I cannot have you sit up all night, pissing all around the toilet every half hour saying you can't sleep. I need my sleep, I work hard. Not all of us can sit on a parapet the whole day and gossip.' Then she turned to the rest of us and switched on a smile. 'Coffee wakes him up. Then he wakes me up.'

Gopi turned red as she went indoors, but when it immediately started drizzling, he relaxed. Sridharan Vakkeel began to laugh. I joined in and soon everyone was laughing, and the tension let up. Gopi pointed towards the door through which Kavitha had gone and whispered, 'Thank you, O Lord Indra. Thank you for this precious gift.' And the rain kept tune on the roof. We knew that after we left, and after the downpour eased, Gopi would look up at the sky and let loose a volley of abuse. He was too old to outshout the rain, he told us, which was still as youthful as on the day he had begun fighting it.

I suppose on the day Gopi dies it will rain big, warm droplets. There will be that understanding and borderline respect which usually develops between long-time foes. Through the steady patter we will almost hear his weak, phlegmy voice: 'Bastard rain. Bugs me even on the day I'm leaving.'

2

THESE NEW-FANGLED WAYS

'This is appalling!' Sunna exclaimed, throwing her hands in the air. 'Now you do it right in front of us, right here! At least have some respect for your grandfather or your father.'

    No one spoke. The family was sitting down to dinner in the usual clearing in the forest. Sunna was exasperated at her teenage daughter, Mista. The bickering between the two was more frequent than anyone cared for, but it was only to be expected. Mista was entering the age where girls and their mothers could hardly sit down to eat together in the same clearing.

    'You're so sure you're never, ever in the wrong. You scare me sometimes,' Sunna went on, but Puchki, her husband, wisely gestured for her to calm down. Young Mista appeared icily unmoved as she continued to slowly roast her dinner over a fire. A bead of sweat appeared on the dip in her throat, lingered around a while and then rapidly snaked down her bare chest to the leaf skirt on her hips.

    'But it's making her sweat!' the mother said to the father, worried beyond measure. 'Do you think this will do Mista any good? You know what fire does; it burns things down! It's as clear as the bright holes in the sky. I talk for her good, you hear me? But of course, I'm the bad one here. Because I'm the only one who talks. You hear me?'

Puchki heard her. But he did not know how to speak to his daughter. He found it insulting to his position in the family to be disobeyed by a girl who seemed to have suddenly grown up. And disobeyed he would be, he was sure, if she wasn't in the mood to humour him. Mista could be cold and strong.

They all watched Mista's piece of meat roast over the fire. It was frightening. The meat changed colour at the points where the flames licked it. It turned dark, like death. It even gave off an ungainly smell. But what was worse was that in the moonlight they could see greyish, slimy smoke snake up from the meat. None of them could understand how Mista could eventually eat that.

'There is nothing wrong in cooking one's food,' Mista spoke quietly. 'It makes food tastier, in fact. You are so against it because you refuse to try it. Because it's new, and you haven't seen it before.' But it was to Puchki she spoke, not to her mother.

Puchki turned and looked helplessly at his father, Fuhara. This old man, the most ancient one in their tribe, was sacred, aloof, and mysterious. No one knew how old he was, because all who had been around at the time of his birth were now long dead. Some even said he was immortal, that he was as old as the bright holes in the sky, because they had seen him die several times and come back to life a little later. Puchki felt that Fuhara saw and understood everything that was going on between Mista and her mother, but he seemed content feeding bits of his dinner to Teesh, their pet wolf.

'But what is wrong with food as it is, Mista? Generations have been eating it raw, the way nature meant us to,' Puchki said, his voice a careful balance of assertion and reconciliation.

Mista said nothing. The flames crackled, and the grey fumes grew thicker. It was frightful when the fumes burned their eyes

The Greatest Enemy of Rain

and old Fuhara started to cough.

'Do you see what it is doing to your father and your grandfather?' Sunna asked with fervour, glancing at Puchki and Fuhara as if to confirm that they were on her side.

Nothing can be done, thought Puchki. The Chungiyas, those slit-eyed inventors who believed in a shallow existence, had gone and created this horrible and deadly thing called fire. Of course, everyone had seen fire before, much to their horror, when it burned entire forests down. But at least those were natural fires, the bright burning tongues of evil that were unbearable when one went too close. Now, these accursed Chungiya 'inventors' had rubbed stones together and mixed dried leaves or something to actually create the stuff! Puchki did not understand the technology, but he was sure it could do no good. Nothing the Chungiyas came up with had ever done any good. Why, everyone knew that fire simply reduced everything in its path into a useless grey dust from which the original component could never be retrieved. But the new generation! Oh, they were forever following mindlessly the trends of foreign tribes.

The smoke made Fuhara's eyes water. Not to be outdone, Sunna had started to cry silently in the semi-darkness.

Just yesterday, Mista had made for herself a new garment out of banana leaves that covered her chest. Even though her mother vehemently forbade her from wearing such bold fashion, she had donned it defiantly when she went to meet Grus, her man friend. Later when Grus and Mista were sitting by the river watching the birds, Zoola, the old witch doctor of the neighbouring clan, wandered into the scene. She smiled at the nice young couple, sat down a little way off, and defecated profusely.

Zoola reported that something strange happened to Mista then. The girl got up and shouted like one possessed, calling

Zoola a graceless old witch who should have died long ago. Even the nice young man was stunned at Mista's outburst. Zoola just couldn't divine what wrong she had done.

No, no one could understand this new generation of youth.

Now, as Mista stonily turned her meat over the flames, Sunna tearfully said: 'Don't listen to me, but please, my daughter, please fear Bassole.' Bassole was their god, prior to which he had been a giant mountain that could look like a bald human head if you wanted it to.

'Stop speaking for Bassole, Mother. Why should Bassole hold anything against a poor flame?' said Mista.

'That's enough,' said Puchki, but all the manliness in his voice sounded hollow. 'Cook if you want to, burn everything down. But I'll not hear a word against Bassole while I am alive. You will not blaspheme while you stay with us.'

He then turned to his infinitely older father: 'O Fuhara, O Father of us all, tell your little grandchild the error of her ways. Light her path with your wisdom.'

They all looked at Fuhara. The ancient one wiped his eyes and cleared his throat. Teesh stiffened in anticipation. Even Mista stopped turning the meat. They waited for the words of wisdom, and Fuhara looked at them, one after the other, with his dim eyes which seemed tired with the weight of all they had seen. But it was an uncomfortably long time later, when Teesh went to relieve himself behind a bush, that they realized that Fuhara wasn't going to speak. Mista began turning the meat again.

In a fit of hysteria, Sunna threw her meal, untouched, toward Teesh. Puchki had lost his appetite too. Only the old man was now happily chewing with his hardened, toothless gums, throwing bits to Teesh every now and then. He stopped to cough whenever the smoke bit his throat.

'O Bassole, forgive my daughter, forgive us all…' Sunna wailed.

'Chuk buhiyachukbuhiya—nachuk, na, nanachuk,' thundered old Fuhara suddenly. The very crickets in the surrounding forests fell silent. 'Nadaahibuhiya, kadaapibuhiya… aaaaaaaah, nachuknachuk!'

Fuhara had spoken! The family looked at one another. They had just heard the voice of the tribe's primordial wisdom, the assertion of their ageless belief system. However, it was in their ancient tongue which none of them understood, and which Fuhara considered a sacrilege to translate. But he had spoken. And then, when Mista continued to turn her meat over the flames, insisting on not interpreting in any manner what she hadn't understood, the smoke hit Fuhara's nostrils again. A fit of coughing overcame him, and he died.

'Oooooooo,' wailed Teesh the wolf.

'Oooooooo,' wailed Sunna, looking up at the burning holes in the sky.

'The Immortal One is dead! Cursed be the fire that killed him,' Puchki exclaimed, looking morosely from Sunna to Mista to Teesh to Fuhara's body. 'O Bassole, curse the Chungiyas, but forgive my daughter! She knows not the consequences of her actions.' He was wondering how to re-establish his obviously waning authority within the family. This wouldn't do.

Mista looked at the dead Fuhara for a while. The next morning the tribe would gather and place the ancient one among rare leaves in a freshly dug pit. They would bathe him in the urine of the mountain goats. They would put sweet red berries at his feet for his journey and smear sacred clay on his forehead to ward off evil on the way. They would inscribe ancient symbols on his bony chest, so that his soul may not linger among the living. But,

Mista thought, when they dance and sing around his grave and click their sticks together to appease Death, Fuhara would, in all likelihood, wake up and dance with them, unable to contain his excitement. Mista knew that was the logical thing to expect, considering what had happened more than once in the past.

With the calm assurance of youth, Mista sank her teeth into her cooked meat.

3

DAYS WITHOUT TEACHER

On the day Saroja Teacher left on her Europe trip her husband acted depressed during the first half of the morning for the benefit of Radha, their chirpy, gossipy maid. With an old Mohammed Rafi number playing lightly in the background, he stared vacantly into the newspaper. Then, so as to not overdo it, he went and took his bath. He fidgeted for a bit, lay down on the sofa, and shut his eyes although he wasn't sleepy in the slightest. He groaned and moaned lightly until Radha, standing with the broom by her side, laughed: 'Saroja chechi will be back in just about a week, Acha. And I'm here to take care of you till then. Do you want some coffee?'

'No,' he said. He frowned like he always did when this young woman called him 'acha', meaning father, in the same sentence in which she addressed his wife as 'chechi', meaning elder sister.

Listening to Rafi punctuated by the swish of Radha's broom, he must have drifted off to sleep because when he woke up after a while he had no idea of the time and his heart was thudding in sudden clueless excitement. In the brief moment it took him to remember the reason for his excitement he noted that the maid had finished her work and left the house. He ran upstairs, yanked his phone off its charger, banged open the bay windows of their bedroom, and descended to the roof of the porch which served as a small balcony.

'Sethu,' he spoke into the phone, 'Teacher has left. Her brother took her this morning. They are on the flight to Bombay. And from there…vooooosh!' The sound he made came out awkward because he hadn't made such sounds in ages.

'Good,' said the voice from the other end. 'How long before Saroja Teacher is back? Eleven days, right?'

'Yes, the twenty-fifth.'

'Good,' said Sethu again. 'Let's be in heaven for eleven days. When shall I come over? Or do you want to go out?'

'No, no,' the old man said. 'People know us. Come over home.'

'Ha ha, you sure are a scared old mutt. Saroja Teacher has kept you on a short leash.'

'Shut up and come,' the old man said. 'And make sure you buy something…premium.'

'Sure.'

'And…and cigarettes. I don't even remember which brand we used to smoke.'

He had chosen to call Sethu from the balcony above the porch not just because his mobile phone received the strongest signal there. From the balcony, he could see the front gates. In case Radha had forgotten something and barged back in, he would be prepared. Through the bay windows he could see Teacher's smiling photograph on the table by the bed. The picture had a frame that was like her—simple, plain, unassuming, and without the least ornamentation. He thought he saw her eyes twinkle and he quickly turned away from the photo.

'Once a drunkard, always a drunkard,' he chuckled after cutting the call. Then he excused himself: 'How else is an old man to handle life when his old woman goes away to see Europe?'

Through the afternoon, he was restless. He hurriedly finished the lunch Radha had laid out for him, as though he had somewhere to be immediately after. He couldn't enjoy his siesta because he had to get up twice to urinate and once to check if someone had rattled the gates. He smiled, telling himself that he was like a young boy on his first date.

When Teacher called him that afternoon he struggled not to hurry through the call. 'Yes. Yes, I had lunch,' he said a little breathlessly. 'Yes, Radha came. Said she'll come at four to wash dishes. From tomorrow she'll cook; yes. No. I'm fine. Are you through immigration?' His wife would notice any change in his voice, any trace of excitement, so he tried to be casual: 'And how's Kuttan? Is he making a fuss with all the waiting?' Kuttan was Saroja Teacher's brother's grandchild, and the littlest member on the trip.

Towards the end of the call, he perfectly balanced a matter-of-fact tone with simple pleasantness: 'Sethu is coming over in the evening. What are friends for? We might go for a walk.'

He knew that Teacher wasn't sure what opinion to form of her husband's earliest friend. Though she seemed quite fond of Sethu most of the time, he knew she found it difficult to place unmarried old men. There was something about them she couldn't explain to herself. How did they live and how were they happy? There was something about this particular unmarried old man that Saroja Teacher would have liked her husband to be cautious about. 'For your friend it's sky above and earth below,' she had said once or twice. 'He has no family to worry about.' Not that she had any way of suspecting what the two of them would be up to during her absence. Surely, they had grown too old for a lot of her suspicions. He chuckled again, feeling absolutely no remorse for his glee at the expense of his wife.

Through Radha's second visit he had to act gloomy again. But this time he didn't have to be as inventive as in the morning as the maid's work was restricted largely to the kitchen. And yet, he suddenly felt a little tense when she giggled as she was leaving: 'I'm off, Acha. I'll come in the morning. Now you be good. Don't do anything naughty.'

Allow her a little more freedom and she'll ruffle the hair on my head and slap my bottom, he thought angrily.

The moment he saw her close the gates he messaged Sethu that all was clear, and he could come over any time now.

Sethu had an indelicate sense of humour, which the old man sometimes found a little bothersome. Look at what the man did today: he had brought a whisky called Teacher's. And so that the old man wouldn't still miss the joke, he made it a point to say: 'I made sure you won't miss Saroja Teacher.' But nothing could irk the old man for too long as they poured out the drink and Sethu opened a packet of cigarettes.

Life did a reverse at dizzying speed. In a second the two old men were back in their early thirties, seated opposite each other at the Carnival Bar and Restaurant, a pint of golden whisky in their midst, fingers trailing smoke, and a short-statured, over-eager waiter (neither could remember his name now) fawning over them and insincerely suggesting the day's special snacks. The old man could hear the ice cubes tapping against the glass. For a timeless time after that they spoke about those days: the days before Saroja Teacher, which the old man referred to as his pre-marriage days while Sethu called them his friend's days of 'freedom'. Drinking after work, on holidays and weekends, with friends, with just the two of them. Philosophical discourses, debates, arguments, emotions, politics, movies and books, fights, bets, vows, revelations, confessions, singing, mimicking, laughing and crying, gossiping and bitching, career talk, brainstorming, advising, talking and listening. It all stopped, as Sethu regretfully put it, 'when you went and made a promise to your wife'.

The old man stared deeply into his glass. 'I was turning into a drunkard. You drank too, but you were never obsessed,' he answered. 'Teacher only told me what I knew in my heart.' Then he found to his surprise that he was defending his wife and his marriage to Sethu, rather vehemently arguing that one needed to grow up and couldn't continue a life of debauchery that is normal at thirty but not at forty. 'There is a natural progression to everything. Even to life. We stole jam from the kitchen when we were boys. But we stopped doing that in our teens.'

'Of all men, you should say this!' Sethu sighed.

Sometime later in the evening Sethu stubbed his toe on the leg of the table when he returned with more soda. The old man massaged a balm onto his friend's toe. For a moment they were like lovers making up after a quarrel—gently running his hands on Sethu's swollen foot, the old man was apologizing, without saying a word, for putting a stop to their evenings many years ago. Without saying a word, he was making up for having married, for having promised his wife that he wouldn't drink any more, for having caused the birth of a son for whose sake he had even quit smoking, and then more or less stopped even going out with his friends, leaving their myriad drunken topics hanging mid-air.

A little later Saroja Teacher called, and he couldn't recall, even immediately after, what they had spoken about. He later hoped he had asked where the travellers had reached—Where was she calling from? Was she tired? What was the time there? But he wondered if she had discerned that he wasn't himself at all. Would she be concerned? He couldn't worry about all that now.

Interestingly, through the haze of his drunkenness, he

remembered how he had once discussed with Saroja Teacher the changes in him after their marriage, the changes in his life and routine. It was during one of their long walks. 'You've made me clean, like the inside of a plantain stalk. I don't drink, I don't smoke, I don't even eat too much! If you rub my cheeks, I'll make a squeaky sound, like your steel plates after washing.'

'I did not impose,' she had laughed.

'No. But you influenced,' he had laughed back.

And the old man knew that over the years he had developed some other habits; like a river that had chosen a different path after its natural course was blocked. He had literally become clean. He bathed twice—sometimes thrice—a day even on winters, washed his hands way too often, and brushed his teeth with such vehemence that his dentist had recently told him he had a mouth full of worn-out teeth. He had frequent fungal infections, apparently because he used too much soap and it dried his skin. He did not drink but he used too much soap, and that they could live with. But he also hated traveling, because his very routine was so delicate to observe, so detailed and difficult that he and Teacher couldn't sustain it in places other than at home. He couldn't have kept washing his hands at a public place every time he touched the hand-rest of an escalator or when someone gave it a friendly shake. He couldn't take a bath in the middle of a road whenever a little dust blew on him. He would stop enjoying any trip the moment he had to struggle at some hotel to wash his hands without touching the basin. He would become almost hostile and irritable if someone burped near him in a bus. As a result, over so many years it had come to be that he rarely went out of his home except in accordance with his schedule: to get milk in the morning, take the garbage out a little later, and usually after that only for their walks in the evenings. Both in the morning and in the evening his outings would be followed by his soapy baths.

'Does your son call often?' Sethu asked suddenly.

'Once in two weeks.'

His son was an electrical engineer in Denmark and called with the punctuality with which Saroja Teacher took her blood pressure medicine. He said this out loud and Sethu laughed. Sethu, who had neither a wife nor a son or daughter, looked a little gloomy for a moment, the old man thought. But then he focused on refilling their glasses.

The old man could not remember when exactly he blacked out. Sometime in the night Sethu must have bid him goodbye and stumbled back to his home, risking his neck on his old scooter. When the old man came to, it was early dawn and the bile was a whirlpool inside him. Then the vomiting began. The first one was so sudden and unexpected that it required him to wash the toilet afterward, through a splitting headache. Later, after taking a pill, when he was still vomiting at regular intervals, he began to worry that Radha would come in soon and discover something incriminating in the living room where they had sat last evening, and connect it to his sickness. It was curious, he thought, how our society could be so sympathetic to an illness and yet so antagonistic to a hangover. After all, many illnesses too were caused by stupidity, carelessness, and overindulgence. How was a heart attack, brought on by years of gluttony and laziness, deserving of sympathy while a terrible headache after just one drinking session such a crime?

Through his weakness that made the present seem like a memory, he inspected the living room and the fridge. He was thankful that it seemed they had cleaned up after their little party and Sethu had taken the garbage in a plastic cover to chuck by the bin near the park. He went back to bed, feeling as though fingers were squeezing his eyes through his skull.

Soon, he heard Radha make her regular sounds as she cleaned the house. Try as he might, he could not keep himself puking once when she was inside, and sure enough she came right into the bedroom. 'Are you unwell, Acha?'

'Migraine,' he groaned. 'Sethu came over in the evening. He brought some fried chicken to have along with dinner. I think it was made in old oil.'

'I knew your friend came,' Radha said. 'I found this under the washing machine.' And she held up a cigarette butt.

'Oh,' he said without batting an eyelid. 'Yes, Sethu still smokes.'

Radha laughed her irritating, girly laugh and told him: 'Chechi is wary of your old friend. She knows he is naughty.'

'You talk too much.'

'Can I get you a digestive and a glass of buttermilk?' she asked. But why did he feel she was teasing?

Before Radha finished with the morning chores, she came up one more time to report—a little triumphantly—that she had found the cap of a soda bottle under the sofa in the front room and wondered how it came to be there. She had also found scraps from a bottle label in the kitchen dustbin.

'Why are you bringing all these to me?' he asked, irritated. 'Get rid of all the trash.'

'Just showing you,' she said, her mirth intact. Then she made three sundry observances in rapid succession:

'Chechi said she'll be calling me once in a while to ask about the cooking and the home. She might call the day after tomorrow.' She picked up the ironed clothes and set them in the cupboard.

The Greatest Enemy of Rain

'It's time to buy new textbooks for my daughter's school. I'm five-thousand short. Chechi used to help every year.' This she said as she was watering the plants on the balcony.

'If you need any snacks for the evening, Acha, do let me know. If your friend is coming down again…' She said while wiping Teacher's photograph.

The old man lay back, tired. Sethu called a little after the maid had left. 'How are you, old boy? You were swimming in it last night!'

'I'm sick,' the old man said. His tone resembled a dog that had ventured out of his master's gates in the night with big, amorous dreams and then dragged himself back in the morning, bitten and defeated. 'Puked a dozen times and counting.'

'There was something wrong with the Teacher's,' claimed Sethu. 'I'm woozy too. Think it's a duplicate.'

The old man abruptly cut the call and went and upchucked again.

It was only by lunchtime that he stopped vomiting. He felt weak and incredibly sad. He pictured his wife enjoying herself in a strange, bright land with her brother, sister-in-law, and nephew. She would be wearing her shades, panting slightly but smiling constantly as she visited the places she had dreamt of all these years. Having been a teacher of English literature, he knew she was fascinated with the places that had inspired her favourite writers, their homes, and other historical spots. Some waterfall that had moved this poet, a certain chair upon which a writer had sat while mulling over his classic, a tree under which some dramatist had first met his lover. Original folios, the value of which he never understood: how did it matter if you read out of the terrible scribbles of a writer's original pages or the same thing neatly printed inside a book? Teacher was also fascinated with the English way of life, their food, what they wore, and their mannerisms, the French painters and singers by the roadside, the Irish and their passion for brewing. This was the tiny corner of her world which did not include him. So, after many years of thinking about it, for the first time since they were together, she had gone off to enjoy herself without him.

In what he viewed as a cosmic balancing act, the old man picked up his lunch and flushed it down the toilet.

At five, he called up Sethu and said: 'The maid knows we drank. She is fucking blackmailing me.' He asked Sethu to lend him five thousand rupees because he would have to ask Teacher for the ATM pin which he perpetually forgot, and there were bound to be questions. Whereas when she would learn later that he had 'helped' the maid, it would only please her. Sethu suggested that he immediately come over with the money. 'No,' the old man said quickly. 'Some guests are coming over. You can give me the money later.' He lied because he didn't have the stomach for what Sethu was sure to bring along besides the money.

By evening, though the old man had quite recovered and was even a little hungry, he couldn't, for the life of him, have imagined another drinking session ever again. In fact, strange sounds emanated from his tummy when he thought about the taste of liquor. He cut some fruit and made himself a cup of strong black coffee even before Radha came in. By the time Teacher called he was up and sprightly.

But it was Teacher who sounded tired and gloomy.

'Yeah, we are seeing a lot of places,' she said without much enthusiasm, and rattled off a list of names of places they had already visited. He recalled many of these names from when she had mentioned them with stars in her eyes during their walks.

'But you don't sound excited. What is it?'

'Oh, nothing,' she said, and then she declared: 'I guess I'm missing home.'

'You only left yesterday!'

'Yes, but I suppose I am too used to home,' she said. 'And you.'

The old man laughed heartily into the phone. Then he asked his wife to forget home and him, that he was getting along quite fine and she needn't worry, that the maid was cooking really good food, that Sethu came in often to check on him. His heart felt like an egg that had been boiled only slightly, warm but still runny.

'This is a dream come true for you,' he made her understand. 'Don't spend your holiday worrying about me. Just experience those places.'

'Yes,' said Saroja Teacher without conviction. 'I only wish we were together.'

The old man was happy for the rest of the evening. He played some happy songs and hummed along. When Radha asked if he was so happy because his friend was coming again, he did not get irritated at all. Instead, he told her that he would give her no less than five thousand rupees, that she was to take care of her daughter's education, and that only good education could give the little girl a bright future. That brainy woman then sniffed around the house to figure out what substance was making the old man so gleeful.

The next morning, he woke up early and went for a walk in the park. Life and health bloomed inside him as he looked at the morning joggers with their ears stuffed with their music and their knees covered in kneecaps. He saw a young girl he had noticed before. She was very pretty but completely indifferent. She jogged around the walkway, her ponytail bouncing up and down, chewing gum and with a white wire trailing off a mobile phone in her hand to ears that had turned pink with the exercise. And then there was that young man on a bench with a novel that he never read, observing the girl every time she circled the round track and passed him. When the wind blew, a small tree by the track showered yellow flowers on the girl—like cupid's arrows—and the old man saw the young man's eyes fill with happiness. He wondered if the girl would notice if the youth did not turn up one of these mornings.

Back home, instead of going straight for his bath, he decided to make himself some coffee. The coffee was so good that it inspired him to do something; something enterprising and smart on his own. Fidgeting around, he found that dust had caked on the curtain rods in the living room. 'That Radha,' he said to himself. 'She keeps dusting the same places over and over, ignoring other places.' He pulled a chair to the window, climbed on it and, with a wet cloth began to clean the curtain rod. 'Teacher should see me now,' he thought as he cleaned every curtain rod in the house. In a moment he was dusting the arms of the sofa and the chairs, thinking he ought to go around the house like this every day with a mop, and clean something or the other. He stopped when Radha came in (or she would search the kitchen cupboards for narcotics), but he opened an old diary and began noting down the spots and things in the house that needed his attention. Curtain rods, the underside of furniture, the sides of windows that faced outwards, doorknobs…he wrote with boyish enthusiasm.

And yet, all through his bubbliness this morning, the old man was aware of some sorrow waiting right outside the doors of his mind. It was a nagging, gnawing anguish—more ache than pain—some problem whose existence was undeniable. Of course, it had to do with Saroja Teacher being away, but it was more than that. It began there and then became something darker. He refused to let it into his mind, but even from outside it made his joy seem unreal, almost fake at times. By noon he was playing peppy songs and watching a comedy movie on the laptop his son had given him, but his mood still waned.

But then, just after the maid had left, Saroja Teacher called. She still sounded gloomy and his batteries recharged as he told her to learn to enjoy her present, to not worry about anything else, to send him pictures of the places she had been to, to describe the foods she had eaten and the people she had met. He gently scolded her when she told him she had refused champagne at the hotel the previous night. 'Everyone who drinks is not a drunkard,' he told her as if talking to a daughter. 'Who refuses champagne?' But she told him that even if she were to have a glass it would be when he was by her side, and that made him almost weep with joy.

Later in the night he stared for long, unthinking, at the pictures she sent him on WhatsApp. The surroundings were exciting—towns with magnificent artsy buildings and clean streets, and nature with crisp waters and succulent greens and cold brightness—but always with a rather gloomy Teacher in the foreground. It was like a lot of things were happening in her life and yet she wasn't completely present.

The old man went to sleep, acutely aware of his sorrow.

In the morning he did go for his walk but the list he had made the previous day of the things he needed to dust in the morning lay on the dining table like a bit of dream he had woken up from. All the vigour of the previous day had left him and his body appeared withered and puny to him as he bathed. He was in poor spirits the whole of that day and the next, and perhaps even the day after that. Sometime in between he started to mark days on the calendar to count the number of ones left before his wife would be back. Through the ocean of pall his only islands of joy were her phone calls, and the life-giving coconuts on those islands were her misery at being away from him. But after each call, the old man was again adrift on the ocean upon his narrow raft, growing restless with nothing to do, making plans of some activity or the other but deciding against it in the middle of making it. A couple of times he refused to answer when Sethu called, and then finally called him back only to mumble and groan. In a few days he was sleeping late and waking up late, and the casualty was his morning walk. Then, with absolutely nothing to do, he did pick up a cloth and begin dusting a few of the things he had listed, but now the chore was done with a certain restlessness, in some desperation, like he had to finish with it quickly and get on with something of greater importance. But this restlessness, which manifested as hurry, was such a needless hurry, for he had absolutely nothing to do after he had finished dusting. Sheer purposelessness hit him in the belly and turned into a molten agony there. One evening, he went down to the garage to wash his son's car and ended up washing only the front and back windshields. He tried watching TV, but each time he turned it on it brought such a cloud into his head that he turned it off again.

This is what happens to husbands of super-efficient wives, he smiled wryly. They just don't know what to do when they're on their own.

Even the old songs he listened to made the sorrow outside his mind knock to be let in. Whenever he began something and fretfully stopped it immediately after, a fresh wave of desperation hit him, a sense of doom that threatened to bring his world crashing down. Saroja Teacher often detected his clammy ill temper in his voice, and she always comforted him by telling him that she was sad, too.

Radha did not bother him for a few days, seeing that he was past the stage of being irritable and had crossed over to a constant, mild misery. But she did have her needs, and after some days, she told him that Saroja chechi had called her and she had told her all was well here so far, and she was only reminding him that it was time for her enterprising little daughter to get her books. She also asked him why he hadn't invited his friend over again after that evening, so she could cook them some snacks. When she began naming the snacks she could make them, he cut her short and went out with his mobile phone on to the balcony.

'Sethu,' he said into the phone, incautiously loud, 'I mentioned that money to you? Yes, the five thousand? Yeah, this evening is great. And…something premium. Better than last time. Okay, okay.'

At the end of the call, he joked: 'And don't bring a duplicate Teacher's. The original one makes me suffer enough.' There was an underlying sway in that weak joke which neither of them would acknowledge; it signified that the old man had given up on a certain decision he had made earlier and was now on Sethu's side and not quite on his wife's side. He had now reached a place from where he could join Sethu in cracking one at his wife's expense. The Devil had won, and they would be drinking to him that evening.

Immediately after the call, the old man told himself that he had been too impulsive and stupid. In the first place, he should have asked Teacher for the ATM pin and withdrawn the money and given it to Radha. After all, he knew, every year Teacher did give something for the maid's daughter. Maybe not the entire amount—which the clever Radha was now extorting—but she did contribute, he was aware. So why ask for Sethu's help in this?

But then, he felt nothing short of exhilaration when he thought of the evening. It was amazing how dramatically his mood improved right after that call. He told himself that he wouldn't overdo it like last time. I shall drink slowly, enjoying each sip, engaging in topics with my old friend and munching good, nourishing snacks. Yet, towards noon, his heart bobbed around like it wanted to fly out of him, and his movements were jerky and fretful. In a moment of genius, he actually called up Radha to ask if she would be good enough to stay a little late during her evening round today to make them those snacks she was talking about. 'Sethu is also bringing your five thousand.'

Of course, he was very aware that after the last drink and all that puking he had vowed to himself never to indulge again, but when had he ever blinked while breaking a vow? He remembered how Teacher had once said, not entirely pleasantly:

'You could do anything at all and convince me it is right. You could—you could go out with another woman and make me agree it was absolutely fine. And the wonderful thing is, there will be some truth to what you say, in the excuse you give. Absolute, undeniable truth. You don't lie. You just discover new truths that cancel the old ones. Is it your gift to talk well and convincingly? I don't know. You just seem to be right all the time. You can convince yourself that just about anything is true and make me feel it too! Even if you are breaking something sacred between us, something we had agreed on and sworn to observe, earlier. Even if you are hurting me deeply. It is so effortless for you to break the agreements between us; you don't even have to consult me before you break them. You can just break them and then tell me why you did it, and like a puppet, I will sit here and understand perfectly. Oh, it's so tiring at times. You see, you never did this

The Greatest Enemy of Rain

or that thing because you believed and we agreed it was vile and untrue and harmful and dishonest to do it, and then one day you went and did it after all, because you had simply discovered another, greater truth! It's like your word to me doesn't matter at all; like I myself don't perhaps matter all that much at all. You know, you could do anything—absolutely anything, even things that are easily known to be vile and wrong—you could do anything and be right about it. How do you do it? You could spend a lifetime with me and yet could surprise me one day.'

Tears rose in his eyes now as he recalled her words and looked at her photograph by the bed. And yet, it wasn't remotely to his conscience that this memory addressed itself: he felt very deeply emotional as he looked at her smiling face, but he had no qualms that he was going to do something that he had sworn to her years ago never to do.

For god's sake, I'm not going to a whorehouse or robbing a bank. I'm just having a drink with my friend. And I can't tell this to you only because you wouldn't understand.

Nothing could convince him now to call off drinking with Sethu. Oh no, that was done and decided. Decided in a moment but decided irrevocably. He was focused on correcting the mistakes of last time. He would eat cheese before beginning to drink, he would keep eating snacks throughout and never gulp his drink, he would drink plenty of water, not forgo dinner however drunk he got...it went on and on. Every preparation, but never a review of his decision to drink.

And by evening, there Sethu was, ceremoniously putting a bag of purchases down to dip his hands into his pocket and take out five thousand rupees. The old man called out to Radha, who came scurrying out of the kitchen where she had been frying something for them, and handed over the money. 'Here's the money for your little girl's textbooks,' he said for his friend's benefit, smiling.

Needless to say, the old man forgot all the plans he had made to drink slowly. Soon, he was gulping down and smoking one glass and one cigarette after another. Radha kept coming out of the kitchen to serve a variety of 'sides', as they called the snacks, all of which only Sethu seemed to be truly relishing. Once the maid even said, 'Acha, you are going to make yourself sick.' But he only laughed at her and when she returned to the kitchen he looked at Sethu. 'You're nearing seventy,' he said, squeaking to mimic his wife. 'You need to be responsible for your own health. Earlier when you went wild you regretted it only after years. Now you abuse your body, you regret it the next moment.'

Sethu laughed loudly.

There came many more jokes about Teacher then, with the old man narrating how much she feared a drunk husband. 'She had a bitter childhood experience with a drunkard uncle,' he explained. 'The man used to sell her books and clothes for money. She projects that memory on to poor old me when I'm just a little tipsy.'

In the spirit of companionship, Sethu supplied a stash of universal jokes on wives and how their husbands got tied to their petticoat strings. But whenever he spoke lightly of Teacher herself, the old man winced inside, smiling outwardly but changing the topic in haste. There was something raw and almost primitive about his friend, and the moment his wife was mentioned in a tone that threatened to become indelicate, he felt something akin to fear and immediately regretted permitting the conversation to turn that way.

After a while Radha stood by the door watching them, and it was perhaps to show her or maybe with genuine concern that

Sethu started to caution the old man: 'Drink slowly, smartoo. You're just gulping it down.'

Smartoo! Sethu used to call him that decades ago, during their early years, after they had both started their first jobs at the same place.

Once the old man had gotten a little bit drunk, his reflexes slowed. Bits of skin peeled off from his lips, especially when he was laughing aloud, and a tiny white thread formed on his lips. This happened all the time but he always successfully hid it, which he was unable to do now. He knew the peeling was because he overused toothpaste.

'There's skin peeling off your mouth,' Sethu said. 'It means you're deficient in certain vitamins.'

'Oh, no, no,' the old man said, 'it's because I brush too much, with too much of—'

'Nonsense, Smartoo,' said Sethu. 'Believe me, we all brush our teeth. This is not that. You should be concerned. I'll have a talk with Teacher....'

With the confidence of a man who was a loner and had taken care of himself for many years, his friend began to tell him about vitamin deficiency and even put down the names of certain medicines on a small writing pad on the coffee table.

For a while it was all fun, with Radha feeding Sethu all the pakoras and fries he could eat. Then it grew dark, and behind the maid's back Sethu indicated to his friend to send her home. When the old man told her she said, 'Oh, I can stick around for some more time, Acha. If you will need anything else. No problem.' She was happy and thankful for the money.

She was back in the kitchen when Sethu said, not exactly whispering: 'She wants to stick around. All right. Maybe if she stuck around the whole night, we could have a roll!'

The old man was stunned! Did Sethu mean what the old man thought he meant? How crass and vulgar! Radha was as young as Sethu's daughter would have been, had he had one. He said nothing, but then from there the little party went downhill for him. He wasn't listening as Sethu went on talking about real estate prices or something. Instead, he was thinking of how far the two of them had grown apart. He was well aware that by their previous standards, a joke such as this one was quite permissible. In fact, there was hardly anything they couldn't tell each other, hardly a topic too sacred to be discussed, hardly a joke they couldn't crack to one another, hardly a person exempted from being targets of their humour and boorishness. But that was decades ago. Sethu had not moved an inch from there, while he had come a long way. From a bachelor, he had come to a husband, then a father, and he would soon be a grandfather—while his friend loitered around the places of his youth, even as his false teeth threatened to fall off.

Or perhaps Sethu had grown up too, and it was only that today, with the alcohol and with Saroja Teacher away, Sethu had slipped back into the past. But in his heart the old man knew that wasn't the case. Sethu always had a coarse side; a side still rough because of his solitude. Discovering that side now was like going down a cave he always knew existed behind a familiar bush.

This wouldn't end well if he let things go on like this. He stood up, stretched, and acting casual, walked over to the kitchen. 'You can leave now, Radha,' he told her firmly. 'We won't be needing anything more.'

He was glad when she left the house smiling, because then he was sure she hadn't heard Sethu's lurid comment. He did not know what he would do if she had. He feared Sethu the way a man in a glass house might fear an urchin who held a stone in

The Greatest Enemy of Rain

his hand. Sethu had nothing to lose! Why, as soon as he had shut the door behind the maid, the man pushed things further: 'Little girl's textbooks, eh? Come on now, Smartoo, what was the five thousand really for?'

'Grow up, Sethu,' the old man retorted. 'And stop calling me Smartoo.'

'Oh, you're angry,' Sethu said, and then fortunately he began to go on again on vitamin deficiencies and real estate prices.

They had finished well near half the bottle when Sethu suddenly remarked: 'Hey, do you remember the pappadoms?'

'Pappadoms?'

'Yes, pappadoms. The porn CDs Sandeep used to distribute. We used to call them pappadoms.'

They laughed heartily at that. This wasn't all that many years ago. It was nearer their retirement, in fact, when a younger man by the name of Sandeep would bring, in a little cloth bag, a set of compact discs with low quality pornography. People rented these from him; the colloquial ones were the cheapest. Then came the American ones, the Russian ones, and the real luxury were the Latin American ones. Indeed, some of the CDs were of such bad quality that you could see nothing on them, but Sandeep did not have a refund policy. They spoke about the fat girl Leena who, they knew, also rented the CDs secretly from him. The old man and Sethu had a bit of an argument about who Leena was, exactly. The old man said she was the branch head's secretary, but Sethu said she was the receptionist.

And then, all of a sudden, Sethu sat back and closed his eyes. When he opened them again, there was a new light in them.

'A little younger,' he said, 'and we might have gone to a massage parlour. You know, the kind where female masseurs relieve gentlemen customers off their aches.'

'What,' said the old man. 'These types of parlours run in our city?'

'City?' laughed Sethu. 'You'll find them a couple of lanes away if you really look. The kind of massages that end in happiness.'

'Hmm,' the old man said thoughtfully. 'Yes, if we were a little younger. Yes.'

'And a little less scared,' said Sethu, looking at the old man.

Scared! Men who never married have no way of understanding, the old man thought. They'll always mistake the delicate compliance of marriage for the stoop of fear. Men who never married will not understand how hardness needing softness to lean on is a beautiful thing. They only know relationships at work and office, where every demand is a challenge, a taunt. Poor souls! They won't even observe and introspect enough to know, for their happiness depends a lot on painting their solitude as freedom.

He stood up, went over to the toilet, returned, and stretched. 'Sethu, if you don't mind, I would like to call it a day.'

'What? Already?'

'I—I'm a little tired.'

'Are you alright, Smar—' Then he looked at his old friend closely. 'Or is it something I said?'

'No, no,' the old man said. 'I haven't been sleeping well. That's all.' But then he saw that his friend was a little taken aback, and something surged into his mind. 'And as for what you said… well, Sethu, you do need to grow up. No one should remain stuck where they were thirty years ago. Some of your comments are crass and unbecoming of your age.' He felt better after saying this.

Sethu stared at him for a bit. Absolutely crestfallen, he stood up. 'Man, how much you have changed,' he said under his breath.

The Greatest Enemy of Rain

He staggered a little to find his balance. Then he leaned forward and picked up his spectacles. Instantly, the old man felt sorry for him.

'Hey, but your comments are not why I'm calling it a day,' the old man hurried. 'I—I genuinely am tired....'

'It's all right, Smartoo,' Sethu said, and a hint of a smile played on his eager, fun-loving face. 'I understand. Okay, you take rest. I'll call you later.'

He was turning to go when the old man picked up the bottle and extended it, saying, 'And take this with you. I won't be needing it here.'

There's no saying why that particular gesture—the old man extending the bottle of remaining liquor at him—changed a sad Sethu into an angry Sethu. 'Of course,' he hissed, suddenly not looking so beaten any more, 'sure, you can't even have a bit of liquor at home. It would be evidence. All I can say is, a man is born with an identity. Some men lose it when they marry and have a family. Sad!'

The old man said nothing in answer to that.

'When you say some things, they're just jokes,' Sethu persisted. 'When I say the same things, I am being crass. I'm not being my age.'

The old man still said nothing. He just watched sadly as his friend lifted the seat of his scooter, placed the bottle inside, locked the seat back on, and pumped the kickstand, huffing, 'The teacher has taught you well.'

That last one stung but the old man held his tongue. He laughed out loud when he saw that his friend was still muttering and cursing as he drove away on his scooter.

But lying on his bed, he felt more miserable than he perhaps had ever felt before. The unfinished party hadn't got him completely drunk, leaving him with a headache too mild to justify popping a pill. The unpleasant ending and the prospect of a sulking Sethu left a tiring ache in his heart. But it wasn't just that at all. It wasn't all that that made him so irreparably miserable.

He looked at the calendar. His wife would come back in just a few days. And yet, that did not provide him the relief and joy it should have. Whoever the god that was sitting up there and deciding his life for him, it was a sick old god; one with grey hair and skin disease and false teeth and a peeling mouth. A dubious god. His god had no idea how to bring his weakly happy, plain, and dismally satisfying life to a nice close. His wife would be back, and then? Living happily ever after had always been the cruelly mocking ending of fairy tales.

He smiled mirthlessly at Teacher's photo at the bedside table as he thought of the countless times they had had the conversation about who would go first. 'If I die first, I hate to think of what you will do,' she would often say. 'Why, you can't even find fresh underwear after your bath!' And he would reply that when you have found a wife as resourceful as Teacher, you don't just go first and leave her be. 'I'm not finished with you yet. I'll bury you and then open a bottle of Johnnie Walker.' During rare sentimental moments he had told her that he couldn't bear the thought of her alone in their son's house in Denmark or with her brother's family. They would take care of her in a drab, dutiful way like a job you did only to emerge blameless. 'After you,' he had volunteered.

'It's not in our hands,' she would conclude serenely.

It now seemed he had feared for a long time, even months before the day she was set to go on her trip, that these thoughts would plague him once he was alone. He would try to hold them

The Greatest Enemy of Rain

away but they would, in the end, barge into his head. And now that he had squabbled with his best friend, misery had begun to feed on its own arms and legs to grow bigger and more grotesque. He switched off the lights and tried to fall asleep.

An outsider would think he was a lucky old man: with a loving wife, an educated, well-employed son who insisted on sending him money every month, a nice warm pension, no particularly serious diseases (except a bit of blood pressure his doctor absolutely insisted he had). Not a single challenge in his evening years. But if he was really lucky, why did he feel miserable? After Teacher comes back, then what? At least if the end of the road was like a destination reached; with some lit lamps, a little dance and song, some goodies, some glory…. He twisted and turned on his bed, thinking that this way of summarizing things had always made him feel bad. Yet, he sometimes couldn't resist doing this.

'After Teacher is back, then what? Like in the fairy tales, will you live happily together forever and ever?'

'Am I lucky or is Sethu lucky?'

'Will I die first or will Teacher, after all? And which would be slightly more bearable?'

'Is everyone's life like this or is it just mine?'

Everyone's life is like this, he chuckled into the dark. At least all middle-class men were like him. Most of their lives are spent preparing for old age. After college, they rush to get a government job. Why? Not because it is interesting or challenging. Government jobs offer 'security' and…bingo! A pension at old age. He thought, I know those that marry early and have a child in a hurry so that the child is employed and earning before the parents retire, can you beat that? Ha haha! A lifetime is spent in preparation for old age, like it is some great occasion. Like it is the supreme goal of life, the ultimate destination—grand old age.

I did it, now my son is doing it. Son, like me, you too do not have a government job. So, wake up; you need to start saving today if you want to keep enough aside for your old age. Join pension schemes, son, invest in mutual funds, take an interest in the stock market figures. Take shit at work because you cannot afford to lose your job. Take shit from your managers. Buy a scooter, not a car. Buy a small car, not an SUV. Be dead now, a zombie, so you can be alive when you are old. Go slog in a foreign land because you have the future to save for!

This, this, this is that time of my life, my old age, for which I accumulated, kept aside, saved up for decades. This eventless, unceremonious, boring charade that was the ultimate Mecca I was aiming for. Heeheehee!

The next morning, he did not even bother to get up. From bed, he called Radha and told her he would be out the whole day, so she could take the day off. 'Go and buy your daughter those textbooks.'

He fingered his phone, wondering if he should call Sethu and make up for the previous night. He probably should, but then he felt if his friend said something nasty, he would probably bark right back and that wouldn't be good. Besides, he still felt an irrational resentment for Sethu and his type.

Teacher called around ten. His head pounding now, he only picked the call after it had rung several times.

'Were you in the bathroom?'

'Yes,' he lied.

'How are you? Are you being good?'

'Extremely.'

'And don't chew poor Radha's head. I'll be back in just a few days.'

'Did she say I was chewing her head?'

Teacher sensed the weather between his ears was particularly bad. She began telling him about how glorious some of the places were, how funny people everywhere are, but about how she felt all alone despite all of that. 'You know, I just want to come back home. Never thought I would be this homesick.'

The old man did not comfort his wife. He did not tell her to enjoy her present or scold her for forgoing champagne during dinner. It almost broke his heart to realize that he was in fact waiting for the conversation to end. He feared he would pick a fight with her if she kept going on. He hated it now when she spoke about how she wished to just come back home. Why was she treating him like a child?

After that he stopped marking the dates on the calendar, so he didn't know how many days he spent in total sulking. One of those evenings, Radha told him about how she had got almost all the textbooks except the social studies one, which would be restocked only next week. One morning, the newspaper man came to collect his monthly fees. When the power went out for one hour every evening, he preferred to not light candles. Sometimes, he opened Teacher's section of the almirah in which they kept their clean clothes and took a deep whiff. What he really got was the smell of mothballs more than anything, but he fancied that he discerned his wife's scent. He wondered at how different she was from him.

That feminine whiff he had always gotten when he smelled her neatly folded clothes told him that never, perhaps ever, had he seen her in a terribly low mood, such as the one he was riding now. Teacher had a more 'positive' outlook on her life. Always calm, she never went into extremes in her action and her temperament. In spite of living in the midst of serious literature, she had always kept humour and never took herself too seriously. Thoughts about the inherent agony of the human condition or the lack of choice in life or some weighty murk like that were not for her. Which was not to say she was shallow. She was very interested in people and their ways of thinking and politics and philosophy. She engaged in arguments with him with gusto. She empathized with suffering when she looked around her or read the newspaper. But when it was time to make dinner, she was always herself again as she went about her business. Her disposition was such that nothing could ever suck her into the dark interiors of the mind. No development in the world could make her slip off her path and plunge her into itself. In fact, when he was brooding, she always attempted to help him feel the light. Now, if she had been around and had known the latest turn of events, the smell of her clothes told him, she would have asked him to call Sethu and make up with him. Yes, most definitely, that would be the one thing she would have asked of him.

So, the next morning—just two days from when Teacher would be home—the old man called up his friend from his balcony.

'How are you,' he asked as his friend cleared his throat.

'After you drove me out of your house,' said Sethu dramatically, 'I did feel rather miserable....'

'I did not drive you out. I was tired, like I said.'

'Ha haha. Relax, old man,' Sethu said. 'I'm joking. It's fine. We all have our lows.'

And then Sethu suggested that he come over one more time before 'the good lady' was back so they could bring the abrupt ending of last time to a happier closure.

'But let's not drink,' the old man said in a hurry.

'No, let's not,' agreed his friend. 'Maybe we'll go out

somewhere. Get some air. Maybe we'll watch a movie. Do something banned.'

'No, let's stick to what's legal,' the old man laughed.

This time when Sethu came he seemed to be in a great hurry. He went through the reconciliation quickly, giving the old man a hug (which, as far as the old man could remember, Sethu had never done before), nodding formally at Radha who asked them if they needed snacks, and then asked if his friend had started taking those vitamin tablets he had suggested, though it seemed he wasn't particularly interested in the answer. Then he said, almost breathlessly, 'So come now. Let's go out. We can take my scooter.'

'But, but, sit down,' said the old man. 'Let's have chai. And where do you want to go?'

'Oh, let's just loiter. We'll check out the movies. Maybe eat some chaat. We only have another day.'

So, after their tea the old man told Radha to lock the home up and keep the keys under the flowerpot by the door. Then they were on the scooter, evading the barrage of a younger world returning from work on their vehicles as the city threw up its final cacophony for the day. Sethu stopped for a smoke. He seemed very friendly with the tobacconist who was perpetually chewing paan himself, and the old man was surprised when he soon discovered the two were actually meeting for the first time then. Sethu asked the man about the movies playing at nearby theatres, but again he did not seem particularly interested in the answer.

After the smoke they got on the scooter again. Through his helmet Sethu asked the old man if they should get something to eat, and they whiled away more time eating chaat from a roadside vendor.

I am not even feeling squeamish today, the old man thought. Look at the dirt under the fingernails of the guy making these golgappas. Yuck! And I am eating them. It's as though I have finally gone back to how I was thirty years ago, before I turned 'clean'. Why, in my present state of mind, I might only wash my face and feet when I'm back home, instead of my usual Dettol bath after a trip like this!

Perhaps, if Sethu had suggested a drink at a nice pub, with loud music and young people dancing, the old man might have agreed, particularly considering Teacher would be back soon, and also because his mood was now not just lifting; he was positively happy.

But perhaps it was fortunate that Sethu did not suggest any such thing. It seemed for today he was more interested in a 'naughty' movie, as he called it: that would be the typical English film that confused love with sex and threw steamy scenes where men and women seemed to suddenly lose control and fling themselves at each other in a way that never happened in real life. The old man was quite fine with such a film. He supposed he was just a little too old for his heart to start beating faster now at the prospect of such scenes, but he was yet not too old to be amused by them.

The two friends decided to watch a 'steamy' film in a theatre comfortably far from home. It would be a good ending to the days without Teacher, and it would make fond memories for later. Sethu found a newspaper vendor, bought a daily, and they began pouring through the cinema section. They selected a movie that had a name suggesting both extreme action and sudden passion, a kind of pun that could only be the output of a sleazy but clever mind. The only trouble was, the film didn't begin until a good two hours later and the old men had run out

The Greatest Enemy of Rain

of ideas about what to do if they weren't drinking.

'Let's go,' Sethu said suddenly, starting his scooter. 'I'll take you to a street you wouldn't have been on before. And I'll take the long way, so we'll while away some time too.'

It was beginning to get dark. Sethu manoeuvred through cramped streets where cows and humans brushed against each other to avoid manholes and open drains. Honks, yells, moos, and barks intertwined. Streetlights were yet to grace this part of the world, it seemed. People spat as the scooter went past and the old man again marvelled that he yet wasn't feeling the compulsion to run to his clean bathroom and scrub himself with Dettol.

'Presenting Curzon Street,' Sethu announced, turning back, as they slid on to a wider street that suddenly had fewer people on it. 'You find all kinds of whores here: transgenders to gays to the economy class to super-luxury escorts to college students looking for pocket money.'

It wasn't that the old man was completely unaware of the existence of such streets and sex workers, as his friend seemed to think. But he let Sethu play the guide here. It was fun. In a moment, however, the old man learned that Sethu was probably a regular here, going by his knowledge of the place. Sethu, discerning what his friend was thinking, said hurriedly, 'Hey, now don't get ideas into your head. I just know this place. It's not like I—'

'Ha! I said nothing.'

They really were in their younger days now as they felt the cold wind against their faces, as they looked at the side of the street where prostitutes of all colours and promises merged with the darkness. On one side there were men dressed like women, on the other it was the other way around. In this corner were girls young enough to be going to school, and in that were women old enough to have school-going daughters had they been living a more mainstream life. But it wasn't as though the sidewalk was full of them. There were plenty, but they were hidden in the darkness. You could just about make them out; they stood and swayed in dimly lit places; you could see them and judge their class and kind if you were a regular.

'Do you know, there are women here who'll offer you a day of married life for a decent fee?'

'Married life? That's new to me,' the old man said, genuinely curious. 'How so?'

'Oh, they are not for sudden or perverted sex,' Sethu said. 'They come home—or wherever—with you. They spend the day with you. They cook for you, eat with you, come to the cinema with you. You can even buy them a saree or a churidar if you're happy, and they'll kiss you for it. Just like marriage.'

'Amazing.'

'Yes. You can make them out by their attire, like you can with all whores. They wear traditional clothes and always have red and white flowers—lilies are a must—in their hair. Their noses are pierced and sometimes their palms are adorned with mehndi.' Then he added quickly: 'At least, that's what I've heard.'

'Amazing,' the old man repeated.

'Truly. From their outfit they look like housewives, but yet there's a touch of gaudiness here or there, just enough to solicit business. Some of them look like brides. Wait, let me see if I can find you one.'

'Oh, I'm fine, really,' the old man laughed. But he was enjoying this ride immensely.

'Then there's the tough whore,' Sethu said. 'This one charges significantly more because you can beat her, put out cigarette butts on her, tie her up, abuse her parents. If you want, she will cry. If you want, you can cry, and she will taunt you all night with dirty expletives.'

'Okay. Okay.'

'It's like the pappadoms, these whores,' Sethu continued. 'There are all categories, and they have dress codes, so their customers know. The lovey-dovey types who spend a day or more if you need; the quick ones if you're the slam-bam-thank you-ma'am kind; the experimental types who, for some extra cash, will let you do just about anything; the very young ones and the experienced….'

'Hmm. God!' the old man said. He knew there were all types of whores on Curzon Street, but his mind hadn't been on such topics for decades. He felt good.

They continued down the lane slowly, moving the way people do in a zoo. Sethu wasn't successful in showing his friend the one-day-of-married-life variety of prostitute, but he pointed out most of the others. The old man was pained when he saw how young some of them were. Many seemed doped or drunk. A few spat on the ground in front of them when they passed without engaging their services. In a few spots, cars and bikes stalled where men in the shadows stood to negotiate and fix deals.

Sethu stopped the scooter at a corner. The old man tensed and muttered an inaudible question.

'Oh, just a second,' said Sethu, walking over to the side of the road towards the yellow wall that lined it, mumbling: 'Just want to show you my favourite sport.'

The old man, standing by the scooter uncomfortably, saw that three youngish prostitutes were watching them from the shadow of a closed tobacco kiosk. Sethu chuckled in their direction and walked up to the wall. Dim light from a shop further away illuminated his movements. The old man's hair stood on end when he realized that his friend was fishing inside his pants. Sethu turned a little away from the direction of the whores and began urinating on the wall. In the light the women—and the old man—saw him draw a crude heart shape on the wall with his piss. The women began to hoot and sway. They giggled loudly and blew kisses in Sethu's direction.

But the little joke came to a very rude end. Out of nowhere there was the sudden blare of lights and a jeep appeared. The sound of men yelling, brakes, a sharp honk. Before the old man knew what was happening, Sethu was shouting for him to take the scooter off its stand and start it pronto. The prostitutes disappeared like vampires at dawn. Two policemen jumped off the jeep, which momentarily blared its sirens for effect. Call it comedy or tragedy, it so happened that for all his desire to just get out of there, Sethu couldn't stop urinating. In one thick stream his pee continued to fall, refusing to act to the situation, the heart sign distorting like a rubber mask on fire. The swearing cops had to actually wait for him to finish!

In the meantime, the old man had fretted so much that he did something even worse. He took the scooter off its stand and reflexively jumped on to the back where he had been riding pillion a moment ago. He fell down in a heap and felt a sharp pain at his shin where the scooter fell on him. The cop nearer to him made no move to help him. Down on the tarmac his phone began to ring and he cut the call from Teacher. But that ringing prompted him to wiggle from under the machine and stand up with a limp.

'Out for a night of fun, grandpas?' said one of the policemen as Sethu finally turned, adjusting his zipper.

'W-we were going for a m-movie,' said the old man, sweating in his bid to muster dignity.

'That's right, officer,' said Sethu. His voice was gruff, as though he had been in the same situation many times before. 'We were going for a movie and I stopped for a leak.' This wasn't the man who had, only seconds ago, yelled for his friend to start the scooter so they could flee.

'Which movie?' the second cop barked.

Sethu and the old man looked at each other. It wouldn't be smart to mention the sleazy name of that stupid movie at a time like this. 'W-we haven't decided yet,' the old man spat out.

'Oh,' said the policeman. 'Why don't we all go over to the station and discuss which movie? Our sub-inspector loves discussing movies.'

'Officer, this is a mistake,' said Sethu even as he was bundled into the jeep after his friend.

'SI sir also loves correcting mistakes,' the cop muttered, yelling for his companion to follow them in the men's scooter, as Sethu reluctantly handed the keys over.

'Officer, what have we done?' Sethu asked, his voice still totally confident. 'What crime have we committed?'

'A blind man could see that you were engaging prostitutes,' said the cop, raising his voice a bit and starting the jeep. 'You were buying a whore or you had finished with one. Let's take you in and get it out of you. Aren't you rather old for this, dear sirs? Don't you have any shame? You look like you are from respectable families. Do your wives and your children know you would be pissing at prostitutes on Curzon Street? Shall we inform them?'

Then Sethu leaned forward and began trying to bribe the cop. It was all extremely distasteful to the old man.

'Later, later,' the policeman said. 'Keep your mouth shut for now. Open it when the SI tells you to.'

And so, a little over an hour to midnight, the two friends were in a police jeep, riding towards the police station on the charge, as the policeman delightedly explained, of engaging sex workers, urinating in a public place, and riding without helmets. Quietly, the old man checked his phone and saw three missed calls from his wife. He WhatsApped her saying he was at the cinema with Sethu and would call in the morning. He hoped she would see the message, for he knew that if she didn't, she would be uneasy that he hadn't answered her calls.

Fifteen minutes later, they drove through the rusted police station gates, loudly crushing a lot of snails on the front porch. The old man got out and wearily looked at the dead snails, all reduced to slime. There were abandoned bicycles, scooters, a car, and two vans on one side of the compound. The place smelt of feverish sweat, and the old man felt sick.

The SI was a surprisingly gentle soul. He was rather short. Perhaps he had an uncle in the department, or he wouldn't have made it in with his physique.

'So, what were you doing there then, according to your version?' he asked Sethu, a gleam of amusement in his eyes.

'We told you,' Sethu said. 'I mean, we told this gentleman here. We were off for a movie and I just felt the urge to urinate.'

'There were three girls accompanying him, sir,' the constable who had brought them contributed. 'He was showing them how pissing is done.'

'Yeeeesh,' said the SI, covering his ears. Apparently, disgraceful details pained him.

'He was also drawing some message on the wall with his piss,' said the second cop. 'We couldn't see what.'

The sub-inspector listened without taking his eyes off Sethu. Then he turned to the old man.

'And you? Were you just an innocent friend caught at the wrong time in the wrong place?'

'He tried to flee with the scooter,' said the constable.

'My dear daddy,' the SI said with genuine kindness. 'Is it your age to be running from the police? You even seem to be injured. Why, you can't even stand straight. Sprained your leg?'

The man began counselling them in his gentlest voice. He told them that of the many men they caught in various stages of degradation at Curzon Street, an abysmal percentage was old. He wondered what makes a man who was at the age when he should be loving, compassionate, and spiritual plunge to such lows. Suddenly, he asked them their names, addresses, where they had worked, and other details, which the constable immediately took down in the dirtiest notebook the old man had ever seen. Then, resuming the sermon, the Sub-Inspector tried to make them see how much their wives would be pained to know where they had been. How much would their children be ashamed. How badly their neighbours would gossip when they knew. The women in their locality would be careful of them afterwards, and they would tell their daughters to be careful too. 'Dirty old men' would be their tag. How perfectly disgraceful, how devoid of beauty that life would be.

'Dear officer,' Sethu said, emboldened that the SI was so civil. 'Do we look like people who visit whores? Do we look that low to you? We were just—'

'AND DO I LOOK LIKE AN IDIOT TO YOU?' the SI thundered, and the rats that had been fidgeting behind the ancient files in the almirahs went silent. Far in the annals of that rotten place, some thug who had been sleeping behind bars woke up and swore. The SI fought to control himself. 'If you were absolutely in the clear, why did you try to run?'

The SI turned and strode into his office, unable to regain control of himself. In a practiced charade, the constable then took over the sermon, continuing with how they had just indulged in an act the consequences of which they hadn't thought about before giving in to their impulse. He told them the police was here only to help and not to harass anyone, and that the SI was also a perfect gentleman who had only lost his cool because they were not admitting to their fault. He said they shouldn't give up hope just yet and he would make the SI forgive them if only they settled the matter and promised never to indulge in such acts again.

'Don't let thing go out of hand,' he said maturely. 'And never get into this kind of trouble again.'

The helpful constable brokered a deal for ten thousand rupees, which Sethu's incessant moaning and groaning brought down to eight thousand.

It was once they were out and on the scooter, crushing fresh snails and heading out the gates to find and ATM, with a cop following them, that the old man felt the pain in his shin. He felt the spot with his hand and realized it was swollen. After they had paid off the cop and refused his offer to be escorted back home, Sethu turned around on the scooter to say, 'You now owe me nine thousand. Four plus—'

'Shut up and drive,' the old man said, letting out a sigh of relief.

Then Sethu started laughing. Into the night he guffawed, not saying a word, slowing the scooter and rocking it in his uncontrollable glee. The old man sat in miserable silence and that made Sethu guffaw more. He could only stop when they broke the journey at a twenty-four-hour clinic, where the old man had to take his pants off for dressing his blue bruise. He also got two injections, at which time Sethu pulled the curtain across

The Greatest Enemy of Rain

his mouth to giggle, much to the chagrin of a young nurse.

Back home at last, Sethu watched his friend limp off the scooter. Succeeding in containing his mirth at last, he remarked, 'But you can't say I bored you when your wife was away, eh?'

'No, I can't,' said the old man, smiling at last. 'I had more excitement than I can digest.'

'Take that tablet she gave for the morning,' said Sethu as he turned the scooter around. 'It's for the pain.'

'Not a word to Teacher.'

'Not a word to Teacher.'

Sethu said goodnight and rode away, yelling that their adventures had now come to a close, and he was returning Smartoo to his wife almost as good as he had found him, if you could ignore a small bruise on the leg.

The old man spent the night in restless dreams, many of which he would recall for months afterwards and smile. He dreamt of Teacher coming back from her vacation and being somewhat indifferent to him. She loved him less, or perhaps she had trouble recognizing him at all. He dreamt of Sethu being pulled away by policemen while he was still pissing. He also dreamt that his leg ached, and in the dream he woke up and moved aside the blanket to discover the leg gone.

And a day before Saroja Teacher was to return, the old man acted a little too gleeful for the benefit of Radha, who was not to discover that his leg was bruised. The pain medication made him sleepy, which made him a tad slow, and he overacted. He put on a peppy Mohammed Rafi number and sat on the sofa, smiling at nothing.

'Aha,' cried Radha. 'Acha is thrilled that his sweetheart is coming tomorrow!'

When Teacher called he told her that the previous evening,

right after Radha had left, he and Sethu had set off to see a nice action movie. He couldn't take her call because he was in the theatre. He felt an empty, sugary happiness when she mumbled that she had thought, when he didn't answer, that he had learned to live without her. 'I thought you had found a girlfriend,' she joked. And then she told him how tired she was from the trip and how she wished to come back and snuggle on her own bed.

'I never thought I will dream so much about coming home,' she said.

Later, Sethu called to enquire after his leg, disturbing a much-needed siesta. 'How's that leg, Smartoo? Is the mark of our adventure a little less blue?'

'It's almost gone,' the old man replied. 'Slight ache at times, but all right.'

'Awesome,' Sethu said. 'You let me know when Teacher goes away to America. We aren't done with Curzon Street.'

All through the afternoon and evening the old man was very excited, tired but excited, and he did not know if it was a happy or a sad excitement. He knew it was on account of his wife coming back, but he couldn't place his feelings at all. His heart was thudding violently as he set about checking the house, putting things back in their places, though Radha had done a very good job of maintaining the home. He took the garbage out because he knew that Teacher would otherwise have to do it as soon as she reached. He searched under the front-room furniture, inside the refrigerator, behind the television and a hoard of other places, but he couldn't be a hundred per cent certain he hadn't left a cigarette butt or a bottle cap for his wife to find. He knew that the world wouldn't come crashing down even if she found something, but it was with boyish thoroughness that he searched to wipe out evidence, nonetheless. Perhaps he was only fidgeting, he thought. He was only intensely restless, and this is what restless old men were like.

Teacher was on a direct flight this time, and for the hours that they flew, the old man was mad with apprehension. He paced the front room, drank cold water, wondered if he should go out and try to find a cigarette shop that would be open. He fretted that the plane would crash somewhere on some mountain and Teacher would be dead. He watched television for some time, but he couldn't concentrate. Music quickly became unbearable. He called her to check if the flight was delayed, but her phone was switched off, and that intensified his sense of doom. He called Sethu and then hurriedly cut the call when the overhead clock told him it was two in the morning. He cut a fruit and then threw it in the dustbin, deciding to drink some more cold water instead. For a moment, he needed alcohol so badly that he almost picked up the phone again to call Sethu.

Then, the old man did something he very rarely did. He prayed. As far as he could remember, the last time he had prayed was when his wife was in the labour room delivering his son, and he had similarly worried himself sick that she might die. There was nothing to indicate such a possibility, the doctor had said it would be a normal delivery, but he had this very strong hunch that it would end in tragedy. In those moments, he remembered, he had hated their decision to have a baby, hated their mothers who had coaxed them to have one. Now he remembered praying at that time that if God had to take someone, He might consider taking the newborn and leave his Saroja Teacher to live. That was the last time, and if he had ever prayed after that he couldn't recall it now. He had never classified himself as a believer or disbeliever, but he simply did not, under normal circumstances, feel the need to clasp his hands together, shut his eyes, and fill his mind with an entity that had never once offered him proof of its existence. But today, after pacing his room for the better part of the night, it was his restlessness, the agony of his wait, that made him pray. He went over to the puja room that Teacher maintained, and sat down before the numerous gods. He hadn't once lit the lamps here as Teacher would have loved him to do in her absence. She had once told him that it was his disability that he couldn't draw comfort from prayer, even especially as he grew old.

He prayed for a while, panting like a man coming out of water for air. And yet, all the time he wondered how people drew comfort from looking at pictures (in two different pictures the same god was drawn differently, indicating history's biggest fraud) while he felt nothing at all. After trying for a bit longer, he decided to do something more meaningful. He switched on the computer and googled the airline's number.

A voice inspired by birdsong wished him good evening and asked him how he wished to be helped.

'I—I'm just enquiring after a flight,' and he offered his wife's flight details. 'I just wish to know if...the flight is on time.'

The bird put him on hold only for a moment and then told him that the flight was on time.

'Is it a normal flight?' the old man asked. 'I mean, is everything...er, as usual?'

'Sir?'

'You are keeping track of the flight, right?'

'I am not able to comprehend your question, sir,' she sang.

'What I mean is, do you only know that the plane took off on time, or are you keeping track of it while it is flying?'

'Sir,' she said, and the sweetness of her voice slipped a bit. 'Are you worried about something? Where are you calling from?'

'Never mind that,' the old man almost shouted. 'Is it a normal bloody flight? Are you keeping track?'

'I-I'll put you to my superior. Please hold, sir.'

The old man cut the call in a hurry. He placed the phone in front of him, dreading a callback, muttering 'I'm mad, I'm mad,' and giggling a little. Luckily, the airline took him for a crank and did not call back.

The next morning, when his brother-in-law's car pulled in with Saroja Teacher smiling through the windshield, he could only smile back weakly. He knew he had dark circles around his eyes, though he hadn't looked in the mirror. Teacher briefly touched his forearm, remarking, 'You look older. What were you doing here while I was away?' And then she invited her brother inside for coffee.

Suddenly, his routine, comfortably boring, eternal world was back in place, as they sat around the small dining table sipping Teacher's strong coffee. His brother-in-law spoke continuously, at first joking about the things he suspected the old man had been up to while the wife was away—a few of the jokes coming uncomfortably close to what had actually transpired—and then he moved on excitedly to how good the trip had been and what the old man had missed. All through, the old man kept looking at his wife for confirmation that she hadn't equally enjoyed the trip. Her eyes confirmed this, telling him how happy she now was, when she had finally reached his side again.

And then, a little later, as she came out of her bath she found him sleeping like a baby, like he hadn't slept for all the nights she had been away. With a smile she let him sleep. She went over to the balcony where the mobile phone's signal was good but where you wouldn't be overheard. Then she called up her sister-in-law.

'Yeah, he is all right,' she spoke into the phone. 'Limping a little on one foot. Ha, no nothing too bad. Probably banged his shin on the bedside. Trying to hide it, but I'll get it out of him.' She waited, turning around to look through the bay windows fondly at her sleeping husband as her sister-in-law spoke. Then she said: 'No, I told you. There's no point. He hates travelling. He'll have to keep washing his hands and taking his baths. He hates the outdoors, basically. And you know what he says: "I'll come to England and Switzerland and Australia, but not to visit. If ever I go to those places, I won't come back. What's the point of seeing those dustless, spotless places and then coming back to our home? This will only make it feel more like a garbage can." Ha haha. Yeah, that's what. Cranky old man he has become.'

The two women laughed at the respective faults of their husbands.

Saroja Teacher checked to make sure her husband hadn't woken. She lowered her voice and said to her sister-in-law: 'Okay, note this now. I have told him that I haven't enjoyed this trip one bit. Had to lie. No, no, it's not like that. Of course, I loved every bit of it. Wished it would go on forever. Heeheehee! But I can't tell him that. You know how he is. He would sulk if I enjoyed anything without him. So, make sure you don't go around telling him how I loved the Alps or the evening we spent dancing on that ship.'

After agreeing on an Africa tour sometime next year, Saroja Teacher ended the call. She went in and woke her husband for breakfast, remarking with a smile that seeing him sleep, one would think he was the one who had just returned from a long trip.

4

SHRAVAN KUMAR'S LAST DAY

On his last day Shravan Kumar woke up fidgeting and angry. He was late again. He looked out of the window of his second-floor apartment, breathing in the brittle air. In the distance the mist sat over the dried lakebed like a ghost lingering over a sleeping face. Soon, Shravan Kumar thought, that lakebed will be full of labourers shitting, one behind each shrub, and then he'd have to close the goddam window.

He spat out into his neighbour's backyard, shut the window, and carried himself to the toilet.

While brushing his teeth he exclaimed, 'Shit fuck!', and kicked the plastic bucket. He had again forgotten to buy bread and milk the previous evening. Now, if he was to walk all the way to the store and back, he was sure to be late to office and then Sitaramji would be glad to sit him down and give him a detailed lecture. Sitarmaji was bearable when he was angry. But when he was pleased at the opportunity to lecture someone, you were really done for. The same old dialogues would tumble out: how he sometimes felt he was running a crèche and not a company, how he hadn't reached where he was by being late to work every second day (Sitaramji's exaggerations were vindictive, false, and unimaginative), how he had a constant headache thanks to his indifferent staff. Yes, the famous headaches! Sitaramji was always having one and there was always a strip of pills at his desk. He would complain the headache had been plaguing him since morning and he would do well to just go home and nap if only he could have counted on his staff to handle the work. It was just as well, he would add, that it was only a sinus headache and not a cluster headache, which, some said, was even more terrible than labour pain.

Shravan Kumar decided not to go out and buy bread. He rummaged through the mess in the kitchen for something that would do for breakfast, but he didn't even find the regular rotting apple or banana in the fruit basket. In sheer frustration he picked up the fish feed and threw it on the floor, thinking that if he was one of the goldfish in his aquarium in the front room, he could've eaten this and not worried about Sitaramji either.

But then he had an idea, and despite being late, despite having to close the window because the laborers shat on the lake bed, despite forgetting to buy the milk and bread, and despite Sitaramji, Shravan Kumar grinned.

Soon he was being tossed up and down in the back of an autorickshaw, on his way to office. He was quite on time, and yet the scowl was back on his face. The dahlias by the road smiled at him, and he cursed the government for prioritizing the planting of flowers on the roadside while sitting on their cracks about the potholes. He cursed at drivers in big cars all alone, contributing to the perpetual traffic jams. He spat when the red lights did not change quickly. He shouted expletives at a beggar who had extended his hand into the back of the autorickshaw to force him to give alms. He gritted his teeth when he realized that he had forgotten to buy some chewing gum before getting on the auto, because now the smell of his goldfish breakfast would stay on his breath till noon.

He bit and snarled at his life because he did not know that he only had ten hours of it left.

In office too Shravan Kumar was irritable and snappy. He sent the peon back with his half-empty teacup, elaborating on the differences between tea and puddle water. He silently cursed when a client called to say they had decided on engaging Sitaram & Co., which should have been great news had it not meant extra work for him. Then, around noon, Sitaramji called him to his cabin and he wished he was dead. The man droned on and on, this time out of happiness brought on by the new business deal, telling Shravan Kumar that he meant to rename the company Sitaram & Sons, where 'sons' implied his staff who he always thought of as family. Shravan Kumar thought that the most unbearable Sitaramji was the happy Sitaramji.

While the boss told him how smart all his employees were, which automatically meant he himself was the smartest one to hire them in the first place, Shravan Kumar was thinking about the time he had joined the company. He had decided at the time that he would work in this dump only for six months, not more, that he would then aim for a minimum fifty per cent hike and a jump to a multinational company, that he would move to a bigger apartment, buy a 350 cc bike or even a small car, and tell his mother back home that it was now time for her to look for a classy bride for him. Nothing had gone according to plan. Instead, here he was, listening to this sentimental fool drone on and on.

The new client made Sitaramji so happy that in the evening he made all his employees stay late to celebrate, ordering samosas and chai from the nearby halwai. 'You are my sons and daughters,' he told them, as the most favoured among them danced around him. 'Oh, this excitement will give me a headache!' The man was so happy that when the samosas and chai were finished he invited everyone to come with him to a pub.

God help us all, Sitaramji seems to be growing happier by the minute, thought Shravan Kumar. Everything led the bossman to some violent emotion. The fact is, he belonged to a generation long gone. A generation when feelings made everybody happy. This was why this place will never grow, Shravan Kumar thought. Never become a big, multinational business. For success you need to move on, not stop to sing victory songs at every small milestone.

He excused himself, though Sitaramji had made it clear that if he wished to be among the favoured employees he must come for a drink. He shook hands with his boss, ran downstairs, and got into an auto, uncannily relieved to flee the celebrations.

Half an hour later he got off the autorickshaw, about a kilometre from his apartment. He needed to do some shopping. He planned to buy a pint of rum, some cigarettes, and perhaps some grilled chicken, because he believed in ending a bad day on a fun note. That would make sure his gloom did not carry to the next day. He meant to take full advantage of the business that he had significantly contributed to winning. He meant to compensate for his bad mood today, which had made him forego the office party. He must translate this high into a promotion and a hike in due course, he thought, walking fast.

His last thought before he was hit by a car was that he mustn't forget the bread and the milk again.

It was an ageing Honda, red before it hit him, black after because the impact seemed to push him into a slightly different universe, one that was truer, harsher, more soberly coloured. The shriek of the tyres, like the whinnying of a horse, came from someplace ahead of him. Shravan Kumar was lifted into the air and when he tasted the warm cold tarmac inside his head, the car was in front of him. A red-black film engulfed the new night and the stream of light from the streetlamp ahead was now a red torrent. He saw a fat man stumble out of the car and simultaneously he noticed blood and teeth on the road to the left of his face. The fat man came running towards him.

'O god, o god, o god,' the man wailed. Then he looked at Shravan Kumar, bent down, and whispered into his ear: 'I'm so sorry, so very sorry! Are you hurt? Y-you are hurt. Very hurt.' Shravan Kumar realized that his lips and cheeks were sewn into his mouth, and the area above his eyes was swelling so fast that it loomed red over his new universe in an instant. The driver of the car tried to squat beside him on the road, but the compression of his big tummy caused a massive roar from his underside, and he stood again in a hurry. 'O god, excuse me,' the man muttered, 'I-I need to…Y-you must get to a hospital.'

Shravan Kumar tried to move and discovered that only his eyeballs could move.

The fat man once again made to crouch but clutched his backside and stood up again. He turned around, and still clutching his bottom, he ran back to his car, yelling, 'My tummy, oh, it must be the prawns!' Farting again, he looked back once at his victim and said: 'You're very hurt. O god, I-I need to get someplace before I soil myself. No one saw. You must get to a hospital. Faaaast!' Then the Honda sped down the road.

Shravan Kumar must have briefly passed out, and when he came to, he saw that he was lying nearer the footpath. On the footpath a little away from his feet was a pile of shit, which he could smell. He wondered if the fat man had again stopped the Honda and stepped out while he was unconscious. He found that even his eyeballs hurt when he moved them, and though he could turn his face a little, it hurt like hell when he did. It was a relatively quiet street. After a while a scooter approached and slowed down. From under the precipices that had replaced his brow, Shravan Kumar saw a middle-aged couple. They stopped by his head and the woman screeched. 'Ou, ou, ou!' she yelled, 'S-so much blood....'

'Turn away, plum,' came a man's voice, 'Don't look. You'll faint. You're not used to—'

'Jesus Christ! His face.... Oh! His teeth!' The woman started to cry. Shravan Kumar could see only the end of her saree, one anklet, and a pair of neat sandals. He got the feeling that she was a tidy woman.

'Don't, plum,' the man told her. 'You will not be able to take it. Don't look.' He crouched down and Shravan Kumar saw that he was a kindly man with a sweaty brow. 'You are badly hurt, young man. You need help.'

'H-hospital,' Shravan Kumar managed through the mess that was his mouth. But did he manage to speak, or did his voice only swim about inside his own chest in an ocean of blood? 'H-hosp... ambula....'

There was the sound of the woman retching.

'Oh, oh dear God!' The man stood up in a hurry. 'Rachael, I told you not to look. God!'

The woman vomited compulsively and some of the hot sprinkle landed on Shravan Kumar's arm.

'There, there, breathe deep, plum,' the man said, his voice dripping gentleness. 'You don't have the stomach for this. Your pupper will get you out of here!'

'T-thank you pupper,' the woman gasped. 'D-did you see his...his m-mouth. O Jesus!' More hot sprinkle.

'Now come, come my plum,' and the man bent low to Shravan

Kumar: 'Young man, you are badly, badly hurt. Now I must get plum, that is Rachael, my wife, away from here; she just cannot stomach the sight of blood, the poor darling. You understand, she's too sensitive to pain. The thing is, when she sees suffering, she feels as if it is her own. She takes the pain of others on her. That is the problem. Why, when she was young, she saw them cut a chicken and has turned vegetarian since.' He started the scooter.

'S-shit fuck,' groaned Shravan Kumar as he heard the pupper and his plum ride away. The intensity of the pain in his face climbed above the frame of his consciousness. He felt absolutely nothing for a while. This new universe was in a way like this tarmac: hard, warm from the day but cold in attitude, unyielding as he seemed to touch it directly with his brain.

Sometime later two young men approached from beyond the arc of the lamp's light. The way they materialized from the moth-infested light, Shravan Kumar wondered if they were at last the agents of death come to take him away. They were heatedly arguing about something until they saw him.

'What the—'

'It's an accident!'

'Hit and run. Is he conscious?'

'I think so, yes.'

'Barely. Barely conscious I guess.'

'M-mouth! My god, his mouth! And f-forehead!'

They bent over him and Shravan Kumar smelled cheap soap. He had mixed feelings about being so sentient even at this point. He again made an attempt: 'H-hospital. Amb—' and a bubble gum of blood exploded at his lips.

'Relax,' said the one of them. 'Lie back. What's your name?'

'Sh-sha,' Shravan Kumar tried. Then again: 'Doctor. Aaamb—'

'Sh? Sha? Must be Shrikanth? Or are you trying to say Shaikh? Shaikh Abdullah or something? But then, could be Srikrishna for all you know. Or, from the other, big part of the world, Shane, Shawn, Shelby...' He was walking around Shravan Kumar, studying him closely. 'Are you from up north? Yes, you look like a North Indian. Or you're just white because of the blood loss?'

'Ooooff!' said the second, who wore glasses. 'How does it matter? It's just a guy that needs help.'

'What's the harm in getting to know someone?' said the first. But then he turned again to Shravan Kumar. 'Don't stress yourself. What's your name? Do you live near here? Any relatives we can inform?'

'I—here... H-help!'

'Boy, you need a hospital fast! And you need to pray. Which god do you pray to?' Then he looked at his friend. 'Looks like a Hindu, though you can't tell nowadays.' He was speaking like a seasoned old man though he was actually very young.

'You are a piece of work. What does it matter?' the man with the spectacles said. 'Come, let's take him. There's a big hospital, fortunately, just about a couple of kilometres on—'

'That's so like you,' said the first. 'So typical. Big hospital, so it must be good. Anything big, foreign, multinational, and you fall for it.'

'So, you want to take him to a clinic? With this kind of injury?'

'There's Dr Bhagavat who lives less than a kilometre from here. Ayurvedic. He is wise....'

'Unbelievable!' the second young man yelled, standing up. 'Being stubborn in an argument is one thing, Ranga. But taking this man to an Ayurvedic clinic is...it's bull-headed.'

'Why can't people like you never appreciate simple,

homegrown goodness? See, this is what I meant earlier. This is a case to point,' the first young man, Ranga, yelled right back. 'The science of Ayurveda is over five thousand years old. It is tried and tested over time. The world is discovering it every day, but we ourselves, we Indians....'

'You don't realize, but you really aren't patriotic, you know that? What you are is delusional,' the second youth pointed out.

'Ha hahahahaha! I am the one delusional. If a Westerner comes with his dollars and waves it in your face, you start wagging your tail thinking he's God himself. A big hospital must be a good hospital. Because it has branches. Because its head office is in New fucking York. But good old traditional medicine, which has been around for centuries, no millennia, which has the smell of my soil, is not fashionable enough for you. Oh no, Indian medicine is only for joint aches and skin disease. And I am the delusional one.'

'Did you just call me a dog?'

'Wagging one's tail is just a phrase. And it's not personal,' said Ranga in a reasonable tone. Of late he suddenly borrowed the tone of the person he was arguing with. It was a technique. 'But the likes of you...you are all curs. Your souls are sold to your capitalist bosses.'

'I'm not being personal either, but let me tell you, this is not Indianism, nationalism, or the rest of your hogwash. This is delusion. Just saying India is great is not love for India....'

'Our country ails because of people like you,' Ranga said, looking at his friend with restless eyes. 'Do you know, five thousand years ago we had invented plastic surgery already? But how will you know? You are the ailment. You, who run away to foreign hospitals, gather foreign acquisitions, listen only to foreign opinions, imitate the whites because in your heart of hearts they still rule over you....'

Shravan Kumar identified the exact moment he passed on to indifference. He cared not for this world, not for its ambulances or hospitals. He suddenly remembered that all his life he had had a curious inability to fear consequences. Sometimes, the consequence of his actions threatened to be dangerous, and he knew that normally he ought to be afraid, but what he always felt was indifference. People close to him had misjudged this to be insensitivity or selfishness. But now, as he lay on that road, the difference was clear: his own limbs felt to him like they were not his, like he didn't care what happened to him now or in the next moment. But since a man cannot be without desire until his last breath, Shravan Kumar did have a desire even now: he wished he was lying under a bush at the side of the road, away from the red glare and the arguing men and the sudden spurt of two- and three- and four-wheelers that were inconvenienced to go around him, like ants avoiding an obstruction on their march. He could have given all his savings, his job, his certificates, only to be moved a foot or two. He lost consciousness again.

When he came to again, he heard the two young men fighting. It seemed the second young man, the more studious and sober-looking of the two, was really giving it to the first. Ranga, after each slap he received, warned the second of upgrading his line of attack to the next level. 'I'm telling you,' he said at his menacing best, 'I won't hold back if you get me going....' In poor Ranga's mind were the countless film stunts he had seen where the hero gets thrashed at first, then notices a bit of blood leaking from the corner of his lips and unleashes his reserved power to turn the tables on the villain, beating him black and blue. But in the unimaginative reality of that roadside, he only kept getting slapped around, never being able to tap into any reserved strength but instead only succeeding in making his friend angrier with his silly, feeble warnings. Shravan Kumar shut his eyes. Whenever the pain along his neck and chest came down a bit, he gasped. He also knew that his leg was twisted out of shape and he dreaded that he would feel its ache too if he did not die soon enough.

The young men were still slapping each other around when a third youth emerged. This guy was holding a mobile phone in his hand, from which white wires snaked into his ears. As soon as he had sized up the situation he mumbled: 'Schmucks! Blowing each other up when a man is dyin' here.' Bending down, he touched Shravan Kumar's neck, careful not to get any blood on his hands, and said: 'Yo man! Yer pulse is strong. Jus' hang in there, kiddoo. Watcha need is a doc, and ya need 'im fast.' He liked rap music.

The youth looked left then right, moving in a rhythm only he could hear, as if to check if some doctor might be hiding under any of the shrubs on the roadside. Then he looked towards the two fighting young men again and shook his head in disgust. He bent low, touched Shravan Kumar's neck again with only the tip of his forefinger, and said: 'Hmm, let's see if I can call for help.'

'Aaamb…,' the dying man pronounced, 'aaa…mmmb!'

'Yo, kiddoo, relax!' But something seemed to be holding this youth back. He looked at his mobile phone, scratched his cheek thoughtfully, and at last sighed. 'Hey man, I ain't got no balance in my phone.'

Shravan Kumar desperately moved his eyes, and his whole face to the extent he could manage, twitching his lips and blinking. He was suddenly not indifferent any more. He did not wish to be moved just a few feet to the bush but to a good, comfortable hospital bed. But alas, the youth who wasn't too much older than a boy did not seem to understand. Shravan Kumar was trying to point at his own mobile phone in his pocket, which had enough balance, but the boy took his actions to be the fits and twitches of pain, which was the inconvenient but unavoidable side effect of life.

'Take a chill pill,' the boy said. 'Lie back. Help will come. If only I had got me a recharge. My bad!'

'M-my p-pho-pho…' gasped Shravan Kumar, simultaneously wondering if his phone wouldn't be as smashed as his body anyway. 'Use m-my pho—'

'Yes, I can't use my phone,' interrupted the boy. 'Hot damn. My bad, bro, as I said. But you stay put. Don't lose heart. Help will be here soon. Okay?'

'My pho…s-shit fuck!'

Then the youth went into a fit of introspection and his conscience began to prick him greatly. 'Look,' he sighed, 'I cannot lie to a dyin' dood, ok? Not that I'm saying you're dying, cuz you're not. Just stay put's all am sayin'. Now I cannot get involved though gad knows I always help. Okay? Always. But today I'm off to see my chick, man, you understand?' He winked at Shravan Kumar. 'No ordinary girl, she. You heard of Ramnatha Reddy, MLA? That bastard's daughter! Yeah, believe me you! I got that gold mine hooked. She'll eat outta my hand, man. Head over heels she is. Totally out, flat out for me. Ha ha! If I keep this goin', I'm gonna be rich, man, riiiiich! I'll buy you a whole hospital, man!'

Shravan Kumar groaned, which the young lover mistook for a murmur of understanding.

'Thanks, man. If I hang around to help now…you know… this kinda thing always takes time, man. The police, the hospital, your own folks, they won't lemme go. And Ranjana hates it if we miss the movie, man. I know you get me…. Can't disappoint the gold mine, you know. Ha haha! I know you wish me the best!'

Shravan Kumar wished for either of two things to happen. He

would prefer it if this youth, who already sounded very intimate with him, went away. Or at the very least, if he himself would lose consciousness or die, that would be an even better thing.

'If only I had found you here yesterday, kiddoo,' the boy went on in a caressing, almost coaxing voice. 'Trust me on this, if this was yesterday, or tomorrow, I woulda called an amby. Heck, why just call it, I woulda come with you to the hospital, man, seen to your care, run behind the docs like a true bro! That's me. That's Akhilesh Avasti for you. The brother to anyone who needs a brother. Ya believe me, doncha?'

'Y-yes,' gurgled Shravan Kumar. 'G-go! G-g-gooo!'

'Ha ha! You want me to rush? You are bleedin' on the road but ya want me to rush for my date!' The boy wiped the sides of his eyes. 'Now that's a heart 'o' gold, me man. We'll meet again, bro. We'll meet on these very streets and then you'll be up and runnin' and we'll have a drink and that drink will be on me cuz by then I'll be riiiiiich! Ha ha! We'll drink at the swankiest pub, bro! A whole round of drinks for the whole mammafuckin' pub will be on us!'

'G-goooo!' said Shravan Kumar again. The teary-eyed youth then went on his way at last, but not before wishing him a quick and full recovery.

Shravan Kumar realized that the other two young men had also left, perhaps after having reached a common ground in their ideas at last. The night was quiet again, and he looked up at the stars and heaved a sigh of relief that generated another blood balloon at his nose. The indifference was back and made even the tarmac feel comfortable.

But then he felt some movement, and he sensed that he wasn't as alone as he would have liked. He felt a cold touch at his feet. He craned his neck against his searing pain and saw that it was a dog. A stray dog with one ear slightly nipped to indicate he had been neutered. He came up, sniffed here and there, then licked a bit of blood off Shravan Kumar's lips.

Shravan Kumar again felt his curious inability to be afraid. He knew he ought to be scared because this dog would howl, now that he had tasted blood, and then a pack of them would come and that would be a death far worse. But he simply looked at the mutt with glassy eyes.

The stray did lick a bit more of Shravan Kumar's blood from near his chest and groin, but then went away to explore something more interesting, and discovering the scoop of shit further down on the pavement, busied himself with it until the spot was completely clean.

Shravan Kumar drifted deliberately under the sepulchre of his own awareness, now not even opening his eyes when he heard people speaking.

'By the amount of blood, this must've happened at least two hours ago,' said an old man's shivery voice. 'Why did no one take him to the hospital yet? I tell you, must be a goon. A goonda. Who wants to get caught in a gang war? Save him and you become the next target.'

In some time, he heard a child crying to its mom: 'Mom, lookit that man's face! Mooom, that's blood!'

Must have been a year later that Shravan Kumar heard a lady shriek: 'If it was a woman lying there would you volunteer to help?'

'Woman!' came a man's shriek in reply. 'Save a woman and she'll later say you touched her inappropriately when she was unconscious. That is why no one saves women any more!'

Another five years later Shravan Kumar heard a group of people in a circle around him.

'I would've taken him if I had brought my car.'

'I have a car, but the upholstery is new. With all that blood….'

'New upholstery? From where? Car interiors have become a con job nowadays.'

A few decades later he heard a priest bless him and beseech God to forgive him for all his sins so that this child of His would come to Him peacefully. He felt a cold fingertip at his forehead and his shoulders.

Another man remarked that in such cases you mustn't touch the victim, as moving them could cause more harm than good. It might be when you touched this victim that he died or was paralyzed for life. He had attended a special course on road accidents last summer….

A doctor came along but said that there was nothing he could do because he hadn't the proper instruments on him as he was on his way to a medical conference, which, by the way, was going to discuss trauma in road accidents among many other important and relevant topics.

A woman said that the poor bleeding man looked uncannily like her son and she would give her kidneys to him if he needed them, or basically do anything to help right now, had not the very son she was talking about been waiting for her as she spoke, on his way to the airport to leave for the US.

Fifty years later, the worms had left nothing of Shravan Kumar and yet he heard a man with a stammer complain that people who spoke a certain language, who were from a certain locality, never looked twice before crossing the road, or indeed before crossing anything in life at all, leaving it to the rest of the world to follow rules and regulations. There were those that said that he was already dead, so it was too late to help now, but why the hell had people who had seen him earlier done nothing? At this, some people pointed out that even last week when a poor beggar had been dying near the railway track, no one had helped, so was all this compassion for this young man only because he was well-dressed and seemed more elite? But the first group said that when the beggar died without help the public ought to have woken up, their conscience ought to have stirred, and they should have helped this time, whether this was another beggar or a rich person. In this manner, the people who were before Shravan Kumar now became a team that was contesting the people who had seen him earlier. There were those that said that the police ought to remove him or the morning traffic would be jammed, but the police only got drunk in the evenings and would be sleeping in their stations. Here, the people became one team fighting against the police. This was until a mature young woman began to say that there was no point in blaming the police, who were themselves only servants to a system that was selfishly and apathetically run by the government itself, and that if only the people united and became a team they would see that they were paying taxes for the government to come to help in situations such as these. What stopped the government from using tax money to set up CCTV cameras everywhere, so such accidents would be spotted immediately in the nearby police stations and victims could be rushed within the golden hour to the nearest hospital? Soon, a small gathering had formed at Shravan Kumar's feet to listen to her.

Ages later, a philosopher was telling people that life was transient. Perhaps this poor young man was on his way home for a harmless little celebration when Fate had struck him down, and much as we might weep for him or try to imagine ourselves in his pain, the universe itself wasn't moved. Things would go on as before even as this man breathes his last. Such was Man's condition on this earth. Meanwhile, a more practical software engineer got the idea for a new app which enabled a person to anonymously send a location to the police when he or she spotted an accident. Someone remarked that such an app would be misused by miscreants who wanted the police to go on wild goose chases all day long while they went about their dark businesses. Someone else said that they were all wasting time talking: if the right authorities were informed, this man's organs could be harvested. They could be precious to many. But he himself did not know who the right authorities were for this, and if only they did not waste time talking, they could try to find out.

In Shravan Kumar's universe, almost a century had passed when he smelt alcohol. It came sharp and sweet, and Shravan Kumar woke up with a start, dreaming of the smell of beer and fries and the sound of music and the sight of dim lights and pretty bar girls.

The road, red-black, swam into his vision again. He realized that someone was sitting near his head. He painfully rolled his eyeballs up and saw that it was a beggar or a drunk or both. A man stinking of alcohol, peanuts, and sleazy cinema theatres. He couldn't sit without swaying.

'Y-you are h-hurt!' he said in a deep voice and his Jesus Christ-beard touched Shravan Kumar's swollen eyebrows. 'I-I'll help. I'll get you to a…to a…'

'H-hospital,' filled in Shravan Kumar.

Another year later, the drunk was still trying to pick Shravan Kumar up. He had succeeded in moving the injured man to the side of the road, almost on to the pavement. He had managed to even stop a passing autorickshaw. He pulled Shravan Kumar into the vehicle, whispering comforting though senseless words all the while.

Through the slits of his swollen eyes Shravan Kumar saw that the driver of the autorickshaw was the same wino, though a trifle cleaner and maybe sober, but he was the same man who was helping him. He, too, was whispering kind nothings and the voice—the same voice—went right to his soul and bridged the gap between indifference and peace.

The saviours might have taken Shravan Kumar off that tarmac and taken him to a hospital where all the doctors and nurses were the same man, and it would have been another miracle which he might have narrated to his grandchildren, had the spell not been broken just then with the cruel and fatalistic wail of an ambulance. The big white van made the entire road and the shrubs along it pulsate under its rotating red light. The driver refused to do anything about the ear-shattering siren. Two paramedics in white jumped out the back, even as an authority figure, perhaps a policeman, came out the front door and began slapping the beggar around.

'Shoo,' the authority figure yelled over the sound. 'Where are you taking the injured man? Get out of here. Scram, you stinking piece of filth!'

The wino dropped Shravan Kumar on the pavement, not gently, but he can be excused because the policeman was shoving him around. Shravan Kumar heard the autorickshaw speed away.

'Fancy that!' the ambulance man said. 'A guy is lying injured and these guys just pack him into an auto!'

Then he turned to Shravan Kumar and a look of intense compassion came over him. 'Sir, you have suffered enough. You now have absolutely nothing to worry. You are at last in safe hands. No hands can be safer.'

One by one he introduced the ambulance crew and they shook Shravan Kumar's hand, which was already dead, so they had to pick it up and shake it. Then he spoke loudly and proudly, like he was singing an anthem: 'We are from the new government's People's Protection Group, or PPG. This is an initiative the world will soon emulate. Each city has a PPG division, much like the fire force or the coast guard. We just patrol the streets in ambulances, looking for people like yourself who need help. We are young, willing to help, and we represent the government's policy of aiding without heeding to the differences of religion, caste, gender, community, language, region, race, social status, profession, place of work, mother-father name, husband-wife name, political leanings, financial status….' Shravan Kumar missed an unquantifiable portion of this speech as he drifted away again. Years later, he came to and noticed one of the paramedics was checking his vitals with sundry machinery and yelling out figures over the sound of the siren (which, though uncomfortable, was mandatory and hence couldn't be switched off, the authority figure explained) to another paramedic who was entering the figures into a hi-tech application in his hand. The authority figure explained how Shravan Kumar's vitals were being read simultaneously by six super-specialist doctors in PPG's different centres as they spoke. These experts were already evaluating his condition so that they would be ready with the treatment immediately as the patient was wheeled into one of the dedicated PPG hospitals. 'PPG,' the authority figure sang, 'Another name for dependability and trustworthiness.'

Then one of the attenders approached with a sheaf of typed papers and a pen.

'This is the form,' he explained. 'We can fill it later, but you need to sign it.'

'Glllb…glooob,' said Shravan Kumar.

'Come on, sign it fast,' the authority figure said. 'We need to get you out of here quickly, but we cannot move you without the signed form.'

'Ssh... Fffcck,' said Shravan Kumar.

'There is no provision for thumbprint,' said the attender. 'India has been declared a hundred per cent literate country, and so thumbprints—those vestiges from the dark and illiterate era of previous governments—have been completely removed from all government documentation.'

'You shook hands with all of us. Surely you can sign a few papers.'

'Due process is uncompromisable. Even the PPG cannot help you if you will not sign.'

'Shall I just say patient refused to sign?'

'Idiot, if he refuses to sign, he cannot be assigned the status of "patient".'

'He will bleed to death.'

'Which is why he must sign quickly. Or I wouldn't hurry him so much.'

'Is he dead already?'

'If he is, then it is a case for the National Deaths and Funerals Bureau, or the NDFB, which is a flagship body under the government that takes care of removal of corpses and the execution of last rites as per the religion, caste, creed, locality, community, gender....'

When Shravan Kumar drifted in for one last time, the ambulance and the men had gone because much as it was their duty to help, it was also imperative that they followed procedure.

Then his boss, Sitaramji, passed on his car. Can't say passed, for the man, to be fair to him, did stop a moment to check on his fallen employee.

'Shravan Kumar!' he yelled, 'What the hell happened?'

Then the man went on about how all this wouldn't have happened if Shravan Kumar had only joined him for the party, which was to celebrate after a good business achievement of which Shravan Kumar himself was a part; how it revealed employee attitudes and mindsets when they refused to participate in a harmless little get-together; why it was the responsibility of every single employee to contribute to building a sense of teamwork within the organization; how it was simply unforgivable that Shravan Kumar had bunked the party considering he, Sitaramji, had always thought of him as his own son.

With his fingers delicately massaging his hurting temples, the boss finally climbed back into his car and drove away in utter disappointment at employees who did not reciprocate his love.

Shravan Kumar felt two streams of liquid meet at his chin and fall down his neck. At that instant his life was a flash, like the staccato dream of a dolphin that lasted only for the second it was out of the ocean, mid-jump, fathomless droplets of moonlight still dripping off its being. He was glad that the Honda had pushed him into this other universe, and he was glad that it would be in this one that he would be buried.

5

THE SOUND

At first the villagers thought it was the cry of an animal. It wasn't shrill then, more like a deep-throated wail. Everyone agreed it came from the centre of the forest that bordered the village in the east. The more imaginative ones claimed it was the cry of the forest itself, crying to the heavens for the sins of the mortals. The more religious ones said it was the woeful expression of an angel banished by God. The scientifically disposed suggested it was just the wind blowing through the leaves, but they preferred not to elaborate and soon tried to ignore it.

No one knows the exact time the sound began. This was because at first it was too faint to be noticed. People heard it in the background of their consciousnesses, but though it was unlike anything they had ever heard (it never stopped for taking a breath!) it wasn't loud enough to make them wonder. Then sometime later it was just loud enough to become unmistakable; a low wail that constantly emanated from where the centre of the forest might have been. The villagers then formed a committee to think about it. When it grew steadily loud—even the deafest old ones could hear it now—they decided that they couldn't go on listening to it and doing nothing. This was the point at which the speculations began. Everyone had a theory about the sound. Everyone realized that the sound was terrifying, though again they never knew when they had grown to fear it.

People rued that a team of young and strong men hadn't gone into the forest to investigate when the sound was still quite faint. Somehow, everyone felt that the louder the sound got the greater was its malevolence. People stopped stepping outside their homes after nightfall. The wind that often blew in from the forest came to be feared and mothers shielded their infants from it. It was now out of the question that anyone could be permitted to go towards the sound to investigate.

When more time passed people realized that they were shouting to be heard when they spoke to each other. They had to pause in between sentences, or their throats would ache. That was when they realized that the sound was very loud indeed. Housewives cut back on gossip and said only what was necessary. Then one day, a petty thief came forward to the committee and confessed to his small crimes. Following his example, several villagers began confessing to sins of various natures. From small thefts to ill wishes and voodoo, to bribery and forgery, to cheating to even adultery, people began to come clean of a lifetime of sins. Everyone felt a compulsive need to repent if the end was near.

And every sin was forgiven by everyone else.

Later, when they realized that no end was in sight and the sound just continued, maybe even louder now, they did not speak of the days of confession. Instead, they began to make plans to deal with the sound without going in to investigate. Maybe we don't need to understand it, we just need to deal with it, they said. The more religious ones held elaborate rituals to appease the gods. Ancient sacrifices were revived and several goats and poultry met their end. But the sound continued. The scientific ones, who had been cynical about the rituals, suggested a unique and ambitious experiment. They got a majority of the villagers to assemble as close to the forest as everyone dared. Then they got them to roar together at the top of their voices, facing the forest, in their best parody of the sound itself. The experimenters hoped to study the reaction from inside the forest when the inexplicable sound from the forest met its match. It was secretly hoped, of course, that at the end of the loud yell from the villagers they would be met with silence. Oh, how sweet that silence would be! But after the experiment failed, many people said that they knew nothing would have happened. The sound continued as they knew it would. Everyone returned to their chores with the uncomfortable feeling that they were all behaving like characters in a dream.

When one of the weaker old women went deaf there was no doubt that the constant sound was the reason.

The more soft-spoken ones had started to communicate through writing and sign language. No one listened to music any more. No one sang while bathing. No one swore or fought with anyone. The village school stopped functioning and the children played all day long, choosing games that needed no talking. The sound had begun to rule their lives. It took on a kind of godly status to some and a few villagers had begun to face the forest when they prayed. More time passed and the village was divided into two groups—those that found God in the sound and those that thought it evil. The committee, though it still existed, was considered redundant, mostly consisting of defeated middle-aged men.

At this time, a putrefying smell emerged from the forest and theories about its origin began to sprout. One side considered it as a sure sign of evil while the other side held that it was merely the smell of animals that had died because of the constant sound. But immediately, the latter possibility yielded more terror: how exactly could the sound have killed the animals of the forest? If it had, what future awaited the villagers? And why hadn't the wild animals come crawling, running, and flying into the village much earlier for fear of the sound? The whole village would have shifted further away had it not been surrounded by the forest. No one dared to go near the forest itself now, even if it was in a direction opposite to where the sound came from.

Thankfully, the decaying smell soon ceased. People were grateful when it was only the sound once again. It was now so very loud that one of the members of the committee suddenly went deaf. The incident was much joked about. Apparently, the man woke up one morning and discovered that the sound had stopped! But his enthusiasm hit a wall when he excitedly ran to tell his wife it had stopped and he couldn't hear a word of her reply. The joke was scribbled on walls so people didn't have to repeat it at the top of their voices. Within the committee it was rumoured that perhaps the sound might target its members specifically. After all, the committee was formed to deal with the sound and it was more than likely that the sound didn't like it. One after the other the members resigned from the committee and it finally ceased to exist. No one missed it.

Then at one time, a new generation of courageous youth decided to find out the source of the sound once and for all. Three of them risked their lives and went into the forest. But reportedly as they went even a little deep into the woods, the sound was so loud that it seemed to physically prevent their progress. In fact, the three young men ran back into civilization like rabid dogs and were mentally unstable for a long time after.

By now, all speech was ruled out. Very serious or complex matters were communicated through writing, for which many carried slates and chalk. For more routine talk a clever sign language had evolved. Through this sign language people reinvented terms for swearing, fights and yells, negotiations and reconciliations, love and lullabies.

As time passed the villagers could not decide if the sound was getting any louder. Many people had gone deaf by now. It seemed impossible that anything could ever be louder than that sound. When it rained the water played on rooftops quietly like in a picture. Even the thunder was known only through its accompanying lightning. On still afternoons the leaves of trees vibrated with the sound. And since they could hear nothing else, many villagers wondered if they too had already gone deaf and the lone sound from the forest wasn't just continuing in their minds. Thus, sound and silence became one. Then slowly, imperceptibly, everyone in the village was convinced they had really gone deaf. Even the animals seemed to no longer be able to hear.

Once again no one could point out the exact instance—nor even the age or era—when the whole village had gone deaf. But slowly, a new peace descended like a blessing. For them, the sound had at last stopped. Life was back to normal and people once again ventured out well past nightfall. The frequent cool breeze from the forest was as pleasurable as it had been a long time ago, before the sound had started. A new committee was formed to decide on matters of law and order. Everyone was happy as there was nothing to fear any more. Of course, it wasn't as if no one wondered whether the sound still went on, or about how loud it now was. Even a long, long time later the villagers wondered if the sound was still there, gradually rapidly drowning everything in its heavy, deep, and steadily climbing wail.

But that was something they would never know.

6

THE ANSWER

Buster 235 was the fifth supercomputer to be commissioned with the near-impossible task of proving or disproving the existence of God. But what was heartening was that even after forty years it had not been decommissioned nor had it burned any of its own key circuits out. There was hope that the Answer would come. And when the Answer finally came the year was…. No. No one could be sure of the year because in the excitement of knowing the Answer no one had quite remembered to keep a record of things. But it was some time in the future, and even if you are reading this in the future it can be safely said that the year was still some time further in the future.

It had all started several decades ago, when some young scientists met some seasoned businessmen, and together, they later met some powerful politicians with a set of complex presentation slides. All prominent nations pooled in funds for the most ambitious project in humankind's history, and thus was founded the first of the Buster series: Buster 104. It was hailed as an illustrious example of international cooperation and the triumph of human curiosity.

At the time the scientists said: 'They tortured us when we said the world was round, but the world was round. They killed us when we said the earth wasn't the centre of the universe, but the earth indeed is not the centre of anything! And even later when we suggested the theory of the Big Bang with immense restraint and moderation, people still insist that there was a god even before the Big Bang. It's time to settle this once and for all. We will have the Answer before long.'

Religious leaders rebutted: 'We have told them a hundred times and we are telling them again: we are perfectly alright when they invent pasteurization or vaccination. But leave God alone, for God's sake. Hmm? Please. They themselves admit that God is outside the purview of science. In any case, we welcome this new initiative of theirs. If their machine works, they will prove that there is a god. If they cannot find God, it will mean their machine doesn't work.'

And then, when the cameras were turned off the religious chiefs chuckled, 'The imbeciles have dug their own graves this time.'

Then there were those profoundly religious types who felt everything deeply: 'If the Answer is not palatable to our history, culture, and ethnicity we cannot guarantee what will happen. Sentiments might be hurt. There could be spilled blood. We might urge a rephrasing of the Question, and our ways of urging may not be very civil.'

But so potent had been the presentation put together by the scientists–businessmen team that politicians the world over agreed to the quest for the answer—no, the Answer—in spite of the risk of polarization and flaring of extremist views.

And thus, Buster 104 was commissioned.

◆

Take any side you will, but you cannot deny that the machine was a marvel. It stood on about a hundred acres of green forest in an isolated place in an undisclosed country. Its main body stood about seventeen floors tall. The project was protected by the costliest and most elaborate security system the world had ever seen. One arm of Buster 104 was a giant telescope that saw into the deepest depths of the universe. Another ended in minute electrodes attached to the brain of a rat, so that it could probe out the ultimate secrets of consciousness. Then there was a third arm that housed a scanning tunnelling microscope that explored the atoms that comprised the earth. And thus, simultaneously exploring the realms of bigness, smallness, and consciousness, the miracle machine would combine data and analyse it, and the distilled result would settle for mankind the question of God, once and for all.

The machine was built at a cost of a billion billion billion hoohoobees (a new currency invented to keep the project's finances neutral), and it was estimated that it would take about fourteen million hoohoobees a year to run. There were reports at the time that the people in a small state in a Third World country went on to die of starvation as a side effect of the cost of the project, but these were dismissed by the intelligentsia around the globe as a rumour. At the thick of these reports a statement was issued from an undisclosed location by the secret management of Buster 104 to reach the world's press, and it read: 'The rumour that the people of a small state in a Third World country died of starvation as a result of the project are categorically untrue.' And that was that.

On the day the giant computer chugged to life and began collecting data from its three core realms, three rationalists were shot dead in a small town in Peru. This prompted the secret management of Buster 104 to issue a statement to the media: 'Three rationalists were not shot dead in a small town in Peru today.'

Later, the media no longer needed statements from the management and began publishing helpful stuff on their own: 'Place of worship not desecrated by masked goons in Guatemala', 'Suspected suicide bomber did not blow up atheists' convention killing 114' and 'World on brink of war on account of the God question? Experts say no', and so on.

Historians many decades later were to classify this phenomenon as a sign of the ultimate victory of man's quest for truth. 'The human race let nothing come in the way of the Answer,' they would write.

♦

Just a few minutes after Buster 104 chugged to life, it went dead because of a minor circuit lapse, but was repaired and started up again. With such a colossal amount of data coming in every millisecond, the machine had to be modelled on the human heart. It rested in between short phases of activity in order not to burn up. This slowed its progress significantly, but mankind was prepared to wait. The Answer would take time, but it would come, some said. The Answer would take our world with it, others said. The Answer will never come, you idiots, still others said.

But just when the world threatened to go back to the boredom to which it was addicted, Buster 104 spat out its first interpretation of all that data. It happened a few months after the computer began its mission, and the interpretation came out in a humongous roll of paper. The roll with the first instalment of the Answer was as large as a double-decker bus, and almost as long, too. It went on to become the symbol of many things. Statues of the giant bus-like paper rolls came to be installed outside scientific institutions. Miniature rolls began to be used along with lime and snake blood during black magic ceremonies. Toilet paper manufacturers were instructed by governments the world over to change the design of their product in order not to inadvertently insult the first glorious output of Buster 104. Extremists began using moving rolls of paper for target practice. Painters began to paint realistic and absurdist versions of cylindrical reams.

But the trouble with the first instalment of the Answer itself was that it came from data that was inhumanly detailed. The facts and figures collated by the telescope itself ran into about five thousand kilometres of paper. Scientists had to sift through the whole thing over the next five years (during which time Buster 104 was shut down for maintenance and cooling off), and three scientists turned so hopeless they resigned from the project. They were allegedly buried in the backyard of the main building to keep vital information from being let out. After a little more than half a decade, scientists were finally ready with an interpretation of the first instalment, which came to be known as 'The First Instalment of the Answer'. It was published for the scientific community in four volumes, and a summary was translated into layman terms for the rest of the world. It read:

> A detailed analysis of the darkest matter, singularity, et al., suggests that nothing, not even light, can substitute all ways of worship to fill pi-meson and the space from one vacuum, galaxy cluster, or molecules of cheese; the cat of Erwin still cannot decide about a) existing, b) not existing, and c) none of the above. Fish.

The International Society of Ardent Atheists (ISAA) sued the management of Buster 104 in several countries, alleging that the entire experience had been a waste of public money. The Chief Justices of all the countries in which the suits were filed unanimously adjourned court and postponed the next hearing for after the Answer was found.

The scientists declared that though the First Instalment may not make much sense to the untrained mind, they were sure that it would really begin to deliver when put alongside later instalments. 'We do not anticipate that the Answer will be simple, routine, or even logical,' declared the officer responsible for public relations. 'The question is the most intricate ever posed; obviously the Answer will take some interpretation. Please leave it to us. Please do not read the words as they are and get confused.'

But there was internal trouble brewing. Some of the core scientists began to question certain fundamentals of the project. While the first of them were buried along with the three scientists who had quit earlier, the uncertainty continued until it was discovered that there was a vital flaw after all. The telescope was fine, the microscope was fine. The vital flaw was in the rat brain. It was analysed and concluded that the rat brain could not represent consciousness in its entirety because it was an ordinary rat's brain, whereas the length and breadth of consciousness had to also encompass the immense and complex regions of insanity. A fully normal brain could not represent consciousness accurately.

At this time four religious elders in equidistant parts of the globe had coordinated episodes of apoplexy following fits of laughter, and had to be hospitalized. Only the first one was in any condition to articulate, and he declared: 'We'll have to sue the imbeciles for human rights violations; you can see they're killing us.' He broke into peals of laughter again and they had to sedate him.

But over the next several months it was discussed, fought out, meditated upon, and decided that Buster 104 had to be decommissioned and another supercomputer commissioned to take it up from there. Several key political heads had to roll. Many scientists disappeared. Several businessmen began to fight bureaucratic battles to retrieve the money they had invested in the project. Some of the less powerful businessmen disappeared too. But eventually it was as clear as the God question that Buster 104 had to be replaced by a higher version.

At first, they thought of burying the rat in the backyard along with the scientists but then, fortunately just in time, a museum was set up in a historical city of the world where relics of our quest for the Answer would be exhibited. The rat became the first priceless piece here. A financial wizard associated with Buster said to the international media: 'The museum will become a revenue stream for the project. It will contribute to the Answer directly.' Off the record he told the journalists, 'It is only fair that it is named after me. It was my idea.'

It took up most of the next decade to set up Buster 198. To the layman it was just the problem of replacing the rat with a mad dog, but scientists knew it wasn't as simple as that. Every individual neuron of the rat had been connected to the computer. Each connecting electrode had to be nanotechnologically detached—several billions of them!—and new ones connected to the crazed neurons of the rabid dog's brain. And since the dog had several billion more neurons than the rat, several billion more electrodes had to be produced anew and installed. So immersed were the scientists that fourteen of them forgot their shots and eventually died of rabies. But one beautiful spring morning, almost ten years after the rat was moved to the museum, Buster 198 shook to life. But there was a new crisis.

It was a crisis of faith. Indeed, businessmen and politicians alike seemed to have misgivings that the Buster project would ever yield anything. Were the religious leaders right, after all?

What were the scientists doing? Replacing a rat with a mad dog would tell us if there is a god? God! Trillions and trillions of hoohoobees were flowing into this mad chase. Were the scientific brothers rather rabid too, eh?

It was scary because one real-estate tycoon from India went on to declare to the press: 'Can you blame me for losing faith? A rabid dog, for god's sake! I have started to wonder if I should ask for a full refund. My money is very, very hard-earned, you know.'

But, fortunately for the project, the director of Buster was a very shrewd man. He had been jobless for some time in his youth, and he feared nothing more and nothing else than being unemployed again. He was a man who always sat behind a huge desk with his face away from the light, so that no one could be sure what he looked like. People only knew that his face was pockmarked heavily and that he always smoked Havana cigars. In order to completely smother assassination bids, he never revealed his name to anybody (he was simply called 'The Director'), and he brought a different falsetto into his voice every time he spoke on the telephone. Some of the more fanatic religious groups had come together to form a clan called The Association to Identify the Director (TAID)—conducting their own strategic and covert investigations—to identify this man and murder him (the word 'assassination' is used for leaders; this would only be a murder, they pointed out).

The Director was much moved by the dissension and decided to act. He picked up his gleaming black telephone and dialled a long-term associate of his—a creative advertising person who lived and worked at a faraway place. This advertising creative head was a man with forty-two piercings on different parts of his body, and thirteen tattoos of varied themes along his arms, buttocks, and tummy. He was called Sammy in creative circles.

The Director used a different falsetto even with Sammy, though they had known each other for so long that Sammy would know his original voice in any case. But the thing was, The Director himself had forgotten his original voice by now.

'Where do barracudas go before their dinner date?' The Director asked.

'The dentist's, to keep their teeth in,' Sammy replied, 'What happened to your voice?'

'Let that be, how you doing, pirate?'

'Am doped. What are you up to nowadays?'

And they went on like that for a bit before The Director came to the point: 'Don't ask me for details. I cannot divulge. I need a campaign, pirate; a sizzler to change some perceptions.'

Let me explain, at this point in the future the methods of advertising had greatly evolved. At some point of time, the public had gotten quite tired of ads. Whether it was online creatives or television commercials or newspaper ads or hoardings, as soon as one came their way, they told themselves: 'Oh, here comes another one!' So the creative people first increased the number of piercings and tattoos on their bodies and then, when that still did not come to their rescue, began coming up with cleverer ways to advertise. But the public rolled their eyes: 'Oh, here comes another really clever one!' Advertising was under the risk of dying. No matter how clever or funny or supposedly moving a print creative or hoarding or a commercial was, people looked at it (or more often turned away from it) with the prejudice that it was only another ad, after all.

Luckily at this time the creative people had started to get along really well with the technology people. Both parties being significantly cunning, they pooled their resources and came out with a great invention. It was called the Convincer. About the size of a small car, the Convincer was a machine that could be made relatively cheap, considering its huge potential for profitability. It worked something like this:

Suppose you wished to sell a shampoo that no one wished to buy. Instead of feeling gloomy, you just needed to come up with a key strategic message (which, in this case would be 'buy my shampoo'), which your creative advertising partner would come up with for you after due contemplation and several presentation slides. Then your technology partner would feed this key strategic message, 'buy my shampoo', into the Convincer. This machine used elements of string theory to convert the key strategic message into subatomic packets of convincing information. These packets were called Mind-Benders. The Convincer then aired the Mind-Benders to satellites up above that beamed them right into the heads of the public. Very soon, the shampoo would begin to vanish from supermarket shelves.

Now, since no one was sure if this amazing machine was strictly legal, in the narrowest sense of that miserable word, they did the next best thing, which was to keep it a secret. The creative partners carried out their conventional practices in parallel—they came up with good old advertising campaigns so that finally when consumer behaviour changed everyone thought it was the campaign that had worked. No one sued anyone, things got sold, everyone was happy. And thus, the importance of advertising was restored.

So, when The Director briefed his old friend Sammy, the latter immediately went into deep thought. But before that he did the first practical thing he had to do: he dropped a message to his technology partner. It read: 'Believe in Buster. Invest in Buster.' This was because though it would cost the Buster project a couple of million hoohoobees, the technology people would take considerable time to convert the key message into Mind-Bender packets. So, he might as well give them the message immediately—even when his phone was still warm from the conversation with The Director—so that they could begin their work already. He could then go into deep thought. Everyone would be happy with the time he saved.

After he had taken care of this practicality, Sammy went berserk. He smoked pot, visited retired whores (he had a fetish for them), tried to instigate bar brawls in sleepy bars, entered a couple of law suits for assault and sexual abuse, tore his clothes on naked nails and then continued wearing them, took tetanus shots, fought with the government on matters of principle, and generally created such a ruckus that the media reported: 'Creative wizard Sammy working on next big campaign. Hints at Buster project, commits nothing.'

He spent about four months on this before picking up the phone and talking to The Director: 'I think I have cracked it. I will make a detailed presentation later, but let me bounce it off you now. It reads: 'Believe in Buster. Invest in Buster'. What do you think?'

The Director said, 'It works, it works, it works,' and then broke down, sobbing. He said Sammy had captured just what was in his heart. It was because of the passion with which Sammy worked that he always went back to him when he needed a perception-changing ad campaign.

'Hey, pirate,' Sammy cut him short, 'Where do antelopes go before their job interview?'

'To the barber, to trim their horns,' sniffed The Director, 'Now get cracking on the ads.'

In the subsequent months the great advertising campaign rolled. It said, 'Believe in Buster. Invest in Buster', and people believed and invested in the project once again. That real-estate tycoon who had misgivings about the project began getting intense migraine attacks for the first time in his life. Very soon he was convinced of how wrong he had been. Then he declared, 'I am being punished for my wrongs. Who can ever not believe in the quest to discover God? Oh my god! Here comes a billion hoohoobees to atone for my sins.' He had no way of knowing, of course, that the Mind-Bender packets were zipping down from satellites up there, deep into his brain.

Buster 198 rolled out smoothly, and investors once again opened their pockets. Buster delved into the brain of the rabid dog and combined this data with discoveries from the universe and from the space inside atoms. The Answer would come soon, the scientists said.

◆

One thing historians would later record as a curious effect of the Buster series is that the various religions of the world came to be unified. In fact, at the time Buster 198 regained its foothold in public minds, all religions started to have one accessory added to their regular outfits. They all started to wear metal helmets whenever they ventured out of their places of worship or homes. Out on the streets you could identify a religious man, woman, or child by that odd metal skullcap. They walked in it, talked in it, dined in it. Be it a Muslim in the Middle East or a Christian in the Americas or a Hindu in India, the fact that he or she was religious was expressed through the wearing of that metal cap. On one level it became a symbol of solidarity of all religions, and a sort of protest against the machine that was investigating their gods. But on a subconscious and clandestine level it was rumoured that the metal cap prevented brainwashing. Indeed,

The Greatest Enemy of Rain

people who wore metal caps religiously, whenever they went out, were not won over by Sammy's advertising campaign at all!

Meanwhile the scientists at Buster 198 were thrilled. Thanks to Sammy's clever advertising, they gave themselves massive pay hikes. After buying expensive cars and villas in an undisclosed location, they also made large deposits in undisclosed bank accounts. 'Whether there is a god or no,' they winked at each other, 'we better be well-prepared to retire after this project.'

At this time there were odd cases of clashes between scientists and religious clans at various places. The media did report these 'minor incidents', which were duly forgotten. In Guatemala, a place of worship had been blown up by punks who had written on its debris with shit: 'IF YOU BELIEVE IN GOD, WHY DO FEAR THE ANSWER YOU MORONS?'

By way of an answer a group of four scientists on a geological expedition to Afghanistan were kidnapped, decapitated, and their heads stuck with white cement between their thighs. Displayed one morning in a local marketplace, the letters on the chests of the corpses read: 'IF YOU DON'T FEAR GOD, HERE'S YOUR ANSWER YOU IMBECILES.'

This was countered as far away as Greenland where one cleric was found dead in a bus stand, a metal helmet forced into a very unpleasant body orifice, with the paper wrap around his head reading: 'IF THE ANWER IS NO, YOU BETTER WATCH OUT YOU UGLY FUCKS.'

The question–answer session continued with a dead woman in Peru with a knife pinning the message to her forehead: 'AND IF THE ANWER IS YES, YOU'LL HAVE NO PLACE TO HIDE, YOU SONS OF WHORES.'

But these were odd, sporadic incidents reported by the media only because each was a response to the previous and the journalists did not want to break the continuity. Uniformly, across the locations of the events, the police were very understanding, and the political leadership was unruffled. No one was arrested. 'Such things happen,' was the refrain. A few intellectuals tried to become famous by saying that the Buster project would one day lead to widespread war, maybe even a world war, but these were countered by other philosophers who claimed that an investigation such as the one by Buster was inevitable; mankind had to know someday. The quest for truth was eternal and it had only come of age now.

Inside the Buster 198 campus the scientists indulged in some willing suspension of their conscience. There was a fellow scientist named Pete who was an underperformer. The man cycled the whole day in the forest around Buster 198, sucking on a lollipop and apparently thinking. It had been initially maintained that Pete was a genius, but when no worthy idea came from his day-long wanderings in the jungle for decades, the other scientists began to whisper.

It was at an opportune time that this whispering began, because just then the Department of the Rabid Dog had been feeling that the consciousness arm had to be upgraded. The fact that it was a dog brain, they were exploring, placed severe limitations on the outcome. Canines, by their very nature, had a very limited experience of reality as compared to humans. So, one day Pete was given a placebo instead of his regular anti-rabies shot and when he started frothing from his mouth and making barking sounds, they disconnected the electrodes off the rabid dog and painstakingly poked them into Pete's brain. The dog joined the rat in the historical museum, while the Department of the Rabid Man was applauded by all at the party to celebrate the installation of the new version, Buster 204.

The media, which was taken by surprise, wrote headlines to say that the Buster project was once again updated, meaning we were that much closer to the Answer now. Faith in the project received a big boost because the central consciousness of Buster 204 was now a human being, albeit a rabid one. Or, out of necessity a rabid one, because a sane one wouldn't quite completely represent our consciousness.

And thus, humanity was once again on its way to accomplishing the near-impossible feat of proving or disproving the existence of God. We were closer, because the Second Instalment of the Answer came shortly after Pete took over. The gist read:

> Lollipops go pop during the rains which God gives whether it is in the Orion or here under the sun which is what leads to more and more hoohoobees for me my salary and hikes in the value of the Azimuthal quantum numbers.

It was considered significant progress that the word 'God' figured in this output. World over, the anticipation for the Answer heated up. The media said: 'Second Instalment mentions god. Scientists interpret Answer is near.'

As part of the euphoria of the project, Pete was honoured by the management with the decision that he could join the rat and the dog at the museum for eternal glory once the project was over. Thanks to Pete, the Department of the Rabid Man was in turn glorified. A direct effect of this was that in some years the Department of the Telescope and the Department of the Scanning Tunnelling Microscope managed to convince the management that their departments were equally important to the project and needed upgrading, too.

Rather briskly, two more upgrades were done. The huge

telescope, itself about fourteen storeys tall, was replaced by another that was twenty-four storeys tall. The media contributed by reporting: 'Another Third World country does not go on to die of starvation as Buster 204 is replaced by Buster 211.' Rather than send the previous telescope to the museum, the country that had contributed the most funds to the Buster project pulled some clandestine strings and sent it to space, from where it was pointed back at earth and used for spying. Thus, wastage was completely avoided.

But while the twenty-four storeyed telescope was being built and the previous one blasted off into space, the folks at the Department of the Scanning Tunnelling Microscope were not sitting idle. Very soon Buster 211 was upgraded to Buster 235, the fifth and final version of the supercomputer that would tell us if God is or if God isn't. The microscope in Buster 235 could blow up the individual electrons inside atoms to the size of a room! The head of that department issued a videographed release to the world that said: 'God is not to be found only inside rabid brains. Just because we investigate inside of atoms, please don't take our contribution to be tiny.'

The religious heads quickly latched on to this. 'Even insiders of this crazy project know that God exists. "God is not to be found only inside rabid brains," the microscope scientist has said, implying, of course, that he believes in God.'

'They are so blinded by religion,' the microscope head retorted, 'that they don't understand figures of speech. I was only talking about the contribution of my department to the Buster project. Look how they twisted my words. This is what religion has been doing for centuries! Twisting the truth.'

'Ha ha,' laughed a head priest somewhere. 'In their own language, this is what they would call a Freudian slip!'

'Heehee,' rued the microscope head. 'Look at those Quakers quoting Freud. Now, isn't that the victory of human reason that they had to leave God aside and talk of Freud? That's like the devil quoting the scripture.'

'Hoohoo,' cried the head priest, 'and the devil is from where, eh? Did you create him in your laboratory, moron?'

'Yikes, there goes another figure of speech,' returned the scientist. 'You're really good at this, you bastard!'

But the Director then called the microscope head and told him to back off: 'You began it all by competing with another department at your own project. Quit that, or you'll have to quit the project.'

After that the microscope head stopped answering to the provocations from the head priest, which the religious leaders took as proof that God exists. But the little powwow between the scientist and the priest began a big new trend in humankind's chase for the truth—betting on God.

'A glorious new chapter began with the fight between the two gentlemen,' historians would write. 'The chapter of betting. Entire betting syndicates were set up—for the existence of God and against the existence of God. Horse racing and match fixing almost perished, making way for this new speculation; you took sides and you put in thousands and sometimes millions from your savings. Entire cities hitherto surviving on the gambling industry had to convert or perish. Casino after casino were updated to the game of God's existence. Organized crime shifted its focus. Governments in conservative countries argued and banned this new game, where it was then played illegally. Since the Answer was yet to come, the bets also revolved around what the next instalment would hold in store. Individual words, like 'God' or 'blessing' or 'existence' or 'mankind', were betted for or against. And when the supercomputer did spit out kilometres of paper, the output was printed on casino websites for the great gamblers to pore over for days, sometimes weeks. Betters became billionaires or beggars at the end of each game. Many started new businesses, many killed themselves. Marriages were made and broken. Inheritances were drawn up, and sometimes families fell apart. New psychiatric disciplines were founded and researched to treat this new form of addiction. The glorious new chapter in man's search for God began a frenzy the like of which humankind had never known before.'

Humankind, as far as I can see, is forever caught up in some frenzy or the other. It may be argued that if not for our penchant for frenzies, we might still be living on trees.

But at this time a betting frenzy did take over the world and many people were murdered or ruined as a result. Buster came up with at least four different instalments of the Answer thereafter, and each time the biggest consequence was for the gamblers, so that one wondered at the very intent behind the project. Academic interest seemed to be giving way to a baser form of material inquisitiveness. Philosophers cried that the whole thing had turned into an unhealthy game. This isn't the glorious celebration of human curiosity we began with, they sobbed. This is just the fatalistic gambler's insane addiction for what comes next.

It was rather depressing, and several people opted for a certain surgery that was in vogue at the time—a certain lobotomy where a small patch of brain tissue would be removed from your head, following which you wouldn't relate to the God question at all. It was felt by many that the agony would only end when curiosity was killed. After the operation they would feel serene and happy, because it wouldn't matter to them in the least whether God existed or not. Some people likened this to the relief you feel when you vomit in the throes of a migraine. The only problem with this new surgery was that doctors were charging the heavens for it, making use of the patients' agony, trying to retire after performing only a dozen of these. Governments across the world discussed regularizing the fee for this operation, but such things take time. In the meanwhile, a farmer to the south of France took his pet parrot out of its cage, removed its feathers, and chewed its head off. When the animal rights people later asked him about it, he explained, 'I was jealous.' Another took a gun and shot nearly everyone at a shopping mall in San Francisco. A blonde woman in Nigeria, a mother of three, wrote an elaborate suicide note and drove her car straight into a big lake.

But then one autumn day, Buster 235 let out to its human benefactors that the Answer was coming!

The day this was announced to the media, the world held its breath. For that day all the betting stopped. Streets were empty for some reason and corporates declared a holiday. But from the very next day, a new buzz of activities began.

Countries that had long-standing border issues with their neighbours were seen to be moving weapons towards lines of control. Whole leagues of nations began preparing for war. Betting reached a crazed pitch. Looting and arson hit the streets in Third World countries. There were hurried, feverish rapes in busy cities. Scientists killed priests and priests killed scientists, and the incidents were not even investigated. In families, orthodox fathers stopped talking to radical sons. Intellectuals became alcoholics. Debates led to fist fights. The only unifying thought was that the world was ending, yet, strangely, no one thought of shutting Buster 235 down. The possibility of apocalypse overwhelmed the possibility of knowledge.

At the side of the giant building at the undisclosed location where Buster was, several acres of ground was cleared to accommodate all the reams of paper the computer would spew out. This would be the biggest output yet, in terms of sheer volume, because the Answer was on it! On the scheduled night, a camera was fixed upon the huge slit from which the paper would flow out. This was telecast live to all the television stations across the world.

The Answer rolled out near midnight, but it appeared on a postcard-sized bit of paper. It only read:

There is a god, but

◆

Satellites from space recorded images of fireworks back on earth and beamed them into television sets live. The side of the world where it was night was lit up because the religious were celebrating. By the next morning fourteen scientists had killed themselves and another forty-two had been murdered. Among the remaining were the ones who squeakily pointed out that there was a 'but' at the end of Buster's message, meaning there would be another part to the Answer, so hold your horses. Some of these scientists were immediately murdered by the religious fanatics, who said that there might be another part to the Answer but there was no denying the fact that science itself had proven, once and for all, that there was a god. The braver of the scientists speculatively completed Buster 235's message in many vainly hopeful ways, risking their lives and limbs:

'There is a god, but not any more.'

'There is a god, but only in the pathetic minds of some of you.'

'There is a god, but…but, well, that god is what you call science.'

Et cetera.

No one paid them much heed, for it was largely agreed, even by the rational camp, that though Buster 235 might come up with really strange stuff to complete its message, the question of the existence of God had indeed been settled. It was all fair and square. An impartial computer, a product of science, had verified the existence of God in a tampering-free project in an undisclosed location. History had been made, or was being made (for there was another part coming), and some people gracefully made up with the ones they had been in a fight with. But these were few.

Over the next few months, while the world awaited the rest of the Answer, tensions mounted. The more religious countries began unnecessarily sabre-rattling, because they were convinced that there was God on their side. The capitalistic countries responded with a gross exhibition of military power. The countries with troublesome neighbours moved their weapons closer to the borders. Even nuclear warheads were deployed in places. It was almost as if the world had to end now, because everyone had predicted that it would.

Most of the places of betting were shut down by the respective militaries of the countries. Betting was banned across the world by international law, any violations to be dealt with severity. Underworld betting syndicates had, in any case, by now killed each other.

However, as historians later scrutinized, betting had given way to something else. Unprecedented donations were made to places of worship by businessmen and rich people, because they were now sure of return on investment. Now that God existed, they did not mind shelling out gargantuan portions of their wealth as offerings to deities, irrespective of religion or location or even tradition. Places of worship became posh, glittering, luxurious destinations with idols being made of the world's most precious stones and metals. All this within months, when even elected governments began diverting funds to temples and gods. Banks started giving away loans to people who wished to build churches. Families sold their kidneys wholesale to construct mosques. Husbands sent wives into prostitution so that they could erect temples. No one opted for lobotomies any more, and the surgeons began specializing in other disciplines. Priesthood became the most coveted of careers and came to only those who could afford to pay large bribes.

In the far south of France that man who had killed the parrot now went on to eat a pig alive. He later sighed, 'It was so beautiful!' Sammy, the creative head, died in a bar brawl where he tried to begin an argument about Buster 235's message. Someone put out the light by breaking a bottle over his head.

It was rumoured that The Director would soon be made the president of a small nation, but it was also whispered that he would be assassinated soon after. It would at that point be justified to use the word 'assassination' for him, because he would be the president of a small nation. Many predicted that the man would disappear before then.

And in the midst of all this, with the world at the brink of an all-ending war, Buster 235 came up with the Final Instalment of the Answer one noon, before it gave out a sigh, let out dark smoke, and shut down forever.

♦

The Greatest Enemy of Rain

There is a god, but he's neither omnipresent, nor omniscient nor omnipotent. You just think all that because he created you.

Quit using an upper-case 'H' to call him out mid-sentence. It is awkward.

You've been wondering if he existed ever since you began, without ever knowing a tiny bit more about him. So over millennia, you have resorted to simply glorifying him in your minds. He has grown to become impossibly powerful and capable in your imaginings. You have attributed qualities to him that you desire for yourselves.

In reality, your god is not omnipresent. The universe is too vast for him to be present uniformly everywhere. There are, at different times, entire expanses where he tries and fails to be present, because he is situated in a more concentrated form elsewhere. Why else do you think things go wrong at all? When you have a supremely powerful, supremely loving God, why do you still kill each other? Why do road accidents happen, why do sinless babies get cancer, why do black holes eat entire stars? These just happen where and when God couldn't be around. He always comes back in a hurry, but often by then the damage is done.

God is not really omniscient. Entire galaxies collide behind his back. See, do you think in his right mind he would create every speck of dust, until he had two whole galaxies ready, only to spoil everything by smashing them into each other? Why, that would be insane even for you. In forecasting he is not even as proficient as your Nostradamus. He doesn't really see things coming or he wouldn't have created anything, because everything will only be destroyed eventually.

To be honest, God isn't omnipotent either. There are tasks that are quite beyond him. That's why he made the laws of nature. So that things will happen automatically. Just think, if every apple that broke off its tree anywhere in the universe had to necessarily be guided to fall to the ground each time by a non-omnipresent God! Our man would have to be running like that rabid dog all the time. Gravity takes care of that. In fact, a lot of things happen on their own, so God can take his siestas, too. Admitted, he is more capable and efficient than humans, but that still doesn't make him omnipotent. No one is omnipotent. And conversely, if God were omnipotent he would also indeed have to be omniscient and omnipresent, too, no? Think about it.

Quit treating God like one of your movie heroes. He is powerful, yes. Loving, yes. And quite a creator. But do not stick him up on the roof of infinity and eternity. Give him some rope, people, cut him some slack.

So the answer is, God exists, but he is not all that you make him out to be.

◆

After this the scientists did not light any fireworks. According to the history books, nothing much happened after this except the writing of the history books themselves. Countries slowly started removing the concentration of weaponry from their borders, thankfully. Slowly the armies even withdrew from the betting hubs, but that industry had nothing to live for any more anyway. Business resumed gingerly and delicately, and businessmen looked at each other with sheepish grins. World leaders seemed both satisfied and sad. The scientists quickly acted like they were

The Greatest Enemy of Rain

busy with some other invention and the religious leaders became very calm. It was all very peaceful.

There were no more suicides, no more murders, though the man who ate his pets had to be imprisoned to prevent further cruelty to animals.

A little later, the historians began penning this all down. After the answer—as they had now started to call the Answer—came from the Buster project, history was the only thing that seemed remotely interesting to everyone. And in between their narration, when the historians sometimes looked out of their windows, they saw the beautiful sunrise and the pretty blades of grass and wondered how much God was responsible for all this.

7

THE SINGING BUTTERFLIES OF DUABAAG

Even as I write this, I stop at times to stare at my hands, wondering how much more they know than I do. These fingers have become long and hard, their nails dull and brittle, but they do not confide in me yet the details of that day and that night (or was it those days and nights). I don't yet know if I really walked down Duabaag—that beautiful, bewitching garden—and heard those strange butterflies sing. I don't know if Aira was really by my side, or if she is still alive and well, gathering butterflies in a place far away. My memory is strangely fogged, as if more by some magic than age and time. And my hands! They say nothing more though I suspect they know more than they're letting on.

I met her on a train journey. This must have been when I was relatively young, early sixties, I would say. With my new-found ability to write poetry, I was in the habit of travelling to strange and lonely places to write. Always having been unmarried, I had lately discovered what to do with all that freedom. That summer I was making for Paavanpur, a forgotten small town in the far east, to which there was no train or bus. This train, chugging towards a big city further away, came the closest to Paavanpur without quite touching the town. But the trick was, it stopped at a certain signal point where the signal was always red for a few minutes. This was to facilitate the odd traveller to Paavanpur. You needed to jump off quickly at that point, in the middle of nowhere, but you invariably got a ride in a truck or a jeep that was making for Paavanpur. All this sounded just right to me (there was poetry in a godforsaken town so difficult to reach), and here I was, rocking to and fro in a dirty train, refusing to urinate because I knew the toilets would stink.

That was when I noticed a young girl sitting opposite me. I noticed her because when the ticket examiner came I learned that she had the lowest berth, which I wanted. The railways had as usual favoured my backache by assigning me the topmost berth.

I looked at her. She was the type whose age you could have estimated if her spectacles hadn't come in the way. Her glasses suggested she was older, maybe about twenty-six. But her pinched face, thin lips, and the gentle down on her forearms told me she couldn't be more than twenty-one. Of course, it didn't matter as all I wanted was her berth.

'Er...excuse me young lady,' I began, and she looked up from her book. I saw that it was a book on butterflies. 'I have backache. Sometimes it gets so bad I cannot move. I was wondering if...'

'Not a problem,' she smiled, and I saw that she had small, rat-like teeth. 'I'll take the top berth. Not a problem.'

Her smile made her look almost painfully young. I remember her seeming inexperience and freshness evoked a deep feeling of pity in me. Wasn't she rather too young to be traveling alone?

Then for some time I fell to thinking about Paavanpur, the town of sunflower fields, from where you needed to walk at least a kilometre if you wanted to buy soap. I had discovered it in a yellowing magazine in our library and had immediately taken a fancy to it. I had further researched it, spoken to people, and finally figured out I might be inspired to write in such a place. As the train rocked towards nightfall, I continued dreaming and must have dozed off when the girl suddenly said: 'Are you going to Paavanpur?'

'Why, yes!' I said, a little surprised.

'I am, too,' she said, and I was more surprised. Why would a young lady go to such a lonely town? Then I thought that perhaps she was interested in butterflies and had come to see them flitting over the sunflower fields. Or perhaps she had an old grandma there. 'You could help me,' she went on. 'I am a bit nervous about that signal where we need to jump off. I fear I'll miss it.'

'Well, I have that fear too,' I told her. 'This is my first time to these parts. All I know is, we'll reach there by about five in the morning. It's good that there are two of us. We'll keep looking.'

We got talking and she told me that her name was Aira. She was a research student. She studied insects, but her special love was butterflies. When I told her that I was a poet, she said that butterflies and poetry are closely related. As the other passengers started to quietly listen to us over the clank of wheels, she showed me the book she was reading. It was itself a garden of butterflies, and I was taken in by the numerous colourful designs on delicate, powdery wings. She would open a page, show me a beautifully enlarged picture of a butterfly, and explain things about it to me. She was a forthcoming young lady. She told me where each insect was found and how rare it was and how it danced when it wished to mate. I saw that she was looking deep into my eyes, probing, like a ship trying to decide where to lay anchor.

As the windows of the train turned into lines of light and night, she asked me about what I did and wished to see some poetry I had written. She talked about a career in studying insects, about her father who did not really understand what she saw in butterflies. She asked me if I was married and why not, how I had heard of Paavanpur and what I expected to find there, told me that she had, indeed, come to look at butterflies, and at last whispered to me about Duabaag.

'Have you heard of this garden called Duabaag?' she leaned towards me, her eyes snaking into mine. 'It's on the way to Paavanpur…that is, if you walk and not take one of those trucks or jeeps. No one knows where exactly it is, or if it actually exists, because I couldn't find it on any map. I have only heard about it. It is probably just a lot of wilderness full of flowers, but I am sure it's teeming with the rarest butterflies!' As her eyes lit up, I felt my own sleepiness fading.

'I have always loved unstudied landscapes,' she went on, lost in me yet seemingly not conscious of my presence. How quickly the new generation opens up to strangers! 'This garden, Duabaag, is surrounded by local superstition. It seems the butterflies there sing, and you mustn't listen to their song or you will get lost!'

She looked around for a bit, looked out the window and told me she hoped I wasn't sleepy and that she was telling me all this only because I had told her I was a poet.

'There is a lot more,' she went on, 'it's all folklore. Lovely folklore, singing butterflies, new flowers you haven't seen, intriguing landscapes that want you to get lost in…but I don't know it all.' Then something childish, almost amounting to guilt, jumped into her eyes. 'Say, why must we hitch a ride? Why not walk the way to Paavanpur? I mean if there are the two of us, we can walk through this garden…it can't be very far, who knows?'

There it was. I had my answer. She had evaluated me in her fresh, enthusiastic way and found me as harmless as a butterfly. She only wished for someone to escort her to Paavanpur because she wanted to explore this garden of butterflies, Duabaag, on her way and she wasn't sure she wished to do it alone. I considered it, remembered that I was travelling light anyway, and smiled. 'Let's see,' I said, like I might to a child. 'If I get a good night's rest, maybe I can. I am an old man, you see.'

She laughed and became immensely happy. She admitted that she had been wondering at the possibility of going to the garden together ever since she learned that I was going to Paavanpur too. She could have reached Paavanpur first and then decided to visit this Duabaag at leisure, but she wasn't sure she would find a guide in that backward town, and she didn't wish to do this alone. 'Besides,' she said, her face flushing, 'I simply can't wait.'

I wondered at her eagerness to see those butterflies. She explained in a frenzy that she wasn't the type to capture them or stick them up in books. She would merely take pictures of them with her small camera and study them later. Who knows, she might even discover a new species or two!

And then she seemed to suddenly remember her solemn duties. It was beautiful to see how she began to take care of me, that selfish girl! She walked almost the length of the train to find me a relatively clean toilet, she shared her dinner with me, and almost tucked me in, persuading the other passengers to switch the lights off. All so that I would have a good night's rest, and be ready in the morning to walk with her to Paavanpur. The more I observed her, the more I was impressed by her commitment to butterflies.

I slept deep and sweet in the lap of my new-found intimacy with a strange girl whose name I had difficulty remembering. There was so much colour and fluttering inside my head that sometime in the night I woke up and wondered if I was drunk. The train moved with such a steady rhythm that I could not tell the direction of its motion at all. I slept again after looking at my watch, immediately forgetting the time I had read.

Before the crack of dawn there her face was, close to mine,

fresh and fragrant. 'Aira,' I said, recollecting her name. I could see she had freshened up and was ready for her adventure, and I wondered if she had slept at all. 'Four-thirty,' she announced. She was dressed in tight jeans and boots, a small camera slung around her neck and a worn map in her hand.

After I was ready, we stood near the door for some time despite the cold, not talking now. Then she said, 'So…are you fine with it? Do we walk it?'

'We walk it,' I said, and she almost hugged me. 'But I do hope it won't be very far.' She smiled so serenely that it turned into one of those rare moments of my life when I wondered what it might have been like if I had a family.

A little past five-thirty we went to get our luggage as the train began to slow down. 'Is this it?' she asked. The train wailed and halted. I leaned out the door and saw that there was a red signal up front, but not a single passenger seemed to be getting off. Then she spotted a signboard hiding behind a bush:

'PAAVANPUR GOING TRAVELOR GET OF HERE'

'This is it!' she said excitedly, jumping off the train and then helping me down. There again—as she took my duffel bag in one hand and helped me down with the other—I wondered if I would ever hear from her once this little journey of ours was over. Obviously not. For now, our mannerisms, the way we spoke to each other, and our perfect understanding would have suggested to a stranger that we were related. Wouldn't be strange if someone had mistaken her for my daughter.

We found the road after we had jumped over a hedge that bordered the railway track, even as we heard the train silently pulling off behind us like it did not wish to mar the calm of the dawn. Aira was straining her eyes to look at her map, holding it up against a dim half-moon. Then she pointed to the direction we were meant to go, and we began walking. 'Are you cold?' she asked, taking a shawl out of her bag and giving it to me. I wrapped it around my neck.

A little down the road we found a tea shop that had just opened, presumably for the Paavanpur-going traveller. She had tea while I refused, saying tea just then would make me run for a toilet, which it might be difficult to find in these parts. She laughed at that, observing how much like her father I was.

Then as we walked down the road, she began about her butterflies again. I was only half listening, thinking more about whether it was safe for a young lady and an old man to be walking down an unfamiliar road. '...and if she is in no mood for love, you know,' Aira was saying, walking a little ahead of me, turning around and walking backward to face me, 'or if she is already done with her love, or if she finds he is falsely excited and he is actually of a different species, then she will put an instant stop to his enthusiasm. And you know how? She will spread her wings and raise her abdomen high up! In that pose he just cannot find the position to couple with her. Ha!' She arched her own little body to demonstrate the female butterfly's rejection of her male lover.

'Where are you staying in Paavanpur?' I asked suddenly.

'Oh, there is only one small lodge in that whole town,' she said. 'Can't recall the name, it's marked on my map. We will in all probability be staying in the same lodge. Unless you have somebody there...no? Say, after you write your poetry, if you feel like, maybe we can come back again to Duabaag. That is, if there is such a place, and if it is as beautiful as I've heard it is.'

'Duabaag of the singing butterflies?' I said, amused.

'Yes,' she replied. 'It's funny but think about it. What if butterflies really sang, and it's just that we cannot hear them?'

'It must be really beautiful here,' I said. 'Myths and folklore are born in beautiful places.'

'I've heard it's unbearably beautiful. The tribal folk on the hills say Duabaag is full of flowers that bloom across seasons. Eternal spring. They say it is bewitching. There is so much beauty that you can get lost in it. I think they quite fear the place.'

'Must be great to write about, if it exists,' I said, then adding, 'Or even if it doesn't.'

'Yes,' she went on, and I saw that she was like young people when they wake up early; fresh and excited at the crust, a little sleepy at the core. 'Apparently those butterflies carry the souls of dead lovers inside them. That's why they sing so sweetly.'

'Wow!' I pondered, some rhythmic words already forming in my mind. 'Say, is it possible to meet some of these tribal people, I wonder? It'll be great to hear the myth of this garden directly from them.'

'Yes,' she said. 'They'll tell us that you mustn't listen to the butterflies sing. It's bewitching. Makes you forget yourself. Ha ha!'

'Mmm, there is poetry there,' I said absently. The mythical Duabaag was forming inside my head. And then a truck slowed by us to ask if we needed a ride and she waved it by. That moment sufficed to make me think that she only had a sixty-year-old to protect her, but her mind was far from such thoughts.

Thankfully it grew a little light very soon. The chill dropped a bit and the sky was filled with white clouds. She told me that if this wasn't all mythology we would soon find a dirt road leading off into vegetation. Duabaag would span about four kilometres. Once we crossed it we would come to this same road again, but we would have cut our journey significantly short. Paavanpur was only a little further from there.

'You did not drink tea back there,' she said, 'because you were afraid you would need to run for a toilet, eh?'

'Yes.'

'You know something,' she went on, puckering up her lips, 'there are many butterflies that never excrete their waste.'

'Are they constipated?'

'No, silly,' she laughed, again walking ahead of me and turning around. 'They use up all their food for energy!'

'Remarkable creatures,' I observed.

'Oh, you'll love them. They're like poetry,' she said again, as if I had never seen a butterfly ever. We walked on like that until the morning was warm enough for me to take her shawl off my neck and hand it back to her. Two more trucks and a jeep passed us by before she suddenly jumped in joy, saying 'There!' and clapping her hands. A small mud path led off the road and disappeared into thick greens. I was surprised that she was so sure of the way. It was almost like she had been here before.

I had to bend as we left the tar road to walk through a natural arch formed by creepers. The mud path snaked through the bushes narrowly and the sleepy leaves brushed us by as she went on chattering ahead of me. The air was so fresh that I could feel it crisp in my nostrils. We did not reach any border or hedge or fence after which it was Duabaag. Duabaag just happened—the narrow path seemed to imperceptibly lead to a clearing which went on turning wider and wider until it was an ocean of flowers extending far up to the horizon.

'Duabaag!' Aira whispered, and I again had the feeling that she had been here before.

'It's not a myth after all!' I said, looking around, drinking the vision in. 'You think this is it?'

'Duabaag!' she sang again, 'Of course. This is it.'

The Greatest Enemy of Rain

It was easily the most beautiful place I had seen. As the land dipped and rose delicately, the flowers formed strange patterns of colour, like bits of a rainbow fallen to the ground. I could see violet and red and yellow dashed into each other. There was very little green, or perhaps the green was drowned by the other colours. Dewdrops stuck to petals, swollen but refusing to fall off if they could help it. The flowers seemed large to me, even those a little way away from me. We walked down the same path that led us right into the midst of the flowers. Aira looked at her map and then looked around her.

'Where are your butterflies?' I said, and she motioned for me not to talk too loud. 'You'll scare them away,' she said, keeping her own voice very low. Her enthusiasm sent a jolt of energy right through me and I felt a few years younger. In any case, all the tiredness of travel and the walk seemed to have evaporated.

We walked on. The mud path was gradually turning grassy but it was distinct, parting the garden in two. I felt the blades of grass grip at my trousers. Everything was fresh from its night of sleep. I was thinking it would be worthwhile to come here again with her the next day, and the next. Poetry? It simply grew here. The air had a very faint aroma that drew you into it. You drank it in, like some liquid. And because that aroma was so very faint, you gave it more of your attention, more and more of your attention so you could discern it, until it took hold of you completely.

When Aira found her first butterfly, she gripped my hand excitedly and then whispered to me that though we had come across a butterfly and that was great news, this one was nothing to get particularly excited about. 'It's everywhere, nothing rare about it. You'd have seen it in the shrubs in your city,' she said, almost apologetically, like a tour guide who was forced to take you through a boring stretch.

We strolled on—it was a particularly bright moment, because the sun seemed to have come up suddenly, like it was looking at us over a wall—and Aira again gripped my hand and showed me a spot amidst the flowers where a group of butterflies hovered. 'Beautiful,' she whispered, taking her camera off her neck and preparing to click. 'Now that's beautiful!' she said again, taking her pictures and walking off the path for a better view. The butterflies sensed the first humans they had seen in god knew how long, and scattered away. She came back to me then, and sighed: 'Those were the kind of butterflies I could stare at for the rest of my life! Say, now that we know there is a Duabaag, how about we come here every day we are at Paavanpur?'

'Sure,' I said, wondering at how childlike she was. She even gave me a quick peck on the cheek in her uncontrollable happiness. To think I had only met her the day before felt like a dream.

We found the next group of butterflies a little further away and these were even prettier and rarer, even to my untrained eye. In fact, they took my breath away. For one thing, the garden itself had grown almost agonizingly beautiful. I saw big, cheerful flowers that I couldn't name, some deep blue in colour and some a fiery red, heavy with their numerous petals, seemingly drowsy this morning, lulled by the gentle breeze. And then, from behind them emerged the butterflies, like a colourful, impossibly slow explosion. I looked on as Aira danced her way to them. I followed her, thinking that the sweet sound made by the breeze must be what had led to the folklore about the butterflies singing.

I sat down on my knees to watch. The butterflies kept moving away from her and she silently pursued them, trying to befriend them, telling them not to be afraid because she loved them. I could hear her gentle voice, dipped in the music of the breeze, talking to them, persuading them not to fly away from her. She held out her camera to them, telling them that it was not any weapon, it was harmless, it would help her see them again and long for them when she was far away from them. When I saw how fond she was of them, she grew beautiful in my soul. I picked myself up and walked behind her, occasionally sitting to rest my feet though they seemed not to need any rest. I wondered if I could just sit there and pull out my notebook and begin writing.

I can't say for how long we chased that particular cloud of butterflies. Aira had got several pictures and just when she decided that she was done and we should move on, there exploded another swarm of them ahead of us. I sat on the fragrant ground, smiling, watching her with pleasure. She would occasionally come back to where I sat and give me a kiss on the cheek to show her gratitude. I assumed that all she wanted was for me to refrain from saying that we must move on, that I was thirsty or hungry or tired, and that we need to reach Paavanpur. But I was far from saying any such thing. Duabaag seemed to have drawn me in as much as it had her.

I was now beginning to see that the butterflies, much like the flowers, were larger than any that I had seen. They had such elaborate dots and lines and patterns on their wings! And they did not just fly around, or flitter around, like the butterflies I knew. They strolled in the air, casually, luxuriously, like they hadn't a care in the world. Aira needn't have tried to befriend them. I was beginning to see that they did not fear her or anything else. They were from a different world where nothing ever went wrong and there never was anything to be wary about. Very soon they were gliding all around her, some even perching on her hair and one or two on her thin shoulders. She ran up to me, asking me to take her camera and take a picture of her with the butterflies around her. I smiled and complied.

We finally pulled ourselves away and walked on, when I said, 'Where is that mud path?' And we searched the grassy ground for it, parting the plants and peering closely to see the faint track. She smiled, 'I think the path is hiding so we stay a bit longer.' She suggested that we walk in the direction our instincts showed us. So we did, keeping a sharp eye for the mud path.

You might find it funny when I say that we never found that mud path again. The garden had indeed made us lose ourselves in it. It was just as well that I wasn't in the least tired, and Aira was in her heaven. We walked, checking out one swarm of butterflies after another, until we came to a small stream. She bent down to drink and I remarked unnecessarily: 'Cannot deny that we are lost. Maybe those natives were right.' But then I took a sip. I had never tasted water this sweet, and it was quite impossible to worry about losing your way here. She said: 'Well, god knows where Paavanpur is.' Everything seemed bigger and a rush of feelings overwhelmed our senses, as we sank deeper and deeper into the submissive pleasure of being lost. It seemed the further things were from us the bigger they got. Arm in arm like drunken buddies, Aira and I walked alongside the stream.

'We'll just walk straight,' I said, 'until we come out somewhere. I only hope we don't land back on the road we came from.'

'Oh, we won't,' she said. 'I'm sure we are going in the right direction. That mud path might have stretched only till there. I'm sure not many people come this way.'

Then she said that it was strange that a stream like that wasn't marked on her map, but then Duabaag itself wasn't. We decided to cross the water. I found the wetness around her ankles strangely moving, I remember. I had sudden visions of being completely lost in this land, where there was no tiredness or hunger or thirst. My memory fades here, I'm only certain that we walked on like that for a time that was immeasurable. I might have looked at my watch several times, but nothing registered in my head. Seven o'clock would have been the same as eight, or ten, or twelve. Aira was lost in the butterflies and I was lost in Aira. I watched her move with those pretty insects, and I wondered once or twice if she was singing. For even when there was no breeze, when the flowers were still as a painting, I heard humming. It pulled at my soul and drew all of me into it. When I was sure Aira wasn't humming, I said: 'You know, I think those butterflies are singing.' I was like a man unable to wake up.

'Don't listen,' Aira yelled back, giggling. 'You'll forget yourself.'

The land around us was lazily undulating into little hills with silent caves swarming with glow-worms. I caught myself thinking that it would be very pleasurable to have Aira on my lap inside one of these caves. I would wring the ends of her jeans which were damp from wading in the stream. A little later I noticed that the sun wasn't always climbing the skies; it seemed to occasionally bob down and then bob up again, like a ball dropped in water. The clouds were now sprinkled with butterflies, some of them large as birds, each showering down their barely audible song in unhindered, soulful melodies.

It seems strange now but at that time it was the most natural thing in the world. Those butterflies really sang. This could be nothing else, I realized—it had to be butterflies singing, for it felt that only butterflies could sing like that. Too dim to be heard without straining your ears, their chorus still filled that world. Their song was mournful but coy, deep like the seas on a strange planet, and very suggestive. It seemed like they were reminding you of something, tugging at your heart with unspeakable little promises. I drank in their song. I say only butterflies could sing like that because that song was like them; too delicate almost to be heard, yet so beautiful it forced its way into your heart with the sharpness of a needle.

I think I asked Aira if it was true that if you touched a butterfly's wings, some of its powdery colours would come off on your fingers, and the butterfly eventually went away and died quietly somewhere. Did the mere touch of a human, however loving, kill the butterfly? I think that's what I asked. But I cannot recall her answer. I can only recall that she looked like she belonged in that place; the sunlight shone through her; and she seemed weightless, as though any moment she might begin hovering up in the air with the butterflies. I noticed that she wasn't beautiful at all. In fact, if you passed her by on the street you would pass her by without noticing her. But she was very young and her youthfulness was as painful to me as the butterflies' song. When she jumped with joy and her shirt rose, I thought of how that navel was where an umbilical cord had once tethered her, to a big mother butterfly. I almost ran to cover her, to pull her white shirt over her belly. Something about her, and about her being there among those flying flowers, seemed to me unbearable; she was jumping in excitement and yet I found her somehow forlorn. If she suddenly ceased to exist, I thought, my world would have turned into a vacuum, but it would be more bearable, somehow.

I wondered if I was making us go around in circles in that garden. If I was the one deliberately turning us into lost wanderers. I dreaded that this might be over too soon. Then I wondered if she was doing the same. That we wouldn't see that mud path if it ran right in front of her. Now, was she very purposefully chasing those butterflies around in a way that we moved around the same set of places again and again? She seemed so much a part of that landscape, so comfortable to be there, that it appeared impossible that she might be lost there. I don't know for sure, but perhaps we came to that same little stream again and Aira wet the ankles of her jeans again. I am quite sure it happened, maybe repeatedly. You tell me this; her ankles were wet throughout the unknowable time we spent there. That wasn't natural, was it? Unless she kept wetting it in that stream.

But thoughts were to me like drumbeats under water. They lacked sharpness and came from far away. Nothing mattered, nothing was imminent, except that magical landscape with Aira in it.

To me she might have been unforgettable in a painting. Yes, you might pass her by on the road without noticing, but I felt that if she were a painting, it would be impossible to look away. She might be depicted in a sculpture, too, in which she might turn into someone else entirely. Carved in marble she would become the symbol of youth. I wondered, as I saw her dance about with her taunting energy, as she clicked pictures of those large butterflies, if she wasn't trying to bewitch me. In fleeting moments, I again had the distinct feeling that she had been here before. She occasionally still came by to kiss me on my cheek, showing me how grateful she was and briefly treating me to the sudden breathtaking warmth of her youth.

Neither of us spoke about getting back to the world and being on our way to Paavanpur.

Then she did the unthinkable. She began to sing with the butterflies! All along, I hadn't quite admitted to myself fully that the butterflies actually sang. Maybe I thought that I was just hearing it in my head. But then she hummed alongside. I saw her lie happily on the ground in a little clearing among the flowers, her body arched against the sky, her eyes shut tight, the melody flowing out her lips like it had a life of its own.

I was now sure that she was bewitching me. She had taken her spectacles off and her hair was loose in the wind. A butterfly perched on one shut eyelid, listening to her and singing with her. And I thought about the coincidence of meeting her on a train and getting off with her at a signal were no one else got off, and her being a butterfly specialist who never captured butterflies except in pictures.

Before I knew it, I had started planting shameless kisses on her eyelids. We seemed to have done away with the need for time to turn familiarity into intimacy. Danger seemed too far away to be persuasive, like snakes at the bottom of a well.

The trouble, I think, was that indifference did not exist in this place. You see, elsewhere in the world the breeze, the leaves, the movement of the leaves in the breeze, are all indifferent to the person observing them. Nature's indifference, long rued by poets, is actually an essential ingredient of sanity itself. The world, moving in its direction in spite of you, will eventually have you return to it, back on track, correcting your course. But it is a different case when the landscape takes note of you, wraps itself around you, and grows on you. When flowers grow larger, so they don't allow distance to fade them in your eyes. When butterflies hum constantly. When a young girl smiles and laughs and hugs you to make you forget you'd only met her yesterday.

She escaped my embrace time and again, singing and giggling, but I chased after her. We had lost her spectacles and her hair was still loose about her. For some time, we quit fooling around and she went back to studying her butterflies but then I lifted her on to my lap and wrung at the ankles of her jeans, like I had wanted to. I remember being hurt that she had stopped running back to where I sat to plant those childish pecks of appreciation on my cheeks. At times she seemed angry with me for the changed nature of my touch, but when I became morose and lost, she playfully clicked pictures of me and hummed with the butterflies right into my ear. I flattered myself with the thought that this was what she wanted, that this was why she had brought me here. At times I thought that she wished to be one with me, to crush her little frame into me and die with me. But the next moment it seemed distinctly like she was desperately trying to run away from me, like she even feared me and thought I had turned into an ugly monster.

I could have sworn that as we ran about that endless garden, totally lost and indulging in each other in strange, unpredictable ways, the skies turned alternately light and dark in sudden succession. I could have sworn that at certain times the sun dimmed because it wasn't the sun any more; it was night and it was really the moon now. I don't know. All I know is that for all that time—an instant or years—the singing of the butterflies continued. That song must have nourished us too, because we hadn't eaten for who knew how long. We had found some deep red berries which I stopped Aira from sampling because I could tell they were poisonous.

At times we couldn't quite see ahead of us because there were so many butterflies all around. Aira had long stopped photographing them. Her camera lay limp around her neck and she had lost her steam at last. I still kept chasing her, sometimes dancing around her and kissing her. She had stopped resisting my advances and now seemed to come to me effortlessly. Either she had given in to my crushing love that had the weight of a lifetime of longing behind it, or she was herself swept away in morbid passion, driven by the song of the butterflies and the haunting scent of that place. Yes, I could believe at that time that she might have fallen for me, for my old breath and cataracted eyes.

She seemed to be melting into me. She seemed to be reducing, diminishing with every act of love, in some sense I cannot explain. There was a moment when I thought she was like a piece of candy that I was turning around in my mouth, melting away as she gave me her sweetness. It was a funny thought and I noticed that I could still laugh while she seemed lost now, sometimes humming with the butterflies and sometimes crying quietly.

Duabaag played with us. When we slept it formed cushions out of fallen flowers for us. When Aira was melancholic most of the flowers were a sunny yellow and a gentle breezed fanned the down on her cheeks. And whenever we had walked enough in one direction, so that we had a chance of reaching a border of the garden, Duabaag sprawled another endless rush of flowers in front of our eyes, so that the garden seemed to extend till the horizon.

Aira spoke only through song now, in a language I could barely hear and never understand. The wetness had reached up to her knees now and made me wonder if she was disappearing beneath the earth, though there was the much simpler explanation that perhaps she was entering into deeper waters or that the stream was swelling with the change in seasons. In any case she was now very diminished, fading into fragrance and song, offering me her love and haunting me with it at the same time.

Then one evening at dusk (it could equally have been dawn) she came close to me, breathed into me, and looked tiredly into my eyes. I looked at her powdery skin and black button eyes. She stood like that for a long time, and I did too, wondering what she wished to say. I heard nothing, but desire once again took hold of me. She yielded one final time and it was clear that she was bidding me farewell.

We slept again as the sun and moon passed overhead and

The Greatest Enemy of Rain

swarms of those huge butterflies fanned us with their wings, their song a lullaby. When I awoke she was gone. And when I sat up, I saw through the flowers to one side an asphalt road snaking away from me.

◆

As soon as I had reached the road and back into the world I once knew, I checked my cheeks to see if I had grown a long, grey beard. It was the same stubble I had when I had disembarked from the train. I looked around and called 'Aira, Aira' in vain a couple of times, for I knew she had gone. I had seen the goodbye in her eyes.

The garden lay to my side like a sea, deep and colourful, not like the womb I came from but the one I had to return to. I walked down the road as the sense of time jumped back into my head. I told myself that in the morning Aira had seen the road too, and in her shame had walked away and out of my life. Nothing else would make sense.

A truck stopped by and I climbed in. 'Paavanpur?' I asked.

The driver was a huge man with a dirty red cap and small, watery eyes. He looked at me curiously, and said: 'Yes, sahib. This road goes only to Paavanpur.'

The truck pulled away and I looked at my hands then, as I do now. Many times I have asked them why I never properly searched for Aira. Sure, I had asked at the one lodge in Paavanpur, but when no one said they had seen a young girl, why hadn't I gone to the small police station I had seen on my way? Why hadn't I spoken about her to some of the locals I had subsequently befriended, and tried to put together a search party? Why hadn't I enquired with the railways about her ticket and tried to see if they could trace her address and get in touch with a father as old as me, who was awaiting her return? Why hadn't I walked down that same road one day on my own, and tried to locate that garden she called Duabaag, to know if she was still there, tired and lost, her spectacles crushed, her camera broken, her jeans shredded?

Sitting in that truck to Paavanpur, I knew I would never be satisfied with not knowing what had become of Aira, but I also knew I would do nothing about it. Perhaps the poet in me saw her turned into a butterfly herself, fluttering about and inducing fatal love with her song. My rational side still says it was just that she had walked out of my life in shame and disgust, and that she was right now, even as I write this, clicking pictures of butterflies on her camera in some other garden. I certainly hope she is. But then when my hands say nothing of what I think they know, and I crack my old fingers and sit down to write, I am almost visited by the fragrance and song of those countless moments we were in Duabaag.

8

UNCLE

Uncle was a lonely old man. Over years of solitude, he had formed a curiously beautiful relationship with himself. He had learned to lovingly take care of himself because there was no one else to do that. When there was a sudden chill in the mornings, he said to himself: 'Here, wear this scarf or you'll catch a cold.' He guarded his health, his surroundings, and his feelings the way a mother guards her child's. On festivals he cooked himself seven different dishes, then lay out a plantain leaf and the dishes in the exact prescribed order, and ate as if there was a retinue of servants waiting upon him. Then he had an extra-long siesta, waking up only towards evening, and when he was on his porch forking the dead leaves from his lawn, he would look sleepy and refreshed at the same time, his hair standing up like white flames and his eyes saggy but with the clearness of a newborn's.

On Fridays evenings he said: 'Cut your nails. They'll soon be growing inwards.' And then he sat on his porch near his covered motorcycle, carefully adjusted his glasses, tempered down the shaking in his fingers with great effort, and began cutting his nails meticulously, perfectly. By the time he reached his toenails it would be almost twilight and he would invariably curse under his breath: 'This is what happens if you wait until evening. You knew today was the day to cut your nails. Now hurry up. I want this done in the next five minutes!'

In his younger days he would simply flush the nail clippings down the toilet, but in old age he had stopped that. Sometimes an odd piece of nail failed to go down with the flush and later bobbed on the water; a dead part of him that had been growing on him until moments ago. It was extremely unpleasant to look at it. So, he began throwing the clippings under a coconut tree at the side of the house, where the wind would disperse them.

What attracted us to Uncle was his motorcycle. We first noticed it during our holidays, when Uncle removed its cover. Then we saw he did this every morning at precisely eight o'clock. It was an ageless Jawa motorcycle, still glistening under the sun. It was magic because there was not a spot of rust on it! It was perfectly clean like not even a brand-new motorcycle could be. Not a speck of dust, not a teeny bit of caked mud on its wheels, not a faint scratch anywhere or a small tear in the linings of its seat. Nothing real could be so perfect, we thought, as we watched from behind a bush outside his gate.

Uncle wiped the motorcycle with two pieces of cloth he kept in an old box. He did a first round of cleaning with one of these, dipping it in some fluid which we could see wasn't water. He went over every bit of steel, every crevice in its body. He almost seemed like a young man when he did this. Fervently, he cleaned the thin space where the seat met the frame. He rubbed the mirrors on either side, but never looked at himself in them. He wiped every spoke in each tire. We held our breath, five boys hidden in that bush, as he finished with the first cloth and then went in for his breakfast. Then he came back in twenty minutes and pulled out the other cloth from his box. With this he was brisker. He just ran it to and fro, polishing the motorcycle as if it were a shoe. At the end, he would stand back and study it with great concentration.

The Greatest Enemy of Rain

Sometimes he would pull out one of the two pieces of clothes again and wipe a certain part. In the end he would be satisfied. He would then pick up the cover, itself a spotlessly clean white bed sheet, and dust it thoroughly. Then he would drape the motorcycle in it fondly, as though the form hidden underneath was for his aged eyes only; as though he couldn't bear the thought of even light settling upon it.

This was his routine every morning, but then we discovered something even more curious. Sometimes, though very rarely, Uncle left his house with a can in his hand. We saw him do this only once or twice in all our days there, across several of our school vacations. He was going to the petrol pump at the other end of town, we discovered. There was a pump which was closer, but people said it sold adulterated fuel. Uncle walked all the way, bent, sighing, ignoring the blisters on his feet and the frowns on his forehead the journey gave him. He bought petrol and came back, never taking a rickshaw, never asking anyone for a ride. The following morning while cleaning the motorcycle he would gently open its tank, look around almost secretively, and pour the fuel in.

'But he never rides it!' exclaimed Pramod, the youngest of us. 'Where does all the petrol go?'

'It evaporates, silly,' said Jake, who thought he knew bikes.

'Evaporates and goes where?'

'Hush!'

Now, when an old man asks to be left alone in a quiet small town, that is precisely what the quiet small town doesn't want to do. People made stories about Uncle; dark tales, funny tales, theories, predictions, even fantastic myths. There was a woman called Shanta who visited the house every evening to clean it. She spread stories about suspicious-looking stones, lemons, straws from bird nests and dead spiders—all ingredients of black magic—that she had seen in the house. To each person she told these stories, she swore she had told no one else, and requested secrecy in turn. She claimed if ever the dark man learned that she had let out the goings-on in that house (or, for that matter, if she even stopped going there to work out of fear), it might anger him and then she might die of warts, like any victim of vindictive magic.

The rumours Shanta spread were taken up by others across town, mostly as jokes. However, some took the stories seriously and the stories grew sinister. All that we heard about Uncle grew in our imaginations, and we thought he was a sorcerer. His mutterings to himself (from behind our bush we observed his lips move even as ours trembled) made us think he had invisible companions. His motorcycle, which looked like no human hand had ever touched it, made us dreadfully curious. When we heard about the petrol he fed it, Prashant, the dreamiest among us, suggested that perhaps he flew it through the clouds at midnight. But little Pramod's brother Suresh tried to laugh this off saying Prashant's vision was inspired by some English film. Despite this, cold chills ran up and down our spines as we observed Uncle morning after morning from across the road.

Being children, the mythology we were fed made us divide the universe into two distinct pieces—good and evil. We quickly decided that Uncle was evil. The very fact that we felt scared of him proved he was evil. It terrified us to think that we were so irrevocably drawn towards him. Consider the fact that every morning now we hid outside his gates to observe him. We lied to our parents about where we were. We made discreet enquiries about him, never letting out too much about our interest in him. All this made us decide that Uncle must be evil. Our fascination and surreptitiousness were proof of his sorcery.

The Greatest Enemy of Rain

We found out that he was called Uncle by everyone. That was his name. Considering his age, even if they had to use a nickname, people ought to have called him Grandpa or something like that. But the fact that he was called Uncle indicated that he was called that for a long, long time (perhaps a thousand years, Prashant said).

One morning, while we were peeking from behind the bush as Uncle rubbed and rubbed his motorcycle's round front light, he suddenly looked towards us. His face wrinkled up in the sweetest smile we had ever seen. One tooth each was missing on his upper and lower gums in front, on different sides. He carefully placed the cloth across the motorcycle's seat and stood up creakily. Then, still smiling, he beckoned to us with his long, twiggy fingers, slowly, as if he were miles under water. Little Pramod shut his eyes tight with his palms. I realized, the hair on the nape of my neck tingling, that five of us couldn't ever have hoped to hide behind one small bush. Or perhaps the bush had suddenly shrunk, so that we stood exposed and naked all of a sudden. You cannot hide from a sorcerer.

Suresh forced his brother's palms off his eyes and they both fled in one direction while Jake, Prashant, and I fled in the other.

'Now we're in trouble,' I said to myself over and over as I ran.

For almost a week after that, we stayed away from that street. And if you believe in magic then it might make sense to you that we took turns dreaming about Uncle each night. But stranger than that, we even heard people refer to him at different times. It was as if we heard 'Uncle', 'Uncle' from the mouths of the unlikeliest people. Pramod and Suresh heard their father talk about Uncle to the milkman in the morning: 'Do you know anything about that old man they call Uncle? Do you supply milk there? Odd one he is. Came to my shop yesterday to buy, you will never guess, machine oil. What's he doing with that, I wonder?' I heard a fishmonger tell a vegetable vendor: 'You went all the way to the city for those? Ha! Don't mind my saying so, those vegetables are nothing special. This is like that Uncle crossing the whole town for a little petrol.' In fact, it seemed that we were learning more about Uncle then than we have ever before.

Prashant dreamt that Uncle's motorcycle was covered in filth from the sewers and refuse from the meat shops. Uncle approached the dirty bike with a sweet smile, took a deep breath, and blew away all the filth. He didn't stop for breath until the whole motorbike was spotlessly clean again. 'You should have seen his face!' Prashant said, almost breathlessly. 'His eyes puffed out and his teeth were sharp, like an animal's. He blew sparks at the motorcycle. I woke up sweating. I'm sure it was no ordinary dream!' Little Pramod covered his ears.

All these references to Uncle and dreams about him in the gap of less than a week! To our minds it was as if the sorcerer was using all the dark magic in his power to draw us back to his house. 'Sorcerers need boys for sacrifice,' Jake said logically. 'To evoke spirits from the dead world.'

The sorcery must have worked, for in a few days there we were again, unable to resist the pull towards him, crouching behind the bush that could hardly hide us all. And there Uncle was, bending low, cleaning his Jawa with his very lifeforce.

'This is the part, here,' we heard him tell his invisible accomplice, 'the cloth doesn't reach. Will need to brush it.'

'Remind me to buy a brush,' he said, nodding. 'A small one. This evening…from that stationery shop. Such as the one artists use.'

'Let's go this evening, let's not keep it for later,' he muttered. In spite of ourselves we grinned and then Uncle looked up.

The Greatest Enemy of Rain

He smiled beautifully once again, and beckoned us to approach him.

This time we did not run. In fact, Pramod was the first to cross the road and go over to the gate. We followed him one after the other and lined up outside his compound, looking through the grill of the gate.

'That's a fine bike you got, Uncle,' Jake said. 'Fine machine; an old Jawa.'

'Yes, it's the companion of my youth,' Uncle said. His voice reminded us of the sweet water of a tender coconut. 'I'm sorry I was talking to myself back then. You must have heard me. Worry not, I'm not insane. Gets a bit lonely, that's all, so I make myself into many old men, so we can all talk to each other and have a ball. Ha ha! Come on in. I like children who like motorcycles.'

You might think this strange, but we opened the gates and walked right in. Each of us later said he felt like he was in a trance. A kind of forced calm, almost like we couldn't help being calm. Just like you cannot escape sleep with a powerful sedative, even if your house is on fire.

Uncle placed the cloth he was using to clean on the handlebar and went inside for a moment. We looked at each other, but no one said anything. Uncle came back out and opened before us a box of boiled sweets. 'It's the first time you have paid me a visit. Here, have some.'

We unanimously rejected the treat and felt proud of our discretion. We might all be under a spell, yes, but we were not about to eat something offered by a stranger, especially one suspected to be an evil wizard. 'Fair enough,' Uncle said, closing the box of sweets without trying to persuade us. He placed it carefully on the ground and picked up the cloth again. 'You know,' he said, 'this motorcycle would easily be the oldest in these parts.'

In the whole world, we thought, our eyes narrow.

'Yet it's the cleanest. I clean and polish it every day. You see, it's my bridge to my youth. Takes me back to the days when she was new and I would ride her across streets and people would stare in admiration!'

Pramod was looking from the motorcycle to Uncle. We had never heard a bike being addressed as 'she'. It was wonderful to hear him talk like the Jawa was a lady.

'In fact,' he continued in his tender-coconut water voice, 'she has been my only constant companion throughout.'

'What's her power?' asked Jake expertly.

'Three-fifty,' Uncle replied.

'Czech, isn't she?'

'Yes, she is from the Republic of Czechoslovakia. What an interesting boy you are!'

'Petrol, right? I think they had a line of diesel bikes too?'

'Oh, she's petrol. Diesel ones need plenty of maintenance.'

That first meeting went on like that, us standing and him crouched near the tyres, with Jake showing off his knowledge of bikes and Uncle more and more pleased to answer his questions. By the time we left, we were quite comfortable. Even Pramod seemed to have warmed up to our new friend. Jake went on talking to us for some time about Jawa bikes, as if the real object of our curiosity had never really been Uncle. Then suddenly, Prashant said: 'You think we ought to have eaten the sweets?'

'No,' I said. 'Just because he talks nicely doesn't mean we need to throw caution to the winds. We've spoken to him only today, for God's sake, for the first time in our lives.'

We swore to each other that we wouldn't reveal our meeting with Uncle to our parents or to anybody. Our new-found friendship would be our secret. As the hours passed, our meeting began to seem unreal. By that evening it was as if we couldn't entirely be sure we had opened that gate and walked in and stood near that magically perfect motorcycle and spoken with Uncle. But we were back the next day, and again Uncle and Jake began talking about bikes. But today Uncle seemed a little dreamy.

'When I was very young—I am an architect, and it isn't just you but everybody who calls me Uncle, you might already know—and this Jawa here was new, you should have seen me! No less than the heroes in the movies. I would be thud-thudding down the streets in my city, or through lanes flanked by fields, you know? How they looked at me, old men, young men, women, girls, children.... I would wear only black silk shirts those days. Completely black, even black pants, but sometimes with my hair coloured golden. And I would ride the Jawa with my shirt buttons undone almost to my navel. A thick gold chain (matching my hair colour) would run down my chest. Oh!'

We let him dream about himself a bit longer. Jake made to ask something but decided against it.

'Say, this is very rude of me,' Uncle suddenly said. 'Wouldn't you like to come in?'

We were all cautious immediately. 'No,' Pramod almost yelled.

'It's good out here in the open,' I said, placing my hand on Pramod's shoulder. 'Cooler.'

'Fair enough,' Uncle said.

'I was incredibly young,' Uncle continued, 'when most boys my age were still studying or wondering what to do with their lives, I had already started earning. It was all success and the admiration of others. Mothers in the neighbourhood would wait for me to grow up, so they could marry off their daughters to me.

Plenty of money, no liabilities, authority at work…and a Jawa, all went perfectly together.'

'Did you then have an accident?' Pramod asked suddenly. 'Did you fall off the Jawa?'

'Why, no!' Uncle suddenly laughed, his breath hissing through the gaps in his teeth on either side. 'Why must I have an accident? Ha haha!'

'I-I don't know,' Pramod stumbled, 'it just seemed like something wrong must have happened then. Something…bad.'

'Ha haha! Fancy thinking that. Well, nothing of the sort happened.'

He liked Pramod's sudden interjection so much that he took some fallen leaves and crafted a small pinwheel for him. Before making it, he had laid the cloth down on the motorcycle's seat. Jake looked at him and asked him if he could pick it up and clean the rear lights.

'No,' Uncle said rather sternly, 'I'll do it right away.'

'Fair enough,' Jake said.

When we took his leave, Uncle told us that he really appreciated us coming. He only had the company of a maidservant who came in for an hour in the evenings. 'She knows nothing about bikes. Indeed, she hates chatting with me.' And then his eyes glinted. 'In fact, I suspect she's a witch.' We all laughed.

One of those days we asked him if he ever rode the Jawa now.

'The last time I rode it was fourteen years ago,' he said, and we were lost in his eyes. 'I was coming back from a wedding reception in my city. The problem was, I had eaten a little too much, and the bobbing of the bike gave me a heartburn. "That's enough biking," I told myself as I rode back. "You can just keep your bike now, but don't ride it." I never rode her after that, but kept her spotless, as you can see.' Then he seemed to disappear behind a dark cloud for some time. We all waited in silence. After some time, he said: 'But oh, what I wouldn't give to ride her once again!'

'You have never ridden her since?' I asked, thinking of the petrol he bought and of Prashant's theory about him flying at night.

'No, that's what I'm telling you,' Uncle said. 'But I have been dreaming about it for some years now. Of late it's become a craving. Sometimes it's unbearable. I just want to get on her and zoom away.'

'But Uncle,' Jake said, 'why don't you try? We could help you. I'm sure you won't fall or anything.'

'Oh, it's not that,' he said. 'I wouldn't even need any help. Well, maybe if someone could just start her for me. I'm not sure I have the strength in my legs for the kind of kickstart required to get her going. I can get on and ride her now, though not too fast or anything. But no, that's not why I hold myself back. I am too old now. Even if I do ride her now I'll be an incongruous old man clinging on to a very powerful machine. Nothing glorious there! I would ride her if I were young again. That's what I dream about. Going back to my youth, in my black silk shirt and gold chain, and also my hair golden and one ring on my left ear…ah! The architect who creates, the strong youth who builds structures that stand tall. That's who I dream of being again when I ride her. I would sell my soul for a moment like that.'

Pramod, who was watching Uncle's face intently, suddenly remarked: 'Well, Uncle, maybe you should pray for an angel to come and make you young, so you can ride your bike again.' Uncle patted his cheek, though we hoped our little friend wasn't sounding like he was mocking the old man.

For nearly a week we stood every morning near the

motorcycle, talking about this and that. We found that Uncle's irredeemable longing to grow young again so he could ride his Jawa was playing on his mind a lot of the time. It repeatedly came up and it was getting rather depressing when he talked about it. His eyes did not flash like a sorcerer's when he dreamt thus, and speckles of spit sometimes gathered at the corners of his lips as he lost himself. We wished he would stop his dreaming, because it made him look old and ordinary. We tried to relieve his sorrow in all ways we could: Jake spoke about new, powerful motorbikes to distract him. I spoke about our small town and the people in it and what they said about Uncle sometimes. He laughed at the stories. Pramod sang his rhymes. And Prashant told us all about his problem.

Prashant had a very curious problem, and we were even more surprised that he had opened up for the first time in the presence of Uncle. His problem was that he had the ugliest visions at the most inopportune moments. He had a very pious family who visited temples a lot. Prashant's problem was that whenever he stood before a deity to pray, horrible images of shit, phlegm, and sore wounds forced themselves into his head. He even dreamt that these were dripping off the idol itself, and that rendered him totally unable to pray. He felt immense guilt and sometimes feared going to temples. He feared the wrath of God, and he dreaded that his face might expose his thoughts to his parents. But it did not end there. Whenever his father went out of the house, he had a sudden vision that they were bringing him back dead from an accident, his body bleeding and broken up. When his mother was washing clothes in the backyard, he was abruptly jolted by a mental picture of her turning blue from a snakebite.

Prashant went on to describe his horrendous and perfectly disgusting visions. He imagined illicit relationships among neighbours (the worst ones involved his own family members), visions of a plane that was flying overhead suddenly catching fire and dropping from the air, dead bodies impaled on branches, an overdressed man's intestines tailing out his anus as he walked. When he saw the curiosity his confession was evoking he even got a little proud. 'Why,' he exclaimed at last in his excitement, 'yesterday when I saw a cow walking down the street, I imagined it had blood on its jaws! It had turned into a carnivore and was eating people.' This last, I suspected, he had made up in that moment.

Uncle listened to him carefully. Then, dusting his speedometer carefully, he said: 'Well, I wouldn't worry too much about these visions. I think it just means you're an imaginative boy.' Then he thought some more and said, 'You know, I might have a solution. When you think of phlegm on the gods, don't try to stop your thoughts. Instead, add more visions of your own. Introduce sewage and earwax. Ha ha! When your dear one is going out, say to yourself, "There he goes, and I will now see him come back dead and broken." Push it, willingly. Just try that.'

Every day after that Uncle would ask Prashant if he had any visions and how he dealt with it. We realized with some relief that Prashant's problem seemed to cure Uncle of his obsession with his youth, at least for the time being. A few weeks after, he invited us into the house once again. This time, we went in eagerly.

Uncle's house wasn't anywhere near as neat as his motorcycle. In fact, almost every corner had piles of clothes that needed to be washed and every windowsill and table held remains of uneaten food. There were a lot of ancient-looking books, some lying open and some stripped off their covers. 'Shanta, my maid, hasn't come for two days,' he explained.

I do not remember what it was, but Uncle always served us

the same drink. Its base was lime juice, but he added cut fruits and a tonic to it. It was his specialty. Then one day he told us about it. 'This recipe was taught to me by a girl named Jithela. I used to stay in a paying guest accommodation in the city, you know, right after my second job. I was easily the best architect thereabouts. I had already designed some noted houses and an apartment and had made a name for myself. The landlady would send her daughter Jithela to bring me my meals every day in the hope that we might fall in love.' Then he ended the story abruptly, 'It was Jithela who taught me how to make this drink.'

'Well then, did you fall in love?' Suresh asked.

'It was very unfortunate, you know,' Uncle said. 'I still feel guilty. It's the most tragic story of all.'

He was lost in a longing you can observe on the face of a hill when the sun has gone down on the other side.

'Try as I might, I couldn't fall in love with that nice girl,' he said morosely. 'She was a good friend, always smiling and very beautiful. She loved me deeply, always dreaming about me and getting me gifts. But what could I do? I could only see her as a friend. A very good friend, yes, but nothing more. Finally, Jithela cried and her mother cried and I left the place for fear of breaking their poor hearts.'

We sipped the drink and thought that it was very sweet, like the poor girl Jithela. Her name tasted sweet and a shade sour and tangy to us. This was the drink Jithela made for him, with lime and cut pears and apples and green chillies and sugar and salt, so that he would sip it and fall in love with her. Jake smiled and we could see that he was thinking that Jithela might now be a very old woman. But though at first we thought that Uncle had told us something especially near to his heart—almost a confession like Prashant's—we soon realized that Jithela was but one of his

The Greatest Enemy of Rain

many stories. In fact, we slowly started to feel that Uncle drew these out of his vast memory reservoir and kept them ready for us when we arrived. He also started to tidy up the house a little, presumably because he now had daily guests visiting him in the mornings. We came after he was done with his bike cleaning and sat with him until lunchtime.

Uncle told us about Jyothi, a junior architect who was quite unlike Jithela. She possessed neither Jithela's childlike innocence nor was she nearly as beautiful. Jyothi was so moved by Uncle's fine work that she would unabashedly flirt with him. 'She even started to dress like a model. I didn't like her.' Finally it had gotten so awkward that he had to send her away, though he saw promise in her as an architect.

He told these stories with gusto, his mind drifting far away from the cane chair on which he sat, his eyes lost in the fog of the years. But when the story was over he would invariably fall into deep melancholia. One day he again began talking of becoming young and riding his Jawa once more, if only for a day, for half a day, for just a few hours. Prashant tried to tell him about how he lately had a vision of a totally bald man whose scalp was ripped off by a strong wind. The rest of us tried to talk about girls at school. I threw in our math teacher's unpleasant habit of digging his nose when he was turning numbers in his head. But though Uncle smiled at these stories, nothing caught his mind.

Then one day when it was almost time for our holidays to end, Uncle suddenly showed us a bag full of lemons. 'What do you think they are for?'

'To make the Jithela drink?' Pramod said.

'Ha ha! Not so many of them, no,' Uncle replied, a shimmer in his eyes. 'These are for magic.' He then placed Pramod on his knees, picked some playing cards, and threw them on a bench.

The cards arranged themselves into a deck, precariously balanced on each other!

'I learned magic when I was very young,' he said. 'Do you know that women are more fascinated with magicians than men? We men think of magicians as tricksters, but women think of them as wizards and sorcerers.' To us it was the most natural and delightful thing in the world that Uncle was a magician.

Even after school started, we would drop in sometimes on Sundays or in the evenings. It saddened us that without our morning visits to look forward to, Uncle was once again becoming a very old man, talking to himself, and pining for his youth. We understood that he was a man who had left a colourful, exciting, and notably successful lifetime behind him, and was now sick with nostalgia. He missed the admiration of people (which probably appeared in very exaggerated versions in his memory), the attention from women, and most of all the wind in his hair as he rode his Jawa. The sad beauty of time threw a dark pall over him, and we saw that one day he had removed all the clocks in his house. We noticed he was practising his magic every day, with more lemons and chalks and needles. He told us that he was trying to evoke an angel who could send him back to his youth for a day and we saw that he was clearly going mad. But all through he kept up the regular cleaning of his motorcycle, though he was growing older by the day. We waved to him in the mornings as we passed by on our way to school. He stopped us once to ask when our next holidays would be, and when little Pramod told him he said, 'I doubt I'll be alive then.'

Sure enough, Uncle did seem to be fading away. Sometimes in the mornings he did not even see us as he bent double by his motorcycle, lost in another time. After playing cricket with the boys on evenings and coming home to wash up and pray, I often looked at the red of the sky and wondered if Uncle would be dead. I felt a sense of relief whenever we went to see him and he was still there. Once we had an unshakeable feeling that he was sick, and we went to enquire after him. He was recovering from a fever.

'You know, when you have a leaky nose,' Uncle said without inviting us inside because he knew we were on our way to school, 'I just observed something curious. Your nose leaks the most when your hands are not free to wipe it! No, don't laugh. Observe the next time you have a cold. The torrent comes down just when both your hands are engaged. I think there is a reason. I think it is the adaptation of the cold virus. Over centuries of evolution, it has gained enough control of our nerves and brain to make this happen. You see, if you cannot wipe your nose in time—say, if just then you are holding a heavy tub of hot water with both hands—then the virus succeeds in making your nose drip just at that moment, so that it—the virus, I mean—has a better chance of spreading and infecting others. You see my point? It has evolved successfully for this. You can see that science has solutions for everything.'

That's how Uncle was, now. His solitude made him make curious observations which he shared only with us. Yet, school and routine had such power, we did drift away from Uncle slowly. There were entire days when we did not speak to him or even of him to each other. There might have been mornings, and I feel guilty when I say this, when we might have walked past his gate without looking in. But then when we remembered him we made it a point to go see him, albeit for a short while, and see how he was doing. Once he said, his eyes gleaming with madness, 'I'm trying my best to please that angel. Just one day of youth is all I ask.'

One day Jake said when we were playing cricket: 'What'll happen to Uncle's Jawa when he is dead?'

We all had visions of the motorcycle neglected, rusted and dusty with spiders crawling on it. The next day we cancelled our cricket session and spent the evening in Uncle's house. He had indeed grown very old, older than we thought it possible for anyone to grow without being dead already. Pramod later said that his skin had become like when you stay in water for too long. He seemed to have lost more teeth because his cheeks had sunk further in. But his eyes gleamed with a new glee. He showed us the stuff of his magic—the patterns on the floor that he had drawn with different colours of chalk and many lemons, a lamp, and a bottle of some liquid. 'I will sit straight and ride my Jawa along the fields, boys, just you watch. And the very crop will bend their heads in awe. No, worry not, I will not be dreaming that I am young again. I will be young again, for real, for just a few hours, you watch out! The ladies will swoon and boys like you will imitate my style and my gestures.'

He told us that it will happen someday soon, maybe some time during the beginning of our next holidays, which were fast approaching. He was following certain dark texts and engaging in very occult rituals to make an angel appear. He couldn't fail. He had stopped eating non-vegetarian food to keep himself pure for the rituals. In fact, he wasn't eating much at all; he was mostly only drinking goat's milk. He had told Shanta to go on long leave and to come back only much later. The angel would be pleased and his wish would be granted. He told us that the side effect of this magical transformation was that just after he rode his Jawa, and had come back home, he would only have time to clean the motorcycle one last time, and then he would lie down on his foldable bed and die. But he was prepared to make that sacrifice. He did not plan to go on living like this anyway, old and alone, not him, because he had had no ordinary life. Someone so illustrious in his lifetime was not designed for the disgrace of old age.

We asked him, in a rather conciliatory tone, if we couldn't just start the motorbike for him so he could sit on it when it was still on its stand. We felt he could dream up the bowing paddy fields, the wind in his hair and the swooning women in his old brain and perhaps then his burning desires would be appeased. But Uncle did not even answer us.

He was still mumbling when we left him, and we were very worried. But on our way out we glanced at the Jawa in its white shroud. We looked at the tyres and saw that even at the point where they touched the ground there was not a speck of dust!

The day our next holidays began we ran to Uncle to make up for the times we had neglected him. 'Any day now,' he told us, eyes bright. But he continued to tell us disconnected things, like the observation about the running nose. One morning he said: 'You must have seen those calendars with landscapes above the dates, right? Those calendars with the incredibly beautiful house by the incredibly beautiful waterfall? Calendars with sceneries of the loveliest spots on earth with ordinary homes like yours and mine. Sometimes a real village with white huts scattered over a green mountainside that looks like a painting? Or trees among the snow? Or a railway track running among fallen flowers…right through a dreamy landscape? I mean photographs, not paintings, though you always first wonder if they are paintings. Because your mind tells you such beauty can't be real. Have you seen those? People give these calendars to each other on New Year's. Hmm, good. Well, the other day I was wondering if the people who actually lived in those places in the calendars, are they happier than us?

You know, what it must be like to live near a waterfall that looks like heaven, or to go for a walk among trees in the snow. Or to sit in a train that is moving through a dream. Do you think they're happier than us? Or would they be sadder than us, with fewer challenges and an overdose of beauty to greet them every morning when they look out the window? Funny things, those calendars.'

To this day I cannot put together all the different, disconnected things Uncle told us and find a pattern. One of those days he pulled out a calendar from a rusty trunk, and it turned out he used to collect them until some years ago. The dates on it were decades old but it had scenes of all kinds of landscapes—forests, snow, green grass, even big water bodies. Just as Uncle had said, you first wondered if they were paintings. And then Uncle said the most curious thing of all: 'If you just lie down in that grass, you have nothing to fear. Such a place will not have snakes or scorpions to bite you. If you sink into that white snow, you will not get frostbite. No? Don't you get that feeling? That these places cannot have anything unpleasant? Ha haha! You could drown and stop existing in those lakes without feeling breathless and thrashing about.'

He told us about the many chants he had learned from his ancient books to make the angel appear. 'Any day now,' he said again. 'You see, angels don't just appear and grant you your wish. They need to be convinced of your earnestness. They have to give a little of themselves, their divinity, you know, every time they make a human's dream come true. Miracles are against the order of nature, like magic, and something has to give to make them happen.'

That day after we had said our goodbyes to him and were on our way back, Suresh sighed and said, 'You think Uncle is mad? He is very serious about this angel business, you know?'

'Mad? Why?' Pramod asked.

'He was yearning to become young so bad and for so long,' I said, thinking aloud. 'Becoming young again once you are old is impossible, and chasing something impossible can cause madness.'

'You think he is mad?' little Pramod asked. 'You don't believe in angels?'

'If you ask me he was always a little mad…keeping that bike spotless like that,' said Jake. 'That was rather impossible too.'

'He took the help of angels to clean the bike?' Pramod asked.

'Those rituals are killing him,' Suresh said. 'I don't think he eats or sleeps.'

'He drinks goat's milk. He won't die,' Pramod said.

'Shut up,' his brother told him.

Only Prashant seemed to understand what Uncle had last said about angels 'spending' a little of themselves to make human dreams come true. He explained it to us in some detail, until we began to wonder if he was going a little mad too. All of us except little Pramod found Uncle's state of mind very worrying, but at times also a little funny. We had a very restless night and were back at Uncle's house in a hurry the next morning.

Today we found his glances furtive, his skin wrinkled beyond measure, and there were spots on his arms. 'It is tomorrow,' he told us, forgetting even to mix our Jithela drink. He had us stand outside, like in the beginning, and we assumed a lot of strange stuff must be happening inside for him to hide them even from us.

'It is tomorrow,' he said again, for the first time being careless as he cleaned the rim of his tyres. 'The angel came at last! He took pity on me and said I could have my little moment of youth.'

Suresh suppressed a little yelp. Then he looked at Uncle with understanding and pity.

'Don't come here tomorrow. Come straight to the road by the fields at this hour in the morning. Of course, I will not recognize you because I didn't know you in my youth. But you'll know me. Oh! You won't miss me, I can tell you that. Hair coloured golden, jet-black silk shirt, thick long gold chain running through crisp black hair on the chest, the roar of this Jawa, polished to perfection...you will not miss me. Slung at my back will be a black leather bag with my architect's instruments, always with a roll of tracing paper peeking out. Everybody will notice me. You can expect a few young girls to swoon tomorrow, boys. I think my youth will be something disruptive in this sleepy little town.'

Our jaws hung in wonder. Jake looked confused. Suresh seemed worried. Only Pramod was lost in Uncle's words, dreaming with the man and looking from him to the motorcycle and back at him again.

'I will have some time, the angel has promised,' Uncle went on, 'though of course, not the whole day. These things are difficult, you know, even for an angel. Though he didn't say it, I expect I will die straight after the event, so I will need you to alert the town. Don't tell people about the miracle or they'll spank you for lying. Or accuse you of insanity. Ha ha! If any of you grow up to be a writer, make a story of this. And don't worry, I will come back to this old, rotten self at the time of my death. By that time the miracle would have worn.' Then he appeared to think about something, and said: 'Get your bicycles along. Wait for me near the fields and then take the shortcut to the market. I will take every long cut just to feel the breeze in my hair. You can thus see me at multiple points, right? Take the small lanes again and come quickly to the cinema theatre and wait for me under the jackfruit tree. I will do the rounds. I expect I will be back here before lunch. I will thank the angel and lie down to die.' There were tears at the corners of his eyes.

We woke up early the next day, not having slept much at all, and were lined up on our bicycles by the golden fields that flank the town. Did we half expect Uncle to grow young and ride by on his Jawa? I do not know. The wind was howling like something special was about to happen, like there was an invisible spirit riding it and tormenting it. There were very few people walking about. Jake said that he was sure Uncle would come riding on his Jawa, old as the mountains but dreaming that he was young. He only hoped the man wouldn't fall off. He most certainly wouldn't survive a skid and a fall, we thought. I wondered if we should have tried to stop him. Suresh suggested we should be at his house right now, helping him, guiding him out of his madness. 'An old man can break his leg, you know, trying to start that thing.' Prashant said he had visions of Uncle lying dead near the Jawa right outside his house. Pramod clutched Suresh's fingers hard and stared down the road.

Some moments later we heard the roar of the Jawa. We knew it was Uncle only because he looked exactly as he had described: golden hair, black shirt, black trousers. The sun gleamed off his gold chain. The young man before us must have been not more than twenty-two years old.

It was a mad, mad time, you understand? There are some of us today who say that it did not happen at all. Little Pramod, who was the only one at the time to believe in miracles, now denies it with a wave of his hand. A middle-aged banker with a bald patch and clear reasoning, he says there is science to show that a group of people can have the same dream, especially in childhood. And there is science to say that some dreams, after many years, appear real. I don't know, I am confused.

But I'm certain we did stand there that morning, the wind

slapping our cheeks, watching Uncle as he passed by without recognizing us. His black leather bag hung behind him, and the roll of tracing paper peeped out. Only, we later thought that he ought to have passed us by in slow-motion like in the movies. Instead, he just rode by, like people always ride by, glancing at the fields with their scarecrows, his bag bobbing up and down as the Jawa bounced over the potholes without creaks or groans.

We stood dazed for some moments after Uncle had disappeared round the bend. Only Pramod smiled. Then Jake suddenly yelled, 'Come on!' and we raced down the other way with our cycles, through mud roads so narrow we almost nicked the compound walls, cutting our ankles on sharp grass and finally emerging at the marketplace. We stood waiting under a rusty flagpole away from the crowd. The market was now quite awake and there were vendors yelling their wares and shoppers bargaining hard. People were already sweating, though it was windy.

And then Uncle arrived: a young man new to these parts, mounted on an old, magically gleaming black motorcycle. Some people looked up at the sound of the bike, and then looked away again. We saw a beautiful young girl who was bargaining with a roadside vendor over a bunch of bangles. She looked up as Uncle passed, and then pointed at another set of bangles, enquiring if they would be cheaper. Someone threw a ball of wastepaper on the road and it hit Uncle's rear tyre and rolled behind him for a bit. As he passed by, Jake waved. Uncle waved back grandly without recognizing us, and that particular motion of his, that wave when I recall it now, did appear to be in slow motion.

We chased Uncle around, cutting through shortcuts again and arriving before him to watch him. Near the town library, we saw that his Jawa had gathered some dust and dirt from the potholes. 'He'll need to clean it for a month to get it back to what it was,' Jake said, forgetting that Uncle was to die before lunchtime that very day. We could feel our knees aching as we stood by the cinema, under a big banyan tree. People had gathered in a queue before the theatre counter for tickets as Uncle passed by. He waved to them and some of them looked up to stare. No one waved back. They spoke to each other after he had disappeared around the corner and went back to waiting for the ticket counter to open.

The morning progressed like that. We spotted Uncle in different spots all over the town, but no one else seemed to pay attention to him. We felt that perhaps such miracles happen every day and no one really notices them. We cycled back to his house, as he had told us to, a little before lunchtime. We looked at the old Jawa parked in the porch, for the first time without its white hood. It looked dirty and ragged, not like a new bike that had suddenly been ridden about but quite like an old one with caked mud almost everywhere. Each of us took turns to feel the warmth of the underside of its fuel tank.

We walked in and were met with the smell of camphor. We found Uncle in his bedroom, spread out on his bed, waiting to die. The sound of sobbing came from the other bedroom, which was strange, because Uncle had always lived alone.

Uncle looked at us angrily, almost accusingly. 'The damned Jawa is all dirty. Just look at it! I feel like striking a match and dropping it into the fuel tank.'

'We'll help you clean it, Uncle,' Jake said.

'Can't you see, I will be dead in minutes? How can I be expected to clean a motorcycle when I'm dying?'

'Er…but how was the miracle, Uncle?' Prashant asked, like he was making an excuse. 'We saw you. You were great.'

'Yeah,' Uncle sighed, looking up towards the ceiling. Then he smiled briefly, 'The miracle did happen, like I told you, didn't it? Finally.'

It was strange because it seemed he was underwhelmed with what had happened. Perhaps he was sad now that it was over, and he would have to die to pay the price.

'Who is crying, Uncle?' I asked, looking in the direction of the sobs.

'Go check it out,' Uncle said, irritated. 'Everybody seems to be complaining!'

We went hesitantly to the other room. We saw it was an angel. He was marble-white and babylike, just like we might have imagined him. There were two tiny wings on his back. He was naked. There was a halo around his head. He was the most beautiful person we had ever seen or would see in our lives. But our surprise at seeing him was overpowered by his sobbing, which seemed to be breaking his heart.

'Angel!' Pramod exclaimed first. 'But why are you crying?'

The angel looked up at us accusingly. His eyes were ethereal, with their clear long eyelashes that were also white 'Why am I crying?' he said, and his voice was sweet, honest, blessed. 'Well, look at your Uncle! After doing all that he isn't even happy.' He blew his nose into the bed sheet, wiped his eyes, and looked at us again. 'You know, we angels burn out like candles whenever we get involved with you humans. Yet we come. We come down into your lives, moved by your dreams, despair, and prayers. It has happened to me before! But I never learn. You want your dreams to come true, but when they do you don't like them any more. Oh, woe is me!'

'B-but, what went wrong?' Suresh asked. 'The miracle did happen, didn't it? I mean, we saw Uncle going around. You made it happen. So, what's wrong?'

'Ask him!' The angel said with near-human frustration. 'My guess is, he expected something more than a miracle. He thought young ladies would swoon and children will run behind him to touch him and touch his motorcycle. He thought the whole town would sit up to watch him pass by. Run behind him, talk about him, remember him driving about town days later. You saw him, didn't you? He was just another young man on a bike. Ha! My guess is that's what went wrong.'

We were speechless. Now, as I write this, I think this final turn of events was what rendered the whole thing more unbelievable to us than the miracle itself. Maybe if it had all ended with Uncle starry-eyed, happily telling us that his life was fulfilled, clutching our hands, bidding us farewell, and if he had then looked heavenward and died serenely, we might have found the whole episode a little less dreamlike.

'Yes,' I said, 'People did not seem too moved. But why?'

'What why?' the angel sniffled. 'God, you are almost as stupid as he is! Who knew he was an old man turned young for half a day? To them he was just another youth on a motorcycle. Big deal.'

He cried silently for some time. Then he blinked away his tears and said, 'You see, I'm sorry we had to meet like this. Normally I'm a very pleasant angel. But this has happened to me before. I'm particularly gullible to this kind of situation. I am easily moved by some human crying and lighting camphor, drinking only goat's milk, and reading strange books and praying to me. So, I come down to earth and make a miracle. The trouble is, as I said we angels spend a little of ourselves every time we go against the order of nature to make someone's dream come true. Very soon I will have to quit my angelhood at this rate. Then I will fall back upon the earth and live as one of her creatures—a millipede or an anteater, likely. Oh!'

I was about to say something but stopped. Pramod looked like he might cry. I could see Suresh thinking that if we didn't leave the room and go home, his little brother really might start snivelling.

'And this old man, who you call Uncle,' the angel said, pointing in the direction of the other room. 'Oh, he is a particularly nasty one. Do you know, he almost yelled at me? Yes, when he just came in now and was an old man again, he actually shouted. He asked me to work some miracle to clean up that motorbike of his! The nerve! I have half a mind to leave him with a curse.'

'No, angel,' Suresh said. 'Poor Uncle, he is just upset. And he is dying, do forgive him.'

'That's not why I will forgive him,' the angel said darkly. 'A curse burns out more of us than a miracle does. I will surely come down as an earth creature if I spend myself in a curse. That's why I'm letting him off without a curse. But you tell him that. You tell him, I made him young like he asked. I can't make people turn their heads. I can't make girls fall in love. And…and he never really asked for those things. He asked me only to make him young…'

With that the angel vanished. We shivered with wonder, disappointment, and confusion. But we ran to the other room to see if Uncle had died.

'Open the damn thing or you'll die of suffocation,' Uncle was telling himself, as he stood by the small window in the bedroom. Then he answered himself: 'Okay, okay. That's what I'm doing. Quit snapping,' After a fleeting moment of embarrassment he said: 'Has he gone, that angel?'

We nodded.

'Well, it was fun at first, the wind in my hair and the black shirt and the gold chain, the power of the bike and all. But then, I don't know, the magic was missing.'

Uncle continued muttering to himself. Then he seemed to recover suddenly, from everything, including the miracle from which the magic was missing. He turned to us and said: 'Can't have it all, I guess. Okay, you boys run along now. Let me cook me some lunch or I'll start complaining. Ha ha! And don't tell anyone what happened. They'll spank you for lying.'

We couldn't ask him if he was not about to die now, could we? We left him as he tottered up to the kitchen, a very old man but certainly not a man dying that day. We walked out as he was putting a vessel on to the stove to cook. We couldn't help wondering if that angel had indeed cursed him after all.

9

SHABARI AND ANITA

When he was a little boy Shabari's handwriting was so bad that his mother thought he would become a doctor. Later, when he scraped his knee playing cricket, she dreamt that he would be a sports star. When he watched stunt movies his mother thought he would be a police inspector, when he sang, he would be a great playback singer. Many years later when he became a mediocre accountant in a mid-level company in our city, his mother claimed that Shabari, being perfectly honest and having no bad habits at all, was the most eligible bachelor in the neighbourhood.

She carefully looked for a girl who would bring out the best in him. Because the best in him was yet to come, she said. And that was how she got him married to Anita, who she knew would take care of him. Then she died happily, and no one understood what she meant when she took her last breath and said: 'Now it's up to her.'

Sure enough, Anita took care of Shabari and understood that he had true potential. She knew that he wished to one day own a car (even if second-hand), and for that she knew he needed a better salary. On the day he was off for his interview with a bigger company, she fasted and performed puja. She lit lamps at temples, gave money to the poor, and chanted mantras all day. She had fed Shabari thick milk the night before and commanded

The Greatest Enemy of Rain

that he go to bed early, so that he would be fresh and sharp the next day.

This new company, with its stature of being a big multinational, offered to hire him at a lower salary than what he was drawing. But Anita said, 'It isn't the salary you draw today. It is the possibilities for tomorrow that will open up,' and so Shabari took up the job. On the evening of the first day of work in the new company, Shabari shed a tear in memory of his mother, who had always seen promise in him till the very end. Anita held him close and later in the night they felt young, like they had just been married.

A decade into their marriage, it was clear that they would have no children. Like many childless couples, they filled their world with each other until one understood the other the way twins do.

'Shabari and I work hard to get Shabari ahead in his career,' Anita told her friends.

But after he had left for work, she would be alone, all alone. She would make herself a fried snack, switch on the television and, curiously, watch men walking down the catwalk on fashion channels. She studied the latest leather jackets, the coolest hairdos, the slickest boots, and wristwatches. She would observe the stylish men in advertisements, imagine the scent of the perfumes that were being sold, and look into the masculine eyes that appeared on her screen, reading them. She would be so lost in this that she sometimes wouldn't hear the cooing of the fishmonger or forget that she had kept milk to boil on the stove. She would observe these beautiful men and try to fathom their beauty, looking for patterns in their appearance and trying to figure out their hidden secrets. Then when Shabari came back, she would get to work on him, especially on special days at his office, like parties or trips.

She would gel his hair, apply cocoa butter on his face, and put cold cucumber slices over his eyelids. 'It matters, the way you look,' she would tell him.

Then one day Shabari said, in a matter-of-fact voice, that his appraisal would happen the next week. The bosses at office would sit together, call the employees one by one, and decide whose salaries to hike, whom to promote, etc. If things went well, they could buy a decent second-hand hatchback by the end of the next month or so.

At this, Anita introduced certain changes. She continued giving him a glass of whole milk at night because he needed to be energetic to keep up with the pace of such a large company. She purchased new clothes for both of them, but more for him as he was the one who went out. In fact, at this time she upgraded his entire wardrobe, having realized from the TV that his dressing style was outdated.

'You'll spoil him,' Anita's friends warned her.

'Oh, and he still misses his mother after all this,' she replied coyly.

In the evenings, Shabari reported to her the happenings at his office in extraordinary detail. After a day with the hunks and the blue-eyed colts of the fashion world, she found her husband a refreshing change. He told her about his immediate boss and the one above that and the one above that and then the final one in this branch (there were countless more bosses in other branches elsewhere). She listened eagerly as he spoke about Lata, who took coffee breaks like her life depended on them; Sapna, who flirted with every man including the one who got them tea; Shekhar, who always smelt of cold balm and had a stuffy nose; and many other characters. He told her that people here were clearly proud of working in such a big place and they showed it by arguing about needless things all day long. Over time, Anita knew all the people in Shabari's office as though she too was working there with him.

We often said that theirs was a different sort of love. It wasn't very passionate at all. Nothing steamy between these two. They shared a calm, steady love that seemed to go beyond this world. An all-pervading, cold, silent love that was like the space between the stars.

On the day of his appraisal Anita applied almond oil on his hair. 'The gel makes you seem a bit too young. You need to look mature today. Capable and mature,' she explained. She mixed tulsi leaves in his bath so he would smell fresh all day. She made him try on seven different shirts until she could decide which one he would wear. She tied his shoelaces for him so he wouldn't need to bend and crease his trousers. She made him carry a small amulet for luck that his mother had given her before dying.

'Woman,' Shabari said, 'you act like it's the end of the world!' He often called her woman when he felt very warm towards her, the way he remembered his father calling his mother years ago.

But when he came back that evening, he looked crestfallen.

In time Anita understood that Shabari wasn't really interested in his work. He wasn't quite cut out for appraisals and promotions, despite her best efforts. He was a rather quiet man who didn't say the right things when the opportunity came, so that many people judged him to lack a certain depth. In a dog-eat-dog world, he preferred to stand apart and watch dogs eat other dogs. He hated office politics and could never step on another's toe to get ahead. If he had an idea during meetings, he would keep quiet and later bring it up in private to his immediate boss, who told it to his boss at the right time as his own idea, claiming all the credit. In office parties Shabari did not dance or sing or clap. During team trips he asked if he could bring his wife along while other men fretted and hid from their wives how drunk they got and what indulgences they allowed themselves. He was simply not the kind they set the ladder for in such companies. They only gave him small, nominal hikes and, in some years, nothing at all.

'I don't think I am suited for office work,' he told Anita.

But Anita wasn't the sort to give up just yet. While her body had become rather plump from all the fried snacks and television, her mind was razor-sharp about how to improve things for her husband. She really started to prepare him for next year's appraisal at work, spending large amounts of their money on updating his wardrobe. She obtained tip after tip from the fashion channels and male grooming magazines. On Sundays she made a special mix of egg yolk, curds, and medicinal leaves for his hair. She made him jog in the lane in front of their house for an hour every morning, feeling his small paunch after the exercise the way a sculptor runs his hands over his work mid-creation. She had also started to mix turmeric (which he hated) into his glass of milk at night, so he wouldn't fall ill often and miss work. When he seemed to grow younger while she herself showed traces of ageing, she dyed her hair. She did not talk when he was reading the financial section of the newspaper because he needed it to sharpen his professional skills. When he was back home from work, she let him choose the channel on TV because he needed to relax. She left him alone when he needed solitude and chatted with him when he needed company.

But for all her efforts, Shabari did not get a promotion the next year either. What was worse, he did not care.

Then one day one of his colleagues said during lunch: 'Shabari, you are growing younger by the day. What's your secret?'

His colleagues thought Shabari would blush as always.

The Greatest Enemy of Rain

But not one of his friends quite expected what came out of his mouth. That question was a turning point, because the usually quiet Shabari launched into a long speech about how his woman took care of him! He had never had such an audience—it seemed like half the office (including two bosses) was around his table as he narrated the stuff that went into his hair and the mixes in his bath and the diet that made his skin glow and the exercise that kept his muscles toned. Everyone looked at each other and then at him and then again at each other. They hadn't ever heard Shabari string so many sentences together, far less speak with such gusto about anything. Lata abandoned her lunch and had two cappuccinos while his speech was going on and Shekhar put his spoon down and began rubbing balm on his temples.

But like all landslides, Shabari finally ground to a halt. They ate their lunch in silence for a bit, as though none of them knew how to react. Some were in awe after hearing him speak at such length, but it was clear that most were amused. Finally, one of the bosses, a particularly thorny character, looked up from his lunch, cleared his throat, and said: 'That was a passionate speech, Shabari. Now we know why you don't blend in here. You ought to be working in some fashion channel.'

Shabari's face fell. While his colleagues tried to hide their laughter, he could feel they were mocking him. He felt slighted, ridiculed. He immediately regretted his outburst. He could've kicked himself then and there for the mistake.

When he came back home that evening, Anita knew right away that someone had hurt her husband. She did not ask him what was wrong. Instead, she fed him his favourite dinner and massaged his tired shoulders. Gradually, he turned to her and began telling her what happened at lunch that day, and he ended his narration with a simple sigh: 'I'm not cut out for office, Anita.

I'm not cut out for pretty much anything. You are wasting your attention on me.'

'No, I'm not,' she answered, and then she began talking, her eyes twinkling in the moonlight that poured in from the window. She spoke for a long time into the night. In the morning there was a twinkle in his eyes too. He called up his office and told the thorny boss he was quitting, and that he would come in a little later today and put in his papers.

Before the end of that month, they had set up Shabari's Grooming Centre for Men. The men at his office were their first and loyal customers. More customers poured in as their name spread. Anita groomed each customer to his specific body shape, eye colour, hair texture, and skin type. She sculpted men according to their personalities, tinkering with their personalities, modifying their behaviour to suit their aspirations. She massaged their heads, smoothened their wrinkles, plumped up their lips, and brought the twinkle back in their eyes!

She groomed each customer the way she did her Shabari. Oh, the way their business roared!

Shabari never regretted giving up his job. It was much more satisfactory being an assistant to his wife, helping her mix her oils and applying her concoctions on waiting faces and heads.

Like the space between the stars, that was their love. She still takes care of his appearance because he is their ambassador; with his eternal youth, he brings in business. On some nights Shabari cries, thinking of his mother and how proud she would have been.

10

MR AND MRS PARIERA

Mrs Pariera thought she knew the exact moment when her husband lost his mind. She often recounted it to her friends over compound walls and at the washing stone by the old well. She cited her knowledge of the moment as an example of her astute observation skills and understanding of her husband's very pulse after their forty-two years of marriage, which, alas, he could not claim to reciprocate. 'Men see nothing,' she said with a sigh that held in it pleasure, confidence, and even some measure of girly coyness. 'In forty-two years, he hasn't once noticed if I don't wear my bindi in the mornings.'

The incident itself happened some years ago, when she saw him wash his hands at the washbasin in the dining room, thrice in quick succession. When she looked on, puzzled, he said his finger had touched the inside of the basin at the first wash, so he had to wash his hands again, but this time he had touched the tiles that bordered the basin, and when you spat some of it landed on these tiles, and so he had to wash a third time. 'That,' she claimed to her friends, 'was the moment my Mr Pariera went mad.'

She had always protected him from harming himself, though he wouldn't testify to that. In the military when he drank rum too fast, in order to impress his peers at parties, she would loudly proclaim: 'Mr Pariera, go easy. I am not in the mood to be cleaning up vomit the whole night.' That would burst his bubble, amidst loudly guffawing fellow officers, but he would ease down on his glass. Every time, every instance in their forty-two years of marriage when he put himself in a risky situation, compromised his mental or physical health, it was she who got him out of it.

'But men will not admit that we rescue them from themselves,' she sighed, 'it hurts their manly pride.'

So, on the morning he washed his hands thrice, she kept an extra-vigilant eye on him to find out if she could detect a pattern. Sure enough, a little later he picked up the day's newspaper from their doorstep and began dusting it with an old towel. Then he again washed his hands, and only then sat down to read. At breakfast she placed Kutti, a little kitten that had strayed into their home a few days ago, on the dining table near Mr Pariera's seat. All through breakfast she saw him eyeing the cat, and she knew that he was wondering if there was cat hair in his food.

But obsessive cleanliness was only the beginning, she soon learned. Madness has a way of growing on itself, as every wife knows. Very soon he began hurrying back to the house when they were some distance away, on their way to the market. One evening she followed him secretly and found that he was coming back to make sure they had locked the house. The next time he wanted to go back, she absolutely forbade him from doing so.

'You are NOT going back to the house,' she said.

'But I'll just come back, Mrs Pariera,' he said. 'You check out for fresh fish in the meantime. I just need to go back. I just have to.'

'NO!' she said mercilessly. 'Or else tell me what you're going back for.'

After a heated exchange that people on the road had started to notice, Mr Pariera admitted that he wished to go back to the house that day, and only that day, because he wasn't sure he had

The Greatest Enemy of Rain

locked the front door. Mrs Pariera assured him that it was always she who locked up after them, and she was sure she had done it this time as well.

'Well, I was also thinking I could use the toilet,' he said with the defiance of a lawyer trying every trick in a courtroom. 'You know, all that barley water you made me drink today....'

'MR PARIERA!' his wife yelled, and this time people stopped to look at them. 'There are enough and more bushes around and I have seen you urinating upon them several times. This whole cursed town empties everything it has upon these bushes. Even if I die here today you are not going back!'

He thought that she looked like a demon from hell. Her eyes were narrow and glittering, and her lips were stiff, straight, and thin. He followed her in a hurry, forgetting that he should at least have made a show of urinating by the roadside to maintain his credibility. That whole day Mrs Pariera did not make small talk with him. This wouldn't do. He was letting the madness grow, and she had to intensify her treatment. She was glad she didn't let him go back to check if the door was locked.

Later, while at the tailor's, she was heard telling the wife of the bank manager: 'That cured him. I had to be a little tough, but he never goes back home now to check the lock. And you know, at the time I lock up I turn to him and say, "Here, Mr Pariera, I have locked up. Remember this. This means you needn't come back today either to make sure!"'

But what she couldn't have foreseen was that he would completely shift his attention to their old black-and-white television set. She had heard him tell his friends often that the television was like his son in old age, because it filled up his evenings and connected him to the present in the mornings. But all that had been in light humour, she knew. Even earlier, people had seen him climb up on the terrace and turn the colossal antenna to get optimal signal, while Mrs Pariera shouted from downstairs the quality of the reception. Everyone had concluded that the couple watched television a lot. To be sure, Mrs Pariera was fond of watching it too, at the rate of one soap a day and a movie on Sundays.

But things were different now.

Now that he didn't have to go back home to check the door, Mr Pariera instead dusted the television set every night before he went to bed. Then, precisely two hours later, he woke up and went to the toilet. But Mrs Pariera did not hear him urinating. Through a chink in the living room door, she saw that he was in front of the television. He ran his hands over the main switch in the darkness to ensure he had turned it off. Every midnight he spent some time there, to be doubly sure that the switch was turned off.

One evening she saw him in front of the television even before the programmes he watched began, staring vacantly. Another day, at the market he bought a brand new cover for the ancient television. The very next day the blessed thing stopped working and the local electrician informed a crestfallen Mr Pariera that it had short-circuited because water seemed to have seeped through its back. The picture tube was completely burnt and repair was out of the question.

'But wasn't that rather drastic?' the bank manager's wife asked Mrs Pariera. 'Besides, now you don't get to watch television either, no?'

'Ah, we have to make our sacrifices,' she replied. 'That's what marriage is all about, my dear. This is my advice to you, too. Men have the seeds of madness and waywardness inside their heads. These come from being men. They will just let these grow, if left to themselves. You have to have one end of the rope in your

The Greatest Enemy of Rain

hands. I have known Mr Pariera for over forty years. I hate to think where he would be if I did not check him!'

But Mrs Pariera stopped short of mentioning to her friend the rather severe bout of insanity that her husband displayed when he returned from the electrician's that day. He rushed into the kitchen and expressionlessly broke some vessels. Their pot in which she kept drinking water was smashed. Stonily, he trampled on her favourite tea set and spat into the bowl of sugar. He even picked up the little pocket Bible she kept in the kitchen and threw it out the window. All the while she stood like an exorcist, her lips a thin line, her arms folded across her huge frame, mumbling constantly under her breath, waiting for the rage in him to let go of him. For almost a week after that they scarcely spoke, but she was glad that his unhealthy attachment to the television set was cured.

Mr Pariera did not buy a new television set, partly because he was saving money to start an antique shop, and partly because Mrs Pariera seemed to be falling sick frequently, and he did not wish to make her uncomfortable. She was often feverish, but she still kept a strict watch over him.

But once when she was talking about his madness and her monitoring of it to a group of ladies outside the mill, the fishmonger's wife said: 'You know, Mrs Pariera, maybe Mr Pariera is just bored, out of having nothing to do.'

Mrs Pariera put down the bag of rice she had brought along to grind, and faced the woman with surprising vehemence: 'My husband is NOT jobless. Yes, he is retired, but in the Army you would have stood up in respect when he strode in, all decked up in his uniform. You ought to have seen the number of stars on his shoulders, the medals on his chest! You would have stood up straight and saluted when he passed a command! Why, even now he is not jobless, as you say. Even now he is busy starting a new business.' The fishmonger's wife winced when Mrs Pariera then added with unmistakable spite: 'A major new business, you see; quite different from selling fish.' After that the women refrained from making any observations about Mr Pariera. They understood that Mrs Pariera had given herself the right to criticize him, but would not tolerate anyone else doing it.

She continued to treat his madness, permitting him to wash his hands only before his meals and leaving him to dust the radio (he had now taken to the radio) only if he also cleaned up the shelf on which it was kept, because that way he dusted the radio less often. She deliberately prevented him from keeping huge reserves of batteries for his torch. Her idea was that if the torch ran out of batteries and the power failed on the same night, they were still not in any grave danger because they lived in the middle of civilization. She even made him clean the mess the cat made, saying it made the mind healthy to take care of pets in old age. Besides, he could, of course, bathe afterwards.

Then, when he spent a lot of time examining if the ashtray was bang in the centre of the coffee table, she did nothing. She did not throw away the ashtray. 'I can read you like a book,' she thought to herself. 'I have read you for forty-odd years. I can read you backwards and forwards now.' She knew he was perfecting the position of the ashtray only to tease her. This was his sense of humour.

But she stopped talking about all this to anyone; not even to the best of her friends who came to visit her when she was ill more and more often.

He had to control himself a lot, but years later he admitted to a friend that he had been a weak man and had cheated on his wife a little, here and there. When she couldn't get up from the bed,

The Greatest Enemy of Rain

he had hidden a big bottle of Dettol and overused it during his baths, until one evening she smelt it on his skin and weakly told him to stop. At her funeral he was seen hurrying back to his home muttering he would be back in a jiffy. When someone asked him why he was going home, he said: 'I'll have to lock the front door myself from now on, you see. And today I think I might have forgotten to lock it.'

The week after her death, his friends report, he bought a new colour television set. They say he also made a few fleeting changes, including beginning to smoke his special cigars as he had done during his military days, and playing rummy with himself in the mornings. In the evening he could be seen rocking slowly on his chair on the porch, bursting the bubbles on some bubble wrap he had got with something new he had purchased. He seemed to be always purchasing something new; usually something electronic or electrical. Some people said that he was revelling in his new-found freedom. Others that he was learning to live alone in his own way. Still others said he was grappling with grief, forming new habits and acquiring new things to deal with his loneliness. Sometime later he began sharing his military rum with friends on weekends. During one such drinking session, someone ventured to ask him if he missed his wife very much. 'Miss her? Of course, I miss her. But I also feel free, free like I always wanted to be.' He was lost to them for a moment. Then he continued, a little absently: 'She was a good woman. She took care of me. Or she thought that is what she was doing. Though, you know, she was a little batty. Always a little batty. Well, not always. I know the precise moment she went mad. It was after lunch on a Sunday, I think. She was looking at me curiously as I washed my hands at the basin. Her eyes followed my fingers. You know, darted, like an animal's. Ha! I knew something was amiss. Then I knew for sure when she began rationing my soap and Dettol, and locking up my towels. She even poured water into the TV's picture tube! Batty but good, Mrs Pariera. Even when she had lost it, she cared for me. Or thought she did.' They did not press him further, because they could see how emotional he had become.

11

THE SHIT OF THE SERAPH

At first the shit was long, ropey, new, like alien fingers. It sat on the windowsill, mocking, like a bold picture framed, glowing under the sun, letting off a morbid, ancient smell that reminded you of hummus. Granda sat right opposite the window on an expensive sofa which Ma had bought because relatives often came to see Granda, and she wanted them to know she never compromised in his care.

'The seraph came again last night,' Granda would explain, hissing through the ghosts of teeth that had long left him. 'Swooped down and did it on my windowsill.'

'How, just how do you climb up on that window, Papa?' Ma would ask, her arms at her hips in an expression of defeat. 'It's so dangerous! What if you fell?'

'The seraph again said it,' Granda insisted. 'There's gold for whoever takes care of the old man!'

'Gold!' Ma exclaimed. Gold was a forbidden word to come from Granda. All his children—including Ma—held it against him, because they believed he had squandered the vast family reservoir of wealth for his selfish business experiments all through his life. 'Tell me about gold.'

Dada sometimes came in and held the newspaper he was reading against his nose. He liked to point out that at about the time Granda turned ninety-two he went completely mad. Dada said it was like the pull of the other world was so strong now that the hinges that fastened Granda to this one were coming loose. He was secretly but very apparently glad that Granda wasn't his father. 'My father had his favourite lunch of rice, dal, and fried bitter gourd, then sighed in his siesta and died,' Dada often said, and we all knew what he believed but didn't utter: that good people died good, peaceful deaths. Of course, he never said that he thought that only sinners lived past ninety and shat on windowsills.

'Ratna!' Ma called out, her voice uncharacteristically loud yet beseeching, not unlike the wail of a drowning woman.

Ratna was our maid. She came in, chubby and quivering, and us children would begin to snigger. Granda sniggered with us, sometimes staring at his doing with glimmering eyes, sometimes winking back at us. 'It's dusted with gold, that shit,' he smiled. 'Go through it. Sift through it. There could be more gold inside, though I'm not sure—'

'You could be quiet, Papa,' Ma said with frustration coiled like a spring inside her, refusing to let it out because Granda had brought her up to be a refined, gentle lady. She would look at the maid and say again, 'Ratna...' That word was a capsule inside which was both authority and request, command and bribe. Sure enough, by evening Ma would have gifted Ratna something—an old but pricey churidaror blanket, a mosquito net, and even a big, ornate wall mirror one time. Ratna would make a face the moment Ma said 'Ratna...' and it would be the face of a person who had to do what she had to do, of one who would obey but must never be taken for granted.

After we were all marched out of Granda's room, Ratna would clean up and carry the cellophane wrapper with Granda's shit in

The Greatest Enemy of Rain

it right through the centre of the house, like an exhibit. That was to show everyone how selfless Ratna was. How accommodating, how sacrificing. The first time or two when Granda did it on his windowsill, she had taken the much easier option of flushing the shit down Granda's own toilet, but later said she could save water by disposing of it outside in the fields. Since we did have a water problem in this high-altitude town, Ma agreed. Invariably, Ratna would pass by Dada watching television in the front room and he would exclaim 'Ugh! Can't you carry it out the backyard?' and with a giggle Ratna would hurry and—come to think of it, none of us ever saw where she finally disposed of Granda's shit, she did it so efficiently. Behind her back Ma would whisper to Dada: 'Let her be. It is nice enough of her to clean it. You know how difficult it is to find someone to do this?'

Rarely, Dada would respond with 'This is why...' or 'My father...' and then that noon we would have lunch with the solemnity of folks at a funeral. Ma wouldn't laugh at Dada's jokes nor mix him his drink in the evening. Sometimes she would grudgingly point out that she had suggested many times it was time they got her father a home nurse and Dada would grunt back asking her how much she thought home nurses cost.

To recap, Granda had begun shitting on the windowsill of his bedroom a few weeks after he went mad. A few weeks later, he began thinking the house was a train and asking us when it would leave the station, about a week after this he began seeing Grandma in the mirror on the almirah, talking to him. After the initial tubular output he soon gave us shit of more pasty consistency which dripped a little on either sides of the window and looked like Dali's Melting Watch. This would be a true nightmare to clean. 'The seraph's stomach is upset. He told me so himself,' Granda said, embarrassed, and Ma quietly hiked Ratna's pay. She also ordered Ratna not to make Granda's favourite raw-mango chutney ever again. Not if he wouldn't stop his antics.

Dada sometimes ventured into Granda's room which was neat but perpetually covered in shadows. He decorously enquired after Granda's health, and you couldn't make out if he was being warm or mocking. Granda held his son-in-law by the wrist, as though to prevent him from running away, and said: 'There was this schoolteacher who lived in a paid accommodation. He got very angry one day because he had found a fly in his chai. He yelled in anger at the waiter in the tea shop, the man with the psoriasis on his fingers, you know? Ha ha, and this waiter replied, "A fly? Then what more do you expect in a two-rupee chai? An elephant?" Heeheehee!' Dada smiled and patted Granda's shoulder, simultaneously freeing himself from the older man's feeble grip.

A month or so after the raw-mango chutney was stopped, Granda was excited one day when Ma opened his door in the morning. 'The seraph is well again!' Sure enough, on the windowsill were monumental turds leaning on one another like sausages tumbling out of a box. 'That's more gold than you can use.' There was pride and fondness in Granda's voice. 'He is benevolent because you take care of me.' Ratna had now started to giggle as she cleaned the shit, but it sounded like she did not really wish to giggle but was forcing herself to do so to remain calm.

'You'll have to stop this, Papa,' Ma said. 'This is disgusting, to say the least. I hope you don't fall off that window one day.' She always added a sentence that showed she was speaking for Granda's own good. She did not ever say that it pained her to take care of him and put up with him.

But in a week or so Granda's seraph was unwell again. Ma

stopped serving pickle this time, and when Granda looked enquiringly at Ratna when she served him, Ma told him, 'You stop your dirty habit and you will get the pickle again.' Though she spoke as if she was talking to a child, there was spittle at the edges of Ma's mouth, and we knew that she was barely managing to control herself. 'There is a toilet attached to your room and if you can climb a window, you can walk up to it.'

During this time Ratna's stature was so high in our household that Dada began to say she was more important than him. Indeed, Ma had started to give away vessels from the kitchen and jars of sugar, lentils, and spices in return for not just cleaning up Granda's shit but also, as Ma put it, 'for preserving the honour of the family'. By the last she meant she hoped Ratna would never mention the windowsill misadventures when she was among other servants and washerwomen. We sometimes heard Ratna say with passion: 'You don't worry one bit, Didiji. For as long as I live, this blemish on the family will never go beyond these walls.'

In about a year Granda was still not dying, and what was worse, he was still at his nightly sport on the windowsill. Ma gave away Dada's favourite dhotis and shirts for Ratna's brothers. In winter she donated another blanket, this one not old at all. Dada bit his lips and watched television.

Every time Ratna had to clear flowy feculence Ma would judiciously remove another item from Granda's meal. Then one day she remembered the way, decades ago, a lifetime ago, Granda would often tell her brother when he was being naughty, 'You are becoming too difficult. Shall we send you away to the boarding school then? They know how to take care of the likes of you.' As Ratna was cleaning up, Ma stood in front of Granda's sofa and spoke to him: 'You are becoming rather difficult, Papa. Shall we send you away to the old age home then? They take good care of naughty old men.'

Granda produced a word which I understood some years later to be a pungent expletive. Then he said: 'And let all the gold go to them, you idiot?' Ma hurried out of that room because if she stayed she would have betrayed with her expression that she understood the expletive, and Ratna would realize that Ma knew.

Then Ma and Dada discreetly visited a doctor in another town. Another town because if they visited one in ours, they suspected the news would eventually leak and folks would know and they would laugh, 'Mounisha's father soils the windowsill. You need to clean shit in the mornings to atone for your sins.' So they met an experienced old physician, and Dada was gracious enough not to leave the burden of explaining their indelicate predicament to Ma. The old doctor laughed and suggested a few tips to train Granda towards less adventurous shitting habits. 'There's no medicine for this,' he said, and warned, 'ninety-three is way too old even for these tips to take effect. You can only try.' And then he told them that his payment may be made at the reception desk.

Dada, Ma, and Ratna together trained Granda, holding him at the toilet once every two hours with the hope that he would run out of shit for the windowsill. But the thing was that as soon as they held him over the toilet bowl he would begin, 'There was one schoolteacher in my youth, I don't remember his name. Only that he lived in paid accommodation. Once he lost his temper in the teashop because he had found a fly in his chai...' By the time he was midway into the anecdote he would scarcely remember what they had got him to the toilet for, and they would bring him back to his sofa and sit by his side, more exhausted than him. After about a week he did begin to shit, right in the middle of his tale about the fly in the chai. Still, he saved some shit for

The Greatest Enemy of Rain

the windowsill. Ratna still had to clear sizeable amounts most mornings, and Ma sternly reduced Granda's rations because it seemed he was being overfed, seeing the quantities that came out of him. 'It's a sin to overfeed the old,' she said to Dada. 'They get attached to food and that makes their passage to the other world that much tougher.'

After the doctor had failed, Ma started to try temples. She and Dada became pilgrims and took short trips (longer ones were impossible as they had to come back quickly or Granda would drive Ratna mad), and Ma told the gods that she would do this for them and that for them if they helped with a solution to her unbearable, unutterable problem. She assured herself that it was never Granda's death that she asked of the gods, only a respite from his dirty toilet habit. She cried before altars as she remembered that he was her father who had given her life and taught her and taken care of her for so many years. Even at home she prayed aloud in the evenings and her voice was again like a spring coiled up inside her throat. She rubbed holy ash and turmeric all over Granda and kissed him at night, telling him to use the toilet or call out if he needed them. I suppose she was losing her mind too, because in return for making the shit disappear, she once gave Ratna a small gold ring!

Ma perhaps regretted this immediately after, but she let Ratna keep the ring. Dada, on the other hand, wouldn't let it go. He began with his caustic jokes that evening at dinner, saying things like: 'Hope I don't turn a shitting seraph in my old age. Because I'm not sure I'll be looked after this well. A gold ring to a servant. Gosh!'

We children couldn't figure out why he was putting Ma more on edge. She did not speak and ate nothing.

Over the next days the tension between Ma and Dada grew.

At regular intervals Dada cracked jokes: 'By the time we are done with your papa, we will be living on the footpath', 'Our children's future is there on the windowsill each morning', 'God help a household where the servant has a share in the family gold'.... We heard Ma quietly cry to someone in the telephone that the ring had anyway come from her family and Dada had scarcely bought her any gold, but she wasn't mean enough to mention that and she hoped she wouldn't be forced to go to that extent.

Once or twice, during calmer moments, Ma tried to reason with Dada. 'Look, we need to keep Ratna happy. This kind of clean-up was never part of the deal. No servant agrees to this. Without Ratna we wouldn't know what to do. You must admit, she even disposes of the stuff so carefully. Even the neighbours don't know. And no water wastage either.'

'So give her your necklace next,' Dada would say loudly, so that Ratna could hear from the back of the house.

Once Ma was so tired of the whole thing that she exclaimed, 'It's all very fine for you to say whatever you want. If Ratna goes, I'll be the one cleaning shit!' That was the only time we heard her refer to shit as shit. The only time her spring went boing. Ma was too refined, too gracious, for life to be doing this to her. When her brother and other relatives came to visit, she tried to impress upon them how difficult it had gotten to take care of Granda without telling them about the disgraceful windowsill accidents. Then Granda complained voluminously how his mango pickle had been stopped, how the one pappad at lunch had disappeared, the half-banana at breakfast had vanished, that there wasn't the slight bit of smearing of ghee on his rotis any more, how he was being threatened with the old age home every second day (in truth Ma hadn't ever dared to mention it again after he had used such language on her), and how he was in fact being starved even

The Greatest Enemy of Rain

when his pension still came in on time and they—the husband and the wife—did not even let him see any of his own money. Granda went on and on to the relatives, the way prisoners talk about the pathetic affairs of prison to visiting human rights inspectors. When he went on like this Ma was torn between letting his outrageous toilet habit slip and her natural grace which kept her from speaking about such terrible stuff. She ended up saying as though about a child: 'Papa's stomach is delicate, you know. The doctor has really put some restrictions on his diet.' And right before all the brothers and the relatives she would bend down and fondly kiss him on his bald head.

When Ratna was scooping the windowsill waste into a cellophane bag, Granda faced her: 'All the gold is for you. For you alone. Are you my daughter? Where's my daughter?'

'Papa,' said Ma, her voice warm with tears of frustration, 'one more word and I'll... I'll...' Ratna led her away from the room as Ma cried on her shoulder.

Then one day the skies came down. There was a huge fight. One morning Dada was slumped on the couch in the living room as usual, and Ratna was carrying our grandfather's shit wrapped in cellophane. But apparently something of immense interest to her was playing on the television. She stood lost in the moment behind Dada, mouth slightly open, shit loosely held in the bag in her hand. Dada's nose twitched and he turned around. His ears grew red and his lips pursed. He switched off the TV and that awoke Ratna from her reverie. Dada yelled: 'Put it on my head then, put that shit on my head!'

Ma came running into the room, positioning herself between Dada and Ratna. At that moment, we could believe the stories that she had descended from an old warrior clan.

'You deliberately won't go around the house,' Dada

continued to yell. 'You have to carry that shit right through the front room, just to spite me. I know. I know we have an old man who refuses to die, we all know that! You needn't blackmail us with that!'

Then he was absolutely quiet and Ma began to cry. Ratna ran out and later came back through the kitchen door to bid farewell to Ma. 'I never meant to blackmail anyone,' were her words before she picked up her things and left. Ma ran behind her and gave her the complete wages for that month, though more than ten days were still left. Ma told her that without her she wouldn't be able to handle her Papa, who was only an old man who did not realize what he was doing. She told her she had given her that ring only because she thought of Ratna as her own sister. She reminded her how they all knew that the children's father had a nasty temper but meant well. She winced when Ratna finally said, 'I can clean shit but sometimes what comes off mouths stinks far worse.'

After Ratna left, a pall descended over the house. Tables, chairs, and doors seemed to cast longer shadows. Most of the time Dada could be heard telephoning his office, pulling someone or the other up for something or the other. Ma cooked like a machine and set things down on the table with a small bang that suggested dispassion. She sent us to school with the usual kiss but now her lips felt like rubber. She never asked us when we returned what our day had been like and what the math teacher had covered in class that day. She and Dada did not look each other in the eye. Dada was forever angry and irritated, and we understood that things were going through a particularly nasty phase in his business. He called out to Ma when he needed tea the way he might call out to a servant: 'Mo, tea!' That's it. And in a moment Ma would appear with tea in hand and set it down

The Greatest Enemy of Rain

with her communicative little bang. 'Mo, my tie,' he would yell on mornings he was going for meetings, and she would appear at his door with four options and not ask him about the meeting he was going to attend. She never wished him luck, she never asked him how his meeting went.

But there was one instance every day where Granda forced Ma and Dada to collaborate. This was during his morning bath. It had been Ratna and Ma before, leading Granda down to the bath in his loincloth. One of them would scrub his back while the other slowly poured water. For his ninety-odd years, Granda was quite a big man. Now, Dada replaced Ratna. He reluctantly put his hand under the older man's arm, carefully avoiding touching any sweat in the armpits, helped seat him on the plastic stool and grudgingly poured the water (which was so scarce at our home that he was justified in only trickling it down on the old man), while Ma scrubbed. We watched at the door, handing out soap and a towel when the bath was done.

One thing that isn't known for certain is whether Granda still did it on the windowsill after Ratna left and, if he did, who cleaned up. When at last he was dead, Ma and Dada said only good things about him. In fact, Ma proclaimed that her father loved her so much, he made sure until the end that taking care of him was never too difficult. It was funny that she should say things so starkly untrue, but I suppose she thought it her solemn duty to speak well of her dead father. But my sister has vague memories, nonetheless, of Ma during the period Ratna wasn't around, at the breakfast table and unable to eat, revulsed and totally green in the face as though she had just come from a task that shook her very soul. We wouldn't know if Ma had simply taken the shit and flushed it down Granda's toilet, not bothering to save water as long as she was forced to do what

Ratna had so kindly been doing until Dada selfishly lost control of himself.

A week later, Ma and Dada had grown so cold towards each other that Dada even began sleeping on the couch in the front room. They obviously hated the time they had to come together to bathe Granda. When the first trickle of water flowed down his spine Granda would begin: 'There was this schoolteacher in my time. He lived in a paid accommodation and he hated flies in his chai.' Ma would pour the water right down grandfather's face and he would be forced to close his mouth. But when they were drying him, he would whisper to them: 'Keep all the gold the seraph gives you. It's the family's, it's for you. Keep it for the children.' Dada could later be heard phoning agencies for home nurses. He would invariably be heard banging the phone down and yelling, 'Such costs! Only the Tatas and Birlas can afford them. And for all that money, they make it clear they won't clean shit!'

But it was wonderful indeed what a heart of gold our maid had. Before the house burned down, before Ma and Dada would file divorce papers, perhaps even before my Ma—who could scarcely pronounce the common word for excrement—might have to clean it with her hands, Ratna came back to us! She stood outside the kitchen window one dawn asking Ma to open the door. She told her that her conscience wouldn't allow her to rest easy when she thought of her Didiji having to clean filth with her pretty, soft hands. Already busying herself with the vessels in the sink, Ratna said loudly that if the man of the house did not want her back, she would like to return the gold ring and the other gifts Ma had given her and leave forever. She went on to say that she was nothing but loyal towards people who were good to her, that she could swallow the bitter words thrown at

The Greatest Enemy of Rain

her in this house only so that she could serve the angelic Didiji again, that she might not have the good fortune of a sophisticated upbringing but she had honesty and goodwill in her heart, which had made her come back to her Didiji.

When I grew up and became a writer, I decided that I would one day write about the story of my grandfather who defecated on many mornings upon his windowsill. But I have become a writer who doesn't like to write too long a story, particularly if it is about a dying man. I shall skip over the months, perhaps the odd year or more after Ratna's return, when Dada was careful not to anger the maid, when Ma was careful not to anger Dada, when Granda continued shitting on the windowsill and telling us a seraph had done it, and when Ratna continued carrying the cellophane wrap through the front room, saving water and giving Dada a whiff of the work she had to do in our house. I shall breeze through the descriptions of how Granda's shit sat like the Stonehenge one day, like mango pulp the other. I shall also skip over the items that Ma kept cutting out or replacing in Granda's diet. Many more gifts passed from Ma's hands to Ratna's—most prominently a vase that was apparently a family heirloom—but I shall skip these too. I shall skip right to the end of my story when, one windy morning, Ratna suddenly pointed out that Granda's windowsill hadn't been soiled for almost a week. It was clear that Granda wasn't well enough to climb up to do his business, and we all knew what that meant.

After Granda passed there was no way of retaining Ratna. Ma reminded her of the time she had joined: 'You were young then, Ratna. And you hadn't come to clean up after my father. You are practically family now.' But Ratna told her that she couldn't bear the thought of not cleaning up after Granda, not bathing him or lighting incense sticks in his room. Every day she stepped into the house, the good maid said, she would miss the old man. I suppose it is the most dreadful work that you do for a man that gets you the most attached to him. In spite of all Ma's pleading, Ratna left. And she left not only our house but all the houses in the neighbourhood and finally even the town itself. Almost like she wished to drift away from all of us, and her past. I remember Dada observing that Ratna was rather overdoing the mourning after Granda's death. 'Why, you might think there was something going on between your old man and her,' he giggled. Granda had been, after all, a very old man whose death had been expected for more than a decade, but Ratna reacted like she was in deep shock when he died. But Dada did not push it because Ma stopped him: 'Your problem is, you do not believe that people can have good souls.'

Measuring the appropriate reaction to death was always something I wasn't very good at. How much of mourning is appropriate, what level of shock is warranted and how many memories of a dead man is one to carry around in the heart? But whatever the impact on Ratna, however genuine it was or not, we never saw her again.

Some months later Dada heard something curious, purely accidentally, at the club for business folk that he used to go to at the time. A half-drunk retired colonel of the military, who now ran a security agency, told him a curious story about Ratna. 'That's the one that used to work at your place, no? Yeah, you told me. The one who drove a wedge between pati-patni for some time. Ha haha! I've seen her, she used work at my neighbour's place too. Well, surprise! One of my clients—stinking rich one, I tell you—has a new neighbour. It's the same Ratna. She has a husband who's younger than her. She's richer than all of us put together. She's building a super-duper bungalow in that super-duper colony. Land alone costs crores there. Of course, no one knows she was a maid once. I took one look at her and recognized her, but I told no one anything! Must have won the lottery, robbed a bank, who knows? Anyway, she can now keep ten maids to clean her shit when she's old.'

12

A DIFFICULT CUSTOMER

They got difficult customers sometimes. This was rare, thanks be to God, but when they got one it really tested them. Their skill, patience, resilience, and commitment, everything stretched to a breaking point. No, we aren't talking about those moody customers who sauntered in very often, as if against their own wish. The ones who came when they had a mere cold, or those who muttered angrily when they were asked to turn their heads or hold up their chins. These were the easy ones. The difficult customer was...well, it was difficult to explain. He came on that rare dark day, complained no matter what you did, demanded to meet the manager or the owner or whoever was responsible around here, demanded a refund and then dismissed it when you agreed for a refund, said he would report you, would write about your business in the media, threatened to finish your career off, and generally did everything short of burying you alive. This was the really difficult customer.

Mr D'Souza was a difficult customer. They had no clue, of course, that he would be a difficult customer when he walked in. He parked his car across the road where it was visible from inside the salon, and it was such an expensive car that anyone would want its owner to be their customer. And then his wife got out of the other side and you saw her invaluable pearl necklace. Oh,

The Greatest Enemy of Rain

how deceptive these rich folks were! Why, less than half an hour later not one person at the salon would willingly have chosen Mr D'Souza for a customer.

Mr D'Souza walked into the salon, his wife on his arm. He was a huge man and fair; he looked like a ripe fruit that made its branch bow. He would have looked abnormally huge if his wife wasn't by his side. She puffed in like a locomotive, huger than him by a good margin, and smiling without reason. The dark mole on her cheeks was strangely threatening and seemed to have a life of its own.

'Haircut,' Mr D'Souza announced, even as they began to fuss around him and found a chair big enough for his wife to wait on. But she stood beside him as he sat on the salon chair and added: 'And a shave. Make it a close one.'

Even the other customers, the less difficult ones, held the duo in some awe. Jake, a young man with some musical contraption snaked into his ear, looked at Mr and Mrs D'Souza from inside the giant glass cap that was treating his damaged hair. He immediately felt that these must be some very special people indeed, for even the two flies that had the irreverence to make their way into this luxurious spa and salon did not dare to go and sit on them. Then there was Lucy, the young lady whose hair fell to her forehead, making her look a bit like a yak. She was waiting for a hair trim and a facial at the women's section. She was trying hard to keep her eyes on the magazine in her hands to keep from staring unbecomingly at the special guests. A few other guests, some waiting, some getting their treatments, suddenly fell to murmuring when the Mr and the Mrs walked in.

The poor barber (his badge claimed he was a 'grooming executive') whom God had chosen to treat the special guest that day was Georgie. Georgie was a frail, tall man with a plume of a hairstyle for himself. Sid, the manager, had made it a rule that all his grooming executives should sport extravagant, coloured hair to inspire customers. Mr D'Souza looked suspiciously at Georgie and muttered as a sheet was wrapped around him: 'Is that clean? Is it washed?'

'Yes sir,' Georgie said, his bent frame bowing further in respect.

'I'm allergic to dirty linen,' said Mr D'Souza proudly.

At the snip-snip of the scissors he began to look troubled and his nose turned a fiery red. 'Oh, wait,' Mrs D'Souza exclaimed, and Georgie stopped abruptly. 'You don't like the sound, Bunny?' She produced two bunches of cotton from the pockets of her tight jeans and shoved them into her husband's ears. Then she looked at the other customers and explained as if it was a common problem: 'Mr D'Souza hates the sound of scissors.'

As Mr D'Souza's haircut progressed, Mrs D'Souza still did not sit down and pick up a magazine. She stood around her husband faithfully, watching the progress on his huge head. Every now and then she would tell Georgie—not looking at him since her eyes were glued to Mr D'Souza's head—to snip a little here and there. Without so much as a glance at the barber she was rolling out a complete thesis on the very special head in front of them, which she seemed to have studied intensely for years.

'Mr D'Souza has always had rough hair,' she said for the benefit of all who were present. 'When he was younger, it was only rougher. You cut too much at the peak, here, and it all stands up. And he is allergic to most oils, so we can't flatten his hair out either. Oh no, oils and gels give him a migraine. But you can cut a lot from the sides, here and here, and from the back. It's good if you cut more here, so the hair won't grow back too quickly and we needn't rush back for another haircut in a couple of weeks.

The Greatest Enemy of Rain

Oh, Mr D'Souza hates salons! He'll come only when it's just too much…oh, no, not there, cut here. No, here, here. H-E-R-E! Yessss. Thank you. Or it'll look like a tuft before the end of this week.'

'Let him cut, Jelly, he knows what he's doing,' Mr D'Souza said as if to a child. Then a little threateningly, he added: 'I hope.'

Jake had taken off the contraption attached to his ears to listen to what was happening. He was chewing gum and tapping on his phone, perhaps sharing what was ensuing directly to his social media. Then he cleared his throat and looked at Lucy. She was still staring at the magazine, her ears pricked up to listen to the D'Souzas.

'Yes, Bunny, he knows,' Mrs D'Souza said, 'but I know your hair more.' Then to the others: 'Once when Mr D'Souza went alone to a barbershop he came back looking like a porcupine!' And she cackled at her own joke, a burp escaping with the sudden pressure, and Jake and even Lucy smiled politely.

'You're going too fast,' Mr D'Souza suddenly said severely, glowering at Georgie in the mirror. 'Slow down, you'll cut off my ear!'

'Yes sir, no sir,' Georgie muttered and instantly the snip-snips went snip…snip.

'Ever since, I go with Mr D'Souza for his haircuts,' Mrs D'Souza continued, unshaken by her husband's sudden display of temper. 'I also go with him to the dentist's, and even to his tailor. Mr D'Souza is such a baby, aren't you, Bunny?'

Jake imagined Mr D'Souza with a feeding bottle in his mouth and shook as he tried to hold in his laughter.

'Look at the back, Jelly,' Mr D'Souza told his wife, 'just above the neck. Is the line ok?'

'Looks fine,' said she.

'And don't use one of your ancient blades,' Mr D'Souza glowered again. 'It leaves red marks on my neck.'

'Yes sir, no sir.'

'Jelly, has he done the sides equally?'

Mrs D'Souza critically studied her husband's whiskers. She took the scissors and comb from Georgie and snipped a touch here, a tad there. Then she stood back to survey her work like an artist, and hesitantly handed back the instruments to Georgie, taking care not to touch him. Then she proceeded to the washbasin and elaborately washed her hands with soap.

Thus progressed Mr D'Souza's haircut, slowly and thoroughly, with constant guidance from Mrs D'Souza and the occasional flare-ups from Mr D'Souza. Georgie was visibly weakening under the pressure. His hands shook a little and he went to drink some water as Mr D'Souza looked at him in the mirror with disapproval. Sid ordered one of the girls working at the salon to ask the esteemed couple if they would have something to drink. When the girl, a birdlike creature with slits for eyes, asked them if they would have tea, coffee, or soft drinks, Mr D'Souza puckered up his face: 'Drink? In a salon, with hair flying all over? Gross!' And Mrs D'Souza discreetly gestured to the birdlike girl to fly away before Mr D'Souza got really angry. Another old customer walked in and sat down to wait his turn.

Mrs D'Souza directed Georgie without looking at him, to cut here, leave a little there, comb this part and see how it looks, balance this side with that, trim the hair in the nostrils and shape the eyebrows, maintain a fixed ratio between the hair on the forehead to that on the top of the head to that at the back and see if it works, cut more from the top of the head since it obviously doesn't work, but not too much, just a little, now let's stop to look. 'Bunny, how does it look? Bunny doesn't know about such

The Greatest Enemy of Rain

things, you can continue.'

Just when Georgie's eyes threatened to spill tears of exhaustion, it was over.

The linen was taken off Mr D'Souza and bits of hair brushed off him. His wife pulled the cotton out of his ears and threw it by the fallen hair. Georgie ran to get a smaller mirror to show what the back of his head looked like. Mrs D'Souza looked at the others in the salon and rolled her eyes. The whole place fell silent as Mr D'Souza inspected Georgie's work. Even the two flies sat quietly on a tuft of cut hair and awaited Mr D'Souza's verdict.

'No,' Mr D'Souza pronounced at last. 'No.'

No one spoke, and it seemed no one breathed.

Sid came running and asked: 'Sir, what seems to be the problem sir?'

'Problem? I don't know, I can't say. You guys are the experts.'

'Sir, is it to be trimmed a little more?' tried the manager.

'You've simply not got it right,' said Mr D'Souza, turning to Georgie and glowering at him. 'I'm not the professional. I can't say exactly what's wrong. It just hasn't met my expectations. Is this your usual standard?'

'Yes sir,' Georgie said. 'No sir.'

Mrs D'Souza had nothing more to contribute. She sat down, resting her massive legs at last, her lips firm and straight. She held her face up high, as if to tell all present in the salon: Yes, this happens sometimes. Now you have to deal with it.

Mr D'Souza turned back to the mirror. Sid took the small mirror out of Georgie's shaking hands and held it up behind Mr D'Souza. Mr D'Souza seemed to have sunk into a deep trance. He turned his head one way, closed his eyes for a while, then turned the other way, and closed his eyes again. When he opened them, he muttered: 'No. Tsk-tsk. No.'

Georgie looked helplessly at Mrs D'Souza who still did not look at him. She had suddenly ceased to be the one who helped with suggestions. She was now the customer, along with her husband, ready with some tough feedback.

'B-but sir,' Sid said, 'if you could give us some clue....'

'Don't know. Just isn't right. This is not how I wish to look.'

'...You know, is the hair to be cut a little more here, above the ears?' Sid went on. 'Or maybe when you have that shave too, as Madam had suggested, it'll look better.'

'What!' exclaimed Mr D'Souza wrathfully. 'You want me to sit for a shave now, after what you did to my head?'

'Just thinking aloud, sir,' Sid managed. 'I'm just wondering what went wrong.'

'What went right, you tell me that,' Mr D'Souza said, his voice climbing and his nose turning red. 'This is not the cut I wanted. In fact, this is not me. This is just not Mr D'Souza.'

Mrs D'Souza cowered and looked at the other customers fearfully, as though to inspire fear for her husband in them too.

'But can we do something to correct it, sir,' Sid said. The average human would get irritated with this manager for not getting even a little exasperated. 'We'll get you another grooming executive.' Without turning around, he motioned Georgie to leave the scene quickly. 'Sir probably didn't like our executive. We'll work it out all over again, until we get it right.'

'Can you put cut hair back?' Mr D'Souza asked, his face like the sky before a thunderstorm. 'The damage is done, isn't it?'

'The proportion is all wrong,' Mrs D'Souza observed thoughtfully.

'The proportion is ALL WRONG!' yelled Mr D'Souza at the door through which Georgie had left.

The old customer who had walked in last whispered

something into the manager's ear. Sid turned to Mr D'Souza, made a small bow, and said with finality: 'May I suggest, sir, that you take a full refund on your haircut?'

'UNBELIEVABLE!' Mr D'Souza's nose was as red as a tomato. 'You think it is that? You think I can't pay your PETTY PITTANCE, your sh-sh-shitty little fee?'

'Now, now Bunny,' Mrs D'Souza said. 'Don't get so mad. Remember, the doctor said you must always be calm....'

'Damn the doctor. Damn them all.'

'I-I didn't mean it like that, sir,' Sid was almost down on his knees now. 'By refund I just meant...'

'Do you know how many people I meet every day?' Mr D'Souza was yelling. 'How many important people? Can you dream up a guess?'

'Now, now Bunny.'

'When they see this, this, on my head, and when they snigger, what do I tell them, eh? That you gave me a full fucking refund?'

Jake went up to Sid and whispered something in his ear. For a while Sid thought to himself, during which time Mr D'Souza continued to fumble and fume until finally his Jelly made him sit down. 'S-sir,' Sid said, slowly, with put-on confidence. 'We'll figure out something. But we need a little time, you know, to confer, put our heads together on what went wrong. Until then can I suggest to sir an apt and engaging recreation?'

'What?'

'Can I suggest to sir a complimentary full-body massage in our special air-conditioned, aromatic massage room? Sir will have Lady Lana and Lady Leanny, both trained and expert masseurs, to work on every muscle and smoothen all the stress that we have inadvertently caused sir.'

Lady Lana and Lady Leanny, two young women with lazy,

hazy eyes who themselves seemed well oiled and syrupy, appeared outside the massage room. Jake and the old customer looked at them hungrily.

'Okay,' acquiesced Mr D'Souza. 'But be sure you have a solution for this when I come back.'

He walked rather eagerly towards the massage room, but then Mrs D'Souza had to step in because a sudden thrill of any kind was bad for his heart. It was decided that Lady Lana and Lady Leanny could leave the room and Mrs D'Souza herself would massage him.

With the couple locked inside the room all the staff and customers of the salon went into a huddle. It was generally agreed that Georgie should be treated with sympathy. He was an unintended victim of the situation. This was a difficult customer, and only God was to blame for assigning him to poor Georgie. Sid announced that Georgie would not be sacked, nor would he receive a pay cut. Poor Georgie, already traumatized, shed a plump little tear, the orange-coloured plume on his head, of which he was very proud, falling grandly on to his forehead as he bowed his head in gratitude. Jake suggested cutting all of Mr D'Souza's hair to give him a completely new look. The birdlike girl said that such a suggestion would only anger the esteemed customer the more. The last customer, the old man, brought his long experience into the idea that they call in a fashion designer to suggest attire for Mr D'Souza that will match his new hairstyle and in fact give him a new personality. He wrote 'new personality' upon a white board that Sid had mounted on a nail for the discussion. Lucy was brought in from the ladies' section to join the discussion. She provided the insight that they should have a separate meeting with Mrs D'Souza and find out what went wrong in the first place. 'Only a woman will finally provide the insight needed,' she claimed.

Meanwhile, all kinds of sounds came from the massage room; the sound of wet slaps on oily skin, grunts from Mr D'Souza, and Bunny this, Bunny that from Mrs D'Souza.

The old customer said thoughtfully: 'Why don't you send them on a cruise? Rich guys are suckers for cruises.'

'What if he or his Mrs has motion sickness?' pointed out Lucy, whose own hair was half cut as she had been called away midway for this important meeting. She felt she was the only one there who thought of these little details.

'Think about what to do with his hair,' directed Sid. 'The problem is his hair. Focus, guys. Focus.' He took the marker from the old man, scribbled HAIR on the board and circled it.

'What can we do?' Jake muttered. 'What's cut is cut. Either you bring a better barber—no offence to this man—and level the rest, or…or…'

'Hair transplant!' said Sid, rushing to his computer and surfing the internet. 'Hair transplant has the right degree of sophistry for such an esteemed customer. It is the only way to replace cut hair, and it can undo any damage already done. Yes, it says here it is possible.'

They all agreed to that because of Sid's enthusiasm, and because he was, after all, the manager of the place. At the end of the day, they all reasoned, Mr D'Souza was his esteemed customer more than anyone else's.

By the time Mr D'Souza came out he was very angry. 'Have you guys thought up anything? And I don't want dumb ideas. Give me practical, doable solutions.'

'Solutions that are doable, practical, not strange fanciful complimentary gifts,' helped Mrs D'Souza, wiping the oil off her hands on the posh curtains outside the massage room.

'Yes sir, no sir,' came out of Georgie.

'And why is that man back here again? I thought he was asked to leave,' yelled Mr D'Souza pointing with his thick, diamond-studded fingers. 'HE IRRITATES!'

Sid motioned for Georgie to vanish and then stood up from behind his computer. 'Sir, while you were enjoying your exotic massage from your trusted beloved…'

'Cut to the chase!'

'Sir, we, all of us here, have come up with the ideal solution.'

'Go on…I haven't got all day.'

'Sir,' said Sid, 'We have a tie-up with one of the finest trichologists in the world, Dr Fernandes. Sir himself might have heard of him. Dr Fernandes runs his own clinic and has solved the problems of thousands of people.'

'Well,' said Mr D'Souza. 'I didn't have a problem before I stepped in here. And I haven't heard of him.'

'Well, yes sir. I mean, no sir. Heh heh. That's why we will sponsor a complete hair transplant by none other than Dr Fernandes himself.' He turned the computer's monitor around so that the special couple could take a look at Dr Fernandes's profile. 'What's more, all of us here will contribute the hair that is to be transplanted on to your pate!'

The last part had not been discussed at all, and everyone was forced to nod. You didn't disagree, you didn't bicker in the presence of someone as rich and eminent as Mr D'Souza.

'Hmm,' muttered Mr D'Souza. 'Jelly, what say you?'

Before she could speak, the famed Dr Fernandes was online. His face appeared on the screen and he said: 'Hello sir. While you were in your massage, Sid phoned me and told me of your condition. Could you please move towards the webcam, so I can study your hair?'

The Greatest Enemy of Rain

Mr D'Souza moved towards the camera grudgingly, suspiciously, anxiously, as if moving in front of it would automatically begin some procedure without his consent.

'Oh, not to worry,' Dr Fernandes said. 'This is an easy case. It's not as if these boys have done a bad job with your haircut. Just that the cut does not suit your face. The unique angle of your hair partition hasn't been taken into account while giving you the cut. But alas! Cut hair cannot be stuck back up now to suit the face, can it? Ha! That's where you're wrong, my dear sir. Indeed, it can be stuck back!' It was obvious that Dr Fernandes had said these same words with similar exclamations hundreds of times. 'I have handled several cases like this. I could come over with my instruments now and we will first procure the best hair off the donors. Then, magically, we will actually stick back hair on your head and make it suit your face!'

'And of course,' Sid added, 'it's all on the house. Anything for an esteemed customer like you, sir.'

'Hmm. Jelly?'

'Well, I don't know,' murmured Mrs D'Souza. Both of them were looking intently at Dr Fernandes on the screen. Then she asked: 'Is a trichologist a real doctor?'

'Course not,' said Mr D'Souza, even as Sid frantically tapped on his keyboard so this exchange would not reach the famed trichologist. 'Which real doctor will specialize in hair, for god's sake?'

'I think we need to consult our real doctor, Bunny,' said the wife.

'I think we need to rethink this whole trichologist idea,' said the husband. 'And the donors are these people? Ugh! How hygienic will this whole thing be?'

'Do you have any options? Any other ideas? Or have you

run out of them?' Mrs D'Souza said, her face contorted in an expression of cynicism that she obviously thought very weighty.

And thus, the idea of a hair transplant was trashed. The staff and customers of the salon huddled inside the women's spa to discuss. Once enough time had passed to make it seem that a good brainstorm had taken place, they came out again and the old customer politely presented his idea to Mr D'Souza: 'Esteemed sir, perhaps, in return for the damage they have done to your hair, these people should sponsor a cruise for you and your esteemed wife. By the time you come back from a long cruise the hair would have grown right back, so that you can meet the important people. I have heard rich people are suck…er…rich people love cruises?'

Mr D'Souza considered this. 'Hmm. Rich people are suck… er…love cruises, you're right,' he conceded. 'But you see, Mrs D'Souza has motion sickness. She can't be on a ship.'

'Aah,' groaned Mrs D'Souza, momentarily fainting and then coming to.

Mr D'Souza was looking at himself in the mirror, saying under his breath: 'It's just that the cut does not suit my face….'

Mr D'Souza began to make some important phone calls. Some whispered that he was calling the authorities, some that it was his lawyer. He now seemed less angry and more resolute. Poor Sid fretfully checked the internet for solutions and made some calls of his own. When a phone call came enquiring about a barber named Georgie from the local police station, everyone was terrified, but the caller said that it was a routine check. Everyone was still uneasy, for a 'routine check' of this kind had never happened before.

Now, Manager Sid was a real leader, or he wouldn't be the manager. When Mr D'Souza's calls began to get the authorities to make routine checks about his salon and an employee in

The Greatest Enemy of Rain

particular, he frantically began thinking of a solution. He ignored the numerous suggestions that were coming from staff and customers alike, and finally jumped up with such force from behind the computer that everyone in the room imagined him naked and yelling 'Eureka!'

'I got it!' Sid exclaimed. 'Let's change the face!'

'Huh?' This came from Mr D'Souza. He looked bored, unyielding, but condescended to raise his eyebrows.

'Sir, excellency, my idea is that your face can be changed!'

'What do you mean?' Mr and Mrs D'Souza exclaimed together.

'Sir, your honour, trust me, it is most routine,' said Sid, making it up as he went. 'We have a tie-up with a renowned cosmetic surgeon who is a real doctor. Like you yourself pointed out, it's not the haircut. It's just that it isn't suiting your grace's face. A slight correction in that nose, a bit of a chipping here on the jawline, and a slightly reduced forehead, a liposuction and a tummy tuck, and we're done! This particular hairstyle will make your highness look like the world's greatest business personality.'

'Hmm,' Mr D'Souza murmured. He had liked the cruise idea itself, and would have taken it up if he did not suffer from motion sickness (which he had passed on to his wife, and she had played along, the good girl). But this wasn't bad either. 'I'm open to it.'

Everyone cheered. Georgie bowed to Mr D'Souza, appearing from behind a curtain, but quickly disappearing again.

A phone call from Sid and about ten minutes later a team of cosmetic surgeons marched into the salon. They were led by the renowned Dr Al, who had completed his degree in a faraway country and had also specialized in a course in business management after his medical education.

'PRESENTING,' Dr Al launched, opening up a manual

before Mr D'Souza, 'the best team of plastic and cosmetic surgeons on the planet! Yes sir, that's no exaggeration. We have cured presidents and Nobel laureates of their stupid squints, poets of their dreamy foreheads, actors of old age, and aliens of their foreign looks. Ha ha, that last was a joke, but our portfolio, sir, is truly considerable!'

He handed out an endless collection of case studies and everyone in the salon stood on their toes to take a peek.

'That's all very fine,' Mr D'Souza said with a small yawn. 'But what can you do for me?' Mrs D'Souza was worried that it might soon be time for Mr D'Souza's nap, and whenever someone came in the way of that he got really hot under the collar. If there was to be a plastic surgery, she might request general anaesthesia, she thought.

'My dear sir,' said Dr Al, narrating in his practised, sing-song voice, 'yours is a simple case of mismatch between hair and face. It must be largely congenital, only exacerbated now by one of the coarser hands here. For Dr Al's Clinic, and our team of experts, this is only a routine procedure. We just need a bit of a correction here, on the bridge of the nose (touching Mr D'Souza's nose with professional confidence), some slight chipping of the jawline, here, and a marginal reduction in the forehead, is all! You will, of course, need to be admitted for a day at Dr Al's Clinic, the finest destination for plastic and cosmetic surgery on the planet.'

It might have worked. Mr D'Souza was rather impressed with the sophistication of the whole thing, particularly the professionalism of Dr Al and his team. He had even begun looking for that stupid barber so that he could forgive him, maybe even throw him a tip, before agreeing to the surgery. It might have worked had Dr Al then not smoothly slid into the various packages and schemes. He naturally launched into some of the most colossal fees on the planet, albeit with thoughtfully worked out deals, such as a complimentary nosejob thrown in with a jawline touch-up and offering the forehead reduction at a fifty per cent discount since Mr D'Souza was obviously a candidate for a long-term and loyal relationship.

'But isn't it all complimentary?' Mr D'Souza asked, suddenly shooing away the junior surgeon who had already begun marking his face with special surgeon's markers.

'Sir!' exclaimed Dr Al. 'Do not insult us, I plead, by asking for the world's finest cosmetic services free of charge. However…' he paused dramatically, 'since this is the result of an admitted screw-up at this sister concern of ours, we can look at some very special deals for you.'

Mr D'Souza looked on patiently as Dr Al conferred with his colleagues, referring every now and then to the elaborate manual in his hand. Finally, the doctors looked up. Dr Al faced his dignified client again: 'Sir, usually Dr Al's Clinic does not go out of its way even for emperors and sheiks. But giving special consideration to your unfortunate experience here, I think we can offer you an extremely handsome deal. While we give nothing free of cost as a policy, in your case we could throw in a breast reduction without charging anything extra!'

There was a stunned silence. Everyone observed Mr D'Souza's nose beginning to go red. Lucy prayed that he might be cured of this condition after his nose job. Dr Al suddenly appeared thoughtful, furrowed his brow, and then said with a smile: 'Oh, we realize that you cannot avail this yourself. Of course…I mean, not for a moment…no. We make yet another concession and agree to serve madam, your esteemed wife, with this service.' He threw a smooth wink at Mrs D'Souza who shrank coyly behind her husband.

Mr D'Souza flew off his handle once again. He yelled that the manager of the salon had first botched up his entire visage and was now lining up the finest idiots on the planet by way of compensation. Sid hurried the team of surgeons out, but not before Dr Al had slid a business card into Mrs D'Souza hands.

'BLITHERING IDIOTS,' Mr D'Souza yelled, his nose now looking like a bee had stung it. 'I'll have your licence cancelled, you nincompoops. You, you…'

'Sweet bun, control yourself. He said nothing wrong!'

'Unearthly duffers, you wasted my day! DO YOU KNOW HOW PRECIOUS MY FUCKING DAY IS?'

He went on with such chosen expletives that everyone's hair stood on end. Sid then decided to make one last attempt at putting out the fire. The situation was out of his hands, so he decided to escalate the issue.

'Sir, a moment; do calm down. Let me call the head office. We will do anything here, absolutely anything, to satisfy you.'

'You have satisfied me enough! I'll see that you shut down. I'll see that that bloody ruffian of a barber is crucified!'

But Sid turned away and placed a call on the landline. For the next five minutes he was totally lost in the call with his head office. Unbeknown to Mr and Mrs D'Souza and everyone else in the salon, this 'head office' was in fact Sid's own home and the boss was his wife. Escalating the issue up to her had never failed in the past. She worked in the human resources department of a large corporate. After the call Sid turned and calmly motioned for Mr and Mrs D'Souza to come to the adjacent room where they could talk for a moment. 'Trust me your excellency, sir, we'll solve it this time.'

Something in his smile, something in the glint in his eyes and the euphoric twist of his lips, made the husband and the wife follow Sid. The trio conferred for what seemed a long time. They then called Georgie in and the four conferred for even longer.

When they came out Lucy, Jake, and the old customer were almost mad with curiosity. One of the flies lay dead on the floor after having waited out its lifetime. The staff was drinking water in turns. But everyone immediately realized that Mr D'Souza would be satisfied right away. Whatever the head office had suggested seemed to be working!

What followed had the beautiful justice of poetry, the curious twist of fate itself, and the simplicity of the world's greatest ideas.

Barber Georgie sat down on the salon chair, the beautiful, coloured plume on his head standing up and proud. Sid picked up the electrical shaver and handed it over to the esteemed Mr D'Souza. The esteemed Mr D'Souza pouted in concentration as he mowed Georgie's plume down. Everyone clapped, and Sid continuously praised Mr D'Souza for the dexterity of his fingers, the sharpness of his mind, and the benevolence with which he was sparing the salon. Mr D'Souza shaved the rest of Georgie's head too until the man was completely bald. They all clapped again, and the ladies then sang a song of praise in honour of the rare and esteemed customer.

Satisfied at last, Mr D'Souza hugged his wife. His nose was slowly becoming less and less red. Mrs D'Souza was happy too, but she only feared that too much of this sudden joy might harm her husband's heart. She turned to Georgie on the chair to say something, then changed her mind, and said it instead to Sid: 'Next time, take care to do only your best for your most esteemed customer.'

'Yes,' said Mr D'Souza with a little yawn. 'Only the best for your most esteemed customer.'

At the end of the shave the staff gathered all of Georgie's fallen hair, gift-wrapped it. and presented it to Mr and Mrs D'Souza. The couple graciously accepted it, blessed Georgie, Sid, and the whole salon, and walked out. As they went to their parked car, Mrs D'Souza warmly held the gift package in her armpit. They even waved as they drove away.

13

THE WOMAN WHO LOVED TO BE RIGHT

Radhamma was well past her middle age when she developed a curious new habit: she became passionate about being right. True, all of us feel a dim bulb light up inside when we tell someone, 'If you eat all that jackfruit, you are bound to get stomach pain,' and then the person clutches his stomach and groans a little later. But for Radhamma, just as she was gracing the shores of old age, turning out to be right became a source of ecstasy. She inwardly jumped in joy and could barely keep herself from clapping her hands when everyone realized just how right she had been all along, on matters ranging from cricket match outcomes to weather forecasts.

In the morning when her husband Chellappan was leaving for the treasury office she would tell him, 'Carry an umbrella, the skies can change colour anytime', and the man wouldn't listen because at that time there wasn't a cloud up there, she found that during the day she actually hoped that it would rain. Part of her mind did whisper to her, 'Radha, you are nasty,' but there was also the part that said her husband ought to listen to her, that he ought to realize she had her reasons to ask something of him, that he deserved the lesson coming to him for turning his nose up at her so often. It said Chellappan was taking her more and more for granted, that he was biased about her ability to reason, that she was sometimes invisible to him. When she looked back, she was convinced that he had never lent her half the ear he gave his old, good-for-nothing friends and drinking buddies. When he came back drenched from work she did run out to the porch with a towel, but she couldn't entirely hide her glee as her tongue lashed: 'I told you. I told you. Perhaps you should listen to me now and then.'

Radhamma told her friend Fatima, a younger woman who lived next door, how Chellappan would come down with a flu for not listening to her. Every time her words came true, she recounted what happened, her eyelids lowered but eyes shining. 'Took the entire rain, all the way from the treasury office,' she would say. 'Told him, particularly because there's absolutely no shelter down that stretch. And he is so intolerant to the first rain of the season! Mark my words, he will be down with a fever by this evening. I told him, told him to take an umbrella. These men! They turn a deaf ear to the wisdom that only us women have.'

Fatima, pausing subtly in the process of spotting weevils among rice grains, would wonder if her friend actually wanted her poor husband to come down with a fever. But she would say, 'Yes Radhechi, Chellappanettan ought to listen to you. You are almost always right about such things.'

'Always right. I am always right about such things.'

'Yes, women have a knack for predicting when it will rain,' Fatima said.

'Not just rain,' Radhamma punched in. 'We are not as stupid as these men think. While they are lost and drifting all the time, we are more observant. So, when we say something…'

'They ought to listen, yes,' smiled Fatima. Fatima was still young enough to miss her own family from whom she had been

The Greatest Enemy of Rain

separated by distance after her marriage. She had an elder sister she particularly missed. Though Radhamma (whom she called Radhechi, or Radha, the elder sister) was far older than her own sister, the woman had, in Fatima's quiet, simple, good-natured soul, occupied a place of love. She liked it when Radhechi was happy.

'You, particularly, Radhechi,' Fatima said, 'You are always right about such matters.'

'Yes, but the man of my house doesn't believe that.' Radhamma's face darkened. 'He thinks he is just shepherding this old cow through life. He will listen to the barber and the milkman, with whom he spends the weekends playing cards and getting drunk, but not his own wife. Now perhaps he will finally have time to think about all this when he is in bed with a burning forehead, sweating and with a stuffy nose....'

Fatima smiled again. Radhechi went into rather graphic details nowadays when she was portraying the plight of someone who had blundered by not listening to her. She painted rather too vivid a picture. So much so that she sounded as though she was cursing the person. Someone who did not know Radhamma as well as Fatima did would think she was insensitive, even vindictive, to curse thus. But Fatima knew that wasn't the case at all! Radhamma only became overly expressive to make her point loud and clear, then louder and clearer. She wanted her words to have an effect, which is perhaps what happens to any person who has felt for a long time that she hasn't been heard out with the respect she deserved. For so long had she been ignored, in her opinion, that she made her words sharp, like shards of glass, so they absolutely wouldn't fail to make their mark.

One evening Radhamma and Chellappan had been invited to Fatima's house for a little celebration. Fatima's husband Rihan was a good-looking man on the sunny side of thirty, and he loved to crack jokes. He was a confident, self-satisfied person because he ran a successful hardware shop in the market. If a young person were to ask Rihan about how to start a retail business, or any small business venture for that matter, Rihan would have enough to talk for three hours. He had the surety and self-righteousness of most self-made men. Which is not to say his success had gone to his head, but he was proud that he had reached where he was out of good trade decisions and an active, sprightly attitude towards his work.

The two couples were seated around the dining table at Rihan and Fatima's house, and Chellappan was helping himself to more pathiri and chicken curry. Rihan mentioned a common friend, Lijo, who was planning to start a nursery for the gardening enthusiasts of the village. The trouble was, as Rihan laughingly pointed out, this Lijo was forever planning new businesses, never quite settling down on one, so that he was the perpetual entrepreneur waiting for one or the other of his 'ventures' to bear fruit. 'His latest is potted plants,' Rihan laughed. 'Says any green initiative cannot fail to bloom because Mother Earth herself will bless him. Ha haha!'

'Oh, sure,' mocked Chellappan. 'Even Mother Earth will lose to our Lijo. Before her blessings take effect our man would have jumped to another business.'

'It is so sad that that boy never comes to anything,' said Radhamma. 'His father was such an enterprising man. I heard he still lives on what the old man left him.'

'More chicken?' Fatima asked her husband.

'Some people never mature,' Radhamma said. 'They keep flitting from idea to idea like boys with new toys.'

'Well, he's young,' said Chellappan. 'I suppose he will

The Greatest Enemy of Rain

experiment some more and then hopefully settle.'

'I don't think youth has anything to do with this,' Radhamma said, her eyes off her plate. 'Lijo is an aimless person. He will keep wandering.'

No one had meant for the conversation to become too serious, but they all humoured her with thin, empathetic smiles. But who was Radhamma to stop there?

'A nursery? Here? Bah! Now we will have to see our friend's son go around with a begging bowl saying "Amma, spare a few coins for a boy who could've been born your son, Amma!" And how will we refuse him? We knew his father for so long. I am telling you, I guarantee you, we'll see the day.'

Now Rihan went rather red in the face because he had brought up the topic and none of them really wished poor Lijo misfortune either.

'It isn't good to see your old friend's son starve,' Radhamma went on. 'But none can take up the burden of another either—'

'Radhamma,' said Chellappan gently. Then he pushed a dish towards her in an attempt to distract her.

'I know. I am always right about such things.'

Later, back at their home, Chellappan thought that when he was washing his scooter and Radhamma was watering the plants in their front garden, it was a nice time to bring up what needed to be brought up. 'Back there you sounded almost as though you hated postman Antappan's son Lijo,' he said, taking care to inject a certain lightness into his tone. 'Poor Rihan felt bad that he had mentioned him.'

'What's there to feel bad?' Radhamma said dryly, almost as though she had been ready with a response. 'It wasn't as though Lijo was in the room. And besides, what I said is true. You just wait and watch.'

'That might be, woman, but do you have to use such harsh words?'

'Harsh words?' Radhamma said. 'Wait and watch. You will see my words were neither harsh nor too much. There were realistic. That is what they were. Realistic.'

'Well, Rihan did look rather taken aback,' Chellappan said. 'He was being light-hearted and you—'

'I don't know what you are going on about. That idiot boy Lijo will come to nothing. We'll all see his nose dragged in the mud. He will keep getting these fanciful ideas until he has completely wasted away his father's money.'

Chellappan took extra care to clean the round front light of his scooter. His wife held the garden hose upright and went on:

'So it would be fine if I had said, "Great, that boy, Lijo, is great! How enterprising, how hard-working! What a genius! His nursery will become the largest in the country and he will be rolling in money soon."' Radhamma's vehement mockery gave her an ugly grimace, Chellappan observed in dismay. '"Oh, dear Lijo boy, you are all set to make your father proud!"'

'All I'm saying, Radha,' Chellappan said quietly, 'is…why don't you use words that are…kinder? Less, how shall I say, hurtful?'

'Because I know the truth,' Radhamma said, closing the tap and folding the garden hose. 'What I speak is the truth, because I can see it. Soft, sugar-coated words will not change the truth. I can see it coming. That boy, he will never come to any good.'

Chellappan said nothing. He was sure that Radhamma hadn't given postman Antappan's son a thought until that afternoon. He hadn't heard her discuss that young man with anyone before then. And yet the moment Lijo's name had casually been mentioned she had worked up such a retinue of damning words for him!

The Greatest Enemy of Rain

Women, Chellappan thought with a wry smile. You can't reason with them. They grow on you after some time, and then you really have to be wary of them.

He occupied himself with his routine chores for the rest of the day, not thinking too much about his wife who expressed her displeasure at the conversation in the garden in subtle ways. She considered it a mini squabble, he knew. After she had heated the water for his bath she went and poured it into the bucket in the bathroom without calling out to him as she always did, which meant she did not care for his lecture of that evening one bit. At dinner she laid the dishes on the table with a stronger than necessary bang. This stood for her gentle but righteous protest at the specific words he had used to point out her faults. There wasn't even the usual prayer together before bed, signifying how rude and needlessly arrogant he had been when he had cut her short in their friends' home that afternoon. But Chellappan was fine with all of this. He knew that she would sulk for the rest of the day, maybe even for most of the next day. He just had to spend some more time with his friends down by the coir factory or in the toddy shop and come back to his wife only when the cloud over her head had cleared.

Chellappan had smartly adapted to Radhamma's bumpy ride past her fifties and early sixties. He had accepted that he could never make her introspect or convince her to change her mind on any issue, big or small. He said whatever he had to when he felt compelled to, and then he knew she would punish him by appearing detached and indifferent for some time, and he knew he had to deal with that time simply by staying away. This approach never seemed wrong to him. Since his philosophy was that happiness depended on not reflecting too deeply, he had arrived at the conclusion that 'digging deep' was in vain. And yet he wouldn't hold back too much. His philosophy also extended to allowing himself the luxury, once in a while, of saying what he felt. Speaking his mind was a need, like eating and breathing, and he had learned to not be uneasy in the least about the negativity of his listener. He did not see why he shouldn't mildly reprimand his wife or single out her faults just because he knew she wouldn't correct her course. It was his need, not hers. Yes, it was convenient to lead close but parallel lives, but he thought he also owed it to himself at times to use the privilege of being her husband to suddenly connect with her and talk to her, especially since he had learned to ignore her afterwards when she responded with prolonged silences and feeble rebellions. He had mastered the art of never letting these conversations snowball into a bigger fight. Indeed, while he couldn't remember any period over their decades together when Radhamma hadn't sulked, he also couldn't recall a significant confrontation that they had had. Every time it was only a half-hearted, incomplete, mildly unpleasant little chat like the one in the garden, never amounting to a stronger conflict that would bring out the deeper differences between them. He couldn't remember having too serious a conversation with her about anything, because he made sure nothing he did gave her a place of greater importance in his routine than what he intended.

'Men and women are fundamentally different,' he would tell his friends over a drink when rarely he felt the need for weighty talk. 'Trying to bridge the gap will destroy your peace of mind. Don't even attempt it.'

Radhamma couldn't decide, if she thought about this long enough, if her husband had become this way at some point in his life or if he had always been thus. But she knew that by now the crack in their relationship was one he deliberately kept narrow but allowed to run deep, as though he wished only to keep it unnoticeable but did not mind it being unbridgeable. At the back of her mind grew a bloom of memories that was always fresh. It seemed like another life that two different people had shared, two people who enjoyed talking to each other and spending time together. Now it seemed unbelievable to her that back then they used to go to the movies together. Up until about eight years ago Radhamma and Chellappan would dress up, eat a generous lunch, and take Chellappan's Bajaj Chetak to the one cinema theatre that was on the way to the city. This day-out that they enjoyed once in about two months had been almost a habit for many years. Chellappan and Radhamma would sit on that scooter with her hand on her shoulder, the picture of a sunny life and a happy relationship. They would watch a movie and come back in time for dinner at home. The next day Chellappan would narrate the whole story of the movie duly to his friends at the coir factory as they worked, though none of them could figure out if his wife had enjoyed it or not.

In whatever little conversation husband and wife had for the next few weeks, little anecdotes from the movie would feature. Radhamma would hum songs from the movie and Chellappan would recall and laugh at some joke. It was clear that both enjoyed the good time they had together, or the habit wouldn't have sustained as long as it did.

Then one day Chellappan said, 'Only a certain kind of film comes to this theatre. How about taking a bus to the city one of these days? We can try out the theatres there.'

But there was an impediment to this plan. Radhamma had a strong streak of austerity that she had inherited from her controlling and conservative mother. And as she aged, her self-discipline began to verge almost on asceticism. She began to cherish the tightness and control that she thought of as her maturity. To her, going to the run-down cinema on the way to the town was already a luxury, considering Chellappan's meagre earnings and their ever-diminishing resources. Even otherwise, she told him, her opinion was that at their age they ought not to be too ostentatious. It wasn't right.

'Ostentation? We are not going to the city to show anybody anything,' he replied. 'Just for a little change of air. Just to check out other cinema theatres and watch some of the latest films.'

But Radhamma became extremely steadfast. 'We will be wasting time and money on me,' she said in the tone of a woman who hadn't left a single inner demon unconquered. 'Frankly, I am not all that much into these films. I'll tell you what. If you want it that much, you go to the city and watch a film and come back.'

'What's the fun in that? If you aren't too eager to watch films, think about all the shopping you can do. It'll be fun, Radha!'

'Fun! Our time for too much fun is over.' Her lips were pursed in displeasure and her eyes got narrow. 'Anyway, let me be. Honestly, my heart doesn't crave all these…new delights. I'm telling you, you take the bus and watch a film and have a great time. I do not mind at all, believe me.'

But of course, Chellappan did not go to the city alone. They continued to watch whatever film played at the second-grade theatre nearby. Once in two months became once in three, then four. Chellappan was bored, not just with that theatre and the movies there but also with the generous lunch, the scooter ride, and in fact the entire chore of going out with his wife. He did not realize that though Radhamma had painted such a dismissive picture of their occasional evenings out, she actually cherished them very much. Once in two months had been enough, but that meagre ration of entertainment was precious to her. Her austerity did not permit anything more, that's true, but anything less made

The Greatest Enemy of Rain

her routine seem bleak. But how was Chellappan to know all that? Because when he gradually lost interest, she wouldn't bring herself to suggest even once that they ought to go and watch a film, that it had been too long now, that she was finding life boring, cold, and frustrating, and that when she had said they were past the age for extravagance, she wasn't recommending such an overdose of monotony either. She couldn't say those things because they contradicted her distaste for all kinds of frivolity. Never let it be said, she resolved, that Chellappan and Radhamma went to watch movies because Radhamma wanted to watch movies. So when Chellappan stopped taking her, Radhamma said not a word, but one oasis in the desert of her days quietly dried up.

For whatever reason, it was the same with visits to relatives' places, going to the market together for supplies, walking in their backyard to look for fallen mangoes, even watching old movies together on their ancient black-and-white television. It seemed that gradually they did absolutely nothing together, except pray before their myriad idols and sleep on the same bed. While Chellappan was out more and more, socializing, drinking, and playing cards, Radhamma became increasingly religious and ritualistic. Though the days stretched before her, she woke up at five, bathed in cold water, and began her prayers, chanting verses from holy books and ringing the sacred bell. She kept her kitchen obsessively ordered. She cleaned the house with a vengeance; to watch her at her chores, one might think she did them out of uncontrollable anger. During the afternoons while her husband took his siesta, Radhamma often walked up to a small lake nearby and sat by it, dreamily observing the patterns the wind made on the silver water. None could fathom her thoughts during those moments, or if she had any thoughts at all.

Then when Rihan and Fatima shifted to the neighbourhood

she began to spend time at their house because she very much loved the childlike Fatima who was also such an unconditional listener. For hours, when Rihan would be at his shop, the two women chatted. Fatima was her answer to Chellappan's time with his friends. Radhamma could go on and on about why her husband was wrong and why all menfolk were wrong and why husbands needed to listen to their wives more. Fatima would listen and nod appreciatively. Though Fatima adored her own husband, she did not in the least mind Radhamma's generalization of men, and that made her generous and accommodating in the older woman's eyes. To Radhamma, Fatima's dedication to Rihan brought out powerful memories and sweet nostalgia. She was fascinated with their way of life. She couldn't explain to herself what held her fancy about the couch on which, presumably, Rihan and Fatima rested while watching television, the small dining table on which they ate and discussed things and laughed and passed the water jug and pickles and rice to each other, the modest kitchen where she pictured Fatima stirring something on the stove while Rihan stood by to sample the curry and tell her if more salt was need. She felt curiously moved when Fatima rarely referred to her husband by name and not as 'Rihanikka' or 'my husband', as custom dictated. On the few occasions that Fatima spoke Radhamma only half-listened, looking around her and absorbing every detail about Fatima's small house.

It is difficult to pinpoint when exactly Radhamma developed her passion for being right, but it was probably a little after she crossed her sixtieth year, perhaps a year after Rihan and Fatima became her neighbours. She wanted others to acknowledge that she was right. At first, the urge was not strong. But then one time a neighbour, who was a milkman, had a cow that was pregnant, and Radhamma casually told her husband one evening: 'I don't

The Greatest Enemy of Rain

think that cow will make it. The way that family treats their cows is so sad.' She did not herself know why she said it. A week later, Chellappan came home from his visit to the post office, and hanging up his shirt on a hook behind the door, he said: 'Woman, you have a tongue with a blackspot. Milkman Nareshan's cow died yesterday. They couldn't save the calf either.'

Radhamma looked up sharply at her husband. His eyes regarded her with interest verging on admiration. A strange quiver ran through her. She had been right! Her husband also knew that she had been right.

'My husband says I have a tongue with a blackspot,' Radhamma beamed at Fatima the next morning. She proudly narrated the milkman incident. And as she narrated it she couldn't imagine how terrible it would have been if the cow and the calf had survived and had been licking each other lovingly now. Her husband would have smirked at her! Suddenly it was unimaginably insulting to her.

'But how did you know the cow would die?' Fatima asked.

'I don't know, I had a hunch.'

Over the weeks, months, and years that followed, she always narrated in great detail to Fatima the incidents that proved she had a blackspot on her tongue, so that whatever she spoke came true. And she got more and more detailed in her narration. There was an incident with one of the villagers—the ladies' tailor—who was ignoring an ugly gash on his ankle, which Radhamma had predicted would soon begin to fester. When it did, she happily ran up to Fatima to tell her, throwing in descriptions of green rot and yellow pus and unbearable pain. One year she said the crop would suffer and the farmers would be hit hard, and after it happened, Fatima listened to her with genuine admiration. Gradually the younger woman too came to believe Radhamma had a knack for predicting things. Perhaps it was true, Fatima thought, that some people are born with tongues with blackspots on them so that the things they said came true. 'Whatever Radhechi says comes true,' she told Rihan. 'I only wish her own husband listened to her more often.'

'Ooohoo,' pouted Rihan. 'Are you saying the good lady is clairvoyant or something?'

'You laugh,' his wife said, 'but such things exist. There are people who have tongues with blackspots. They speak and those things really happen, word for word.'

Rihan humoured his wife, but he was a staunch rationalist. He was also one to be intensely amused at people's follies. He loved to single out such follies among his friends and laugh at them.

On that afternoon when Radhamma transformed the rather well-to-do but entrepreneurially fickle Lijo into a beggar, Rihan later told his wife, 'The prophet has made her prophecy. Now even if the almighty himself had other plans for that poor Lijo, he has no option but to push a bowl into his hands.'

'Well, you watch,' his wife retorted. 'Radhechi will be proven right.'

'His nursery business might flop,' Rihan said. 'But I doubt he will go around with a begging bowl. Not just yet at least, I hope.'

'Whatever Radhechi says isn't to be trifled with. Why, yesterday she casually said my new saree would lose colour when I washed it and—'

But we leave Rihan and Fatima to their friendly banter about beliefs and logic. The thing with Radhamma and her prediction about the postman's son and his nursery was that, as anyone who knows Lijo would tell you, it was destined to come true anyway. In a few months it became a joke around the village that Lijo was selling his nursery wares cheap and no one, obviously, was buying them. People laughed that Lijo's plants had become fodder before they bloomed. Radhamma made it a point to gracefully remain silent on the issue and not stake claim upon yet another of her victories, but her chin slightly tilted upward, especially when she was watering the plants and Chellappan was washing his scooter. In a tacit understanding, Fatima, like a faithful assistant, told the other neighbours about the little conversation they had and how, at that time, the rest of them had thought that Rachechi had been too vociferous about what would happen to Lijo and how, as always, it had turned out that she had been right. The two women thus collaborated, one being the oracle, the other spreading the word.

When she reminded her husband of how her prediction had come true, Rihan was a touch out of humour. 'Well, she knew and we knew Lijo would fail. Everyone knew Lijo would fail. But now that he failed, she is the only one so happy about it.'

It went on for a few more months like that. Chellappan was acutely aware that his wife thought she was turning into a visionary, but he kept himself from fanning the flames with his observations. He deliberately left his umbrella behind, and when it did rain he refused to acknowledge a miracle had happened. These things were called coincidences, he knew, and to make anything more of them was just nonsense.

One of those days he happened to meet Rihan outside the rice mill. The two men moved in different circles and shared the typical relationship of men brought together by their wives' friendship. When they met outside their neighbourhood on rare occasions like this, they spoke a few words to each other that came from the meagre information they had about each other. On this occasion, they fell to speaking about their wives.

'My wife thinks she is right always,' Chellappan said with a grimace. 'Of late she thinks she has supernatural powers.'

'Mine supports the view,' Rihan laughed. 'I let her be. Anything that keeps them happy.'

'Yes, but it gets on my nerves sometimes. This thing of, "Look I was right again, what do you know?"'

'Ha haha. It's all right Chellappetta. I'm sure Radhechi doesn't mean to hurt anyone. She is just looking for endorsement all the time.'

'I just ignore it,' Chellappan said. 'Makes me feel stupid to even acknowledge her empty fantasies.'

The two men went their separate ways, both toying with similar thoughts.

We aren't sure if there are certain tongues with invisible black dots on them but it is almost certain that there are little gods up there who draw daily sustenance from the humour that our condition offers them. A few days after Rihan and Chellappan spoke, a group of these gods decided to get rather naughty. They began tugging at strings that would cause great pain, puzzlement, relief, regret, and a host of other mixed emotions in a particular puppet of theirs down below. Perhaps what they enjoyed the most was the inability of a woman who thought of herself as almost a visionary to see what lay under her nose.

The catastrophe that befell Radhamma began with news of a civic protest in the city. The protest was against the government on some political or ideological matter. Every day Chellappan read the newspaper out loud and they watched on television how the protest was rapidly upsizing into an agitation, with people even burning buses and hurling stones at the best looking glass facades of the city.

Then one evening Fatima casually mentioned to Radhamma

The Greatest Enemy of Rain

that Rihan was set to visit the city to discuss prices of wares for his shop with some distributors.

'What! Going to the city at this time?' Radhamma said, her eyes wide. 'Don't you know the city is burning?'

'Burning?'

'You don't read the papers?' said Radhamma. 'Curfew is on. Everyone is killing everyone. Buses are being torched, buildings are being pulled down. Ask him to stay put.'

That night when Fatima asked her husband if he could postpone his visit to the city, Rihan said without turning to her, 'Who filled you with these worries? Yes, there is some agitation going on, I heard, but that is only in some parts of the city. Where I am visiting there is nothing.'

But then when Fatima told Radhamma of her husband's resolve to go, the older woman was emphatic in her pronouncement: 'It is youthful brashness that is making him take a wrong call. Consider this the advice of an elder sister who cares about the two of you. Tell Rihan to wait until the curfew is off. You never know when things turn uncontrollable in such situations.' In the evening she told Chellappan about this too. 'I think you should talk to Rihan about this. It isn't safe to go to the city right now.'

'He is a grown man,' Chellappan said in the bored voice he reserved for discussions he thought they needn't have. 'He knows where to go and where not to go. Let us give advice only when asked.'

With a sense of purpose that quite exceeded neighbourly well-wishing, Radhamma then began to quietly but strongly counsel Fatima on why she must put all her efforts to keep Rihan from going to the city. She couldn't explain why she felt so strongly about this. Rihan and Fatima were, after all, only neighbours and not really her siblings or children. And all said, it wasn't as though everyone in the city was really dying. In fact, with their own inclination to exaggerate, the media hadn't so far reported any fatalities; only a few hospital admissions of those injured in stray stone pelting. Besides, Radhamma also knew that Rihan was far more informed and streetwise than she was. Yet, with remarkable vehemence she tried to control his going to the city through the sway she held over his wife. She grew rather desperate, in fact, as though some irreparable harm would plague her personal self if Rihan went to the city. It might have been easy to conclude that she believed in her own power of prophesying to such an extent that she was burning with concern for the safety of her friend's husband. But what would pick holes in such a conclusion would be her undeniable disappointment at not being listened to. Perhaps it was true that she simply could not accept that Rihan wasn't putting off his trip just because she had premonitions of danger. How could Rihan so callously disbelieve the blackspots on her tongue?

Like a mother bird forcefully flocking her playful chicks into the safety of her wings, Radhamma persisted with her friend. 'You have to make him see sense. Every day, every day there are stories of arson. Just today they set fire to a bus parking lot. No one died, thank God for that, but can you say when someone will, in such circumstances? It isn't safe to go now. Why can't Rihan put his visit off by a week? I don't understand.'

'Oh, Radhechi,' wailed poor Fatima. 'I have tried my best. He doesn't even take me seriously when I argue.'

A strange light, frosty yet fiery, shone in Radhamma's eyes. 'Of course,' she seemed to chew each word before spitting it out, 'what we say doesn't matter. They don't think we are worth listening to. They think we are their toys.'

'There is nothing I can say that will make him listen,'

The Greatest Enemy of Rain

Fatima said tiredly. But then she spoke out those consequential words, cautiously and with a foreboding of disaster: 'He will go tomorrow, no matter what.'

'WHAT?' Radhamma yelled, her eyes pinpoints. 'The stupid man! Tomorrow? He will DIE if he goes!'

Silence thundered for the next few seconds. Then, through tears, Fatima said: 'Radhechi! H-how could you?'

But the tongue with the blackspot could then only manage to quiver out the words 'Fatima, I—' before the younger woman turned around with a wail and ran indoors.

At that moment Radhamma would have done anything to take back the words that had shot out of her mouth. But she had spoken and now her young friend had, for the first time, turned away from her in rage and despair. In a moment Radhamma wasn't worried any more about Fatima's man going to the city. Suddenly it wasn't about the possibility—wasn't it the certainty?—that her words would come true. It was only about how she could now repair the damage done to her precious friendship with Fatima. Not for an instant could she think about not coming over and chatting with her through the day, sitting inside the house on the diwan next to the television, or standing by in the kitchen as Fatima stirred at the stove. Radhamma's own eyes spilled a few tears at the prospect of the all the pathiri and chicken curry she would miss if she couldn't patch things up.

Back in her home she telephoned Fatima, but her friend did not speak at all. She came out of her house to check if Fatima would come out to pick the dried clothes off the clothesline, but Fatima had already done it when she wasn't looking. There was no way her friend was giving her a chance to speak, to clarify, apologize. When Chellappan woke up from his siesta Radhamma hesitantly told him what happened.

'I told you, I told you, you were going overboard,' he said angrily. 'You stupid woman!'

'I—it just came out like that. I didn't mean it.'

'They are such decent neighbours. You absolutely had to spoil everything with your…your…what are you, an astrologer? You and your stupid prophecy game!'

'It isn't that bad, probably,' said Radhamma weakly. 'I am sure Fatima will be fine soon. She will forgive me. She has that in her—'

'Oh, of course. I don't know about her but do you know what that Rihan thinks about your dim-witted…dim-witted talent? Your famous blackspot? He thinks it is rubbish. He has told me so.'

Then, fearing this would break out into a full-blown fight, Chellappan threw on a shirt and went off to play cards.

Meanwhile in Fatima's home things had turned sour. As soon as her husband came from his shop his young wife threw herself tearfully at his feet, begging him not to go to the city until the agitation was over.

'What are you saying!' Rihan tried to find some sympathy in his heart for the crying Fatima but couldn't. 'Do you think this is a joke? I have already set up meetings. People are waiting for me. I absolutely have to go tomorrow. Whether you send me away with a smile or with tears.'

'You will…if you go you will…OH!'

But Rihan, who had already begun packing his bag, easily figured who was responsible for his wife's behaviour. He suddenly lost his temper. He began by telling his wife how she was bound to go mad because of the long hours she spent with that insane neighbour woman, how that madwoman's husband was himself struggling to keep her in check, and how she had now made his own, Rihan's own, wife equally mad, and how Fatima would do well to stay away from that woman if she valued her own happiness and sanity. It was hubris, he claimed, that made one think one's words could shape destiny. That woman ought to read something in her spare time and not think up nonsense. All through this Fatima only cried, clasping his shirtsleeve at times to keep him packing his bag. Then Rihan told her that it was important to him, though maybe not to her, that he go, that his business was important to him, and that if he stopped earning them a living, then all of a sudden it would become important to her too. Then, he said, this Radhechi of hers would blame him too, and would eagerly 'predict' there'd be a begging bowl in his hands.

Then he began asking her exactly what Radhamma had told her. 'Did she say I would be caught in some kind of violence? That I would be beaten up? Tell me, Fatima, what did she... PREDICT? Tell me, Fatima, did she say your poor husband would just die if he did not listen to her? Ah! So that's it, is it? I'm gone, I'm dead, destined to be killed because a woman with a supernatural tongue has spoken.'

Fatima began to loudly appeal to God to forgive her any transgressions she might unknowingly have committed, to forgive them if they hadn't been thankful enough for the happiness granted them. Even as Rihan was proclaiming that he sometimes felt he had married a six-year-old, or a doll perhaps.

At some point in the night Rihan violently freed himself from Fatima's feeble grip on his sleeve and made to rush to Chellappan's house. 'I'm going to tell that man to keep his wife in chains,' he yelled. 'So the others can live in peace!' Fatima fell at his feet again and he finally calmed down. But neither slept that whole night.

The next morning might have made for an interesting painting. Rihan with a bag at his shoulder making for the market road from where he would hail a tractor or jeep to the city, his hair standing up in tufts, his face smeared with talcum to bring on a false brightness to counter the lack of sleep. Fatima, still wailing, her eyeliner smeared down one cheek, her eyes tired. At the neighbouring window an almost invisible Radhamma, one with the shadows of dawn, looking out remorsefully....

Outside his gate Rihan stopped when he saw Chellappan, who was coming back from the nearby shop with bananas wrapped in a newspaper. Both wives held their breath. But the two men greeted each other stiffly though decorously, and spoke for a bit. Then as Rihan went his way, Chellappan called out: 'Telephone me from there. I need some supplies too. Will pay you when you're back.'

'Of course,' Rihan yelled back. 'I'll check into a lodge and give you a call.'

Radhamma grasped onto this. All through the day she was asking her husband, 'Did Rihan call you?' and 'But he said he will call after he checks into a hotel. Do you know which hotel? Do you have their number by any chance?'

'But he is a dead man, isn't he,' Chellappan finally said, cruelly. 'How can a dead man call?'

When the telephone rang in the evening, Radhamma ran from the kitchen to answer it, but Chellappan had closed and locked the door of their bedroom where the telephone was. When he came out she asked: 'Well?' They looked at each other for a while, and then Chellappan said: 'Your words are yet to come true. The man is alive. I was giving him a list of stuff I need from the city, and I would miss out things if you breathed down my neck. That's why I locked the door.'

The Greatest Enemy of Rain

All through the next day Radhamma tried to catch Fatima's eye, but the young woman wouldn't yield. When Radhamma passed by the house under the pretext of going to the shop for sugar and oil Fatima was at the window, as though unblinkingly waiting for her husband to return early, but she shut the window when Radhamma seemed to be lingering. When Fatima was at the porch of her house sweeping off the dried leaves Radhamma ran up to the dividing wall between the houses, but the younger woman was far swifter as she ran in, leaving her work half done. At lunchtime, seeing his wife so distraught, Chellappan said, 'You ought to go over and request Fatima to forgive you. What is said is said. Now there's no use sulking over it.'

When Fatima was drawing water from the well in their backyard in the evening, Radhamma ran up to the wall again, as there was no way the young woman could drop the rope and run away before drawing the filled bucket all the way up.

'Fatima, listen to me for a moment,' she said through tears. 'I didn't mean what I said. Take these like the words from a sister who—'

'Sisters do not kill their sister's husbands,' Fatima pronounced, her nose stuffy and her eyes burning.

'F-Fatima, I—'

But there could be no talk at all, no apologies for words spoken hastily. Fatima was a molten mix of anxiety, sorrow, and anger. Each passing second she looked at the telephone. It made her shudder involuntarily every now and then. But Radhamma could only react to being repeatedly scorned. Rushing back into her house she spat out, 'Fatima's taking it too far, way too far.'

'Oh?' said Chellappan, picking up the newspaper to indicate disinterest in furthering the topic.

'I have never claimed I am clairvoyant, have I?'

'Oh, never at all. Not once.'

'I don't know what everyone's about. Sometimes what I say comes true. Like the weather or the ending of a movie. That doesn't mean all my words have to come true. There is this saying about some people having a blackspot on their tongues, isn't there? I didn't create that. There is a belief like that. That doesn't mean that a person with this blackspot is a god or anything.'

'Are you sure about that?'

She turned angrily at him: 'I don't know what you are going on about. Fatima is aggrieved, I can understand. What's your problem? If every word I said turned true then I would be the world's most powerful person, no?'

Chellappan concentrated on the newspaper, which he always kept close for a reread in times such as these.

'Those words just escaped me,' Radhamma went on. 'What to do now, there's no taking them back. And that Fatima! She's way too haughty! I didn't say it deliberately, after all. It just came out. She knows that. Now what can I do to make amends? Do I have to fall at her feet?'

'That might be a good idea.'

Then, sensing that his wife might be looking for a nasty fight in order to pin the blame on someone, Chellappan drew the conversation to a close by putting his shirt on and going out.

But from that moment on Radhamma walked as though in a dream. She stopped chasing Chellappan to the phone whenever it rang. She quit trying to catch Fatima's eye. In fact, she spoke not a word to anyone, not to her husband, nor to the other neighbours, the gossipy woman who came to sell pappads, the fishmonger with whom she usually loved to bargain, not a word even to Fatima herself when, a couple of days after Rihan left, she ran directly into the younger woman in the narrow lane behind the two houses. Both women quickly avoided each other's eye and walked past.

In the afternoons Radhamma sat by the lake. She sat on a small mound so that she could look down at the water. At the centre of all the green waterweed a clearing of silver water was shaped like a drowsy eye that was looking up at the clouds. In it a single grey swan glided this way and that. Radhamma saw in this afternoon picture an eye turned heavenward, tired but searching, forlorn but restless. She shook her head to clear the torpor. Then she dragged herself back to the house, closed the door with a bang, lay down beside Chellappan, who was enjoying his afternoon siesta, and slept till late in the evening.

Chellappan shook her awake. 'Wake up, wife. I just got a phone call from Prakashan. Malathi is going through another attack of breathlessness. Prakashan asked if we could go over for a few days. They need help.' Prakashan was Chellappan's brother, a librarian in the neighbouring township. His wife Malathi was prone to asthma attacks, and often, when they were severe or lasted for days, he would call Chellappan and Radhamma to ask if they could come over for a few days.

'I-I didn't hear the phone ring…' Radhamma said groggily.

'Yes, you slept like the dead. What is the matter, woman? Did you drink something strong? Ha haha. I told Prakashan we could come over. I thought it'll be good for you—a change of scene, considering the circumstances.'

They quickly threw a few clothes into an old duffel bag, gave a spare key to a neighbour (in better times that would have been Fatima) and requested them to water the plants in three days if they weren't back, and by late evening were sitting on the last bus to the city. In less than three hours since Radhamma woke up, the couple was having dinner with Prakashan and Malathi.

'Hey, Radha, will your sister-in-law ever recover from her breathing difficulty?' Chellappan needled his wife as he stuffed more rice into his mouth. He turned to Prakashan, who was a small, dark man with bright eyes, 'You see, my wife is a great soothsayer. If she says Malathi will be okay, you folks have nothing to worry about.'

Radhamma looked up from her plate and smiled. 'The sun will rise in fifteen seconds,' she said, looking out of the window. All of them looked out of the window. But the crickets continued to chirp in the dark. 'Oh no. What I said did not come true. I must not be a soothsayer after all.'

'Are my brother and sister having a fight?' Prakashan asked pleasantly.

'We'll help them fall back in love,' said Malathi, and they all laughed. Malathi was a fair, slim woman who looked permanently exhausted. Radhamma thought that apart from her usual tiredness she looked fine. Perhaps the news that they were coming over to help had already cured her of her asthma.

Over the next day, Chellappan kept trying to irritate Radhamma by talking about clairvoyance and blackspots on tongues and the slaying of people through mere words. But Radhamma seemed to be in a good mood. She got along very well with the soft-spoken Malathi who, in spite of the intent of her sister-in-law's visit, wouldn't let her do too much of the housework. Malathi continued to cook and sweep the porch and seemed embarrassed when Radhamma snatched the broom from her and asked her to take some rest. 'I'm all right, Radhechi. These men are merely making a fuss. I'm sorry you had to come over.'

'Oh, that's fine, Malathi,' said Radhamma with a deep sigh. 'I needed to get out of our house anyway. It was…turning stifling.'

For a moment it looked like Radhamma would launch into

a sombre narration of past events, but Malathi did not press her when it seemed obvious that Radhamma had decided against speaking further. It seemed that Radhamma was tiredly turning a page in her life and wishing for her immediate past to be forgotten.

In fact, Radhamma seemed to grow healthier and somehow younger through the day. In the evening she went for a stroll and bought, for Malathi's kitchen, a few supplies from a nearby shop. She cooked her special brinjal dish for dinner. She still spared only the unavoidable minimum words for her husband, but she smiled a little more often. The clouds of the past days might have cleared had the naughty gods left her alone. But the very next morning brought along a shock that was easily the nastiest she ever had in her life.

When the telephone rang in the front room and Prakashan yelled out that it was for Chellappan, she perked up her ears. She walked out of the kitchen to the front room to find that her husband had turned pale. He almost dropped the receiver from his hand as he turned and, dry as a fallen leaf, looked up at his wife to stammer, 'Y-you are a witch after all!' Radhamma looked at him with big, scared eyes. She took two steps back and came to a stop at the door frame to the dining room. She did not hear her husband but deciphered the meaning as his dry lips formed the words: 'Rihan is d-dead. Radha, Rihan is dead. This…early this morning. He—oh my god!'

It was just as well that Malathi had come up behind her and held her, or Radhamma might have slumped. They made her sit down and both Prakashan and Malathi kept hounding Chellappan, asking who had died. Chellappan managed to tell them it was a young neighbour but, mercifully, he did not explain all the dark details about Radhamma's prediction and Fatima's estrangement following her fears.

'I—I have to go,' Radhamma eventually managed. 'I need to go to Fatima.'

Within the hour Prakashan had arranged a taxi for them and Radhamma sat at the backseat, staring all through the journey at the artificial grapes that hung from the rear-view mirror, watching as it bobbed this way and that, tiresome and mesmerizing. She kept swallowing and sighing. She did not remember later if Chellappan had been speaking, or if he spoke just once. She wondered if he had really been telling her about Rihan, about how he died. Something about Rihan not dying in any agitation but because of some tipper lorry that suddenly swerved to avoid a bicycle. Or did she dream it up? She couldn't even later recall if she had gotten carsick and if they really did stop someplace so she could vomit. Her agony pulled the passing scenery outside the window—the breezing trees and shops and people and asphalt and her yesterdays—into herself, wrapping the day and the world around her in the direction of her motion, until the day and the world became a tunnel through which she sped, whether backwards or forwards she couldn't make out. The driver's burly head, her husband's glances from the front seat, the words 'Rihan…he's dead', and the wind blowing through her hair created such a feeling of unreality that Radhamma couldn't even pray. She did not know for how long she sat thus before the car pulled up outside the gates of her home. She got out swaying, turned and walked to Fatima and Rihan's gate and threw it open. In a moment she heard the taxi start and speed away, and Chellappan was by her side, talking to her. She caught only a few fragments of what he was saying: 'No one, absolutely no one', 'Careful', 'Fatima is young', 'Rihan should have, you know…', and more. Next thing she knew her husband was knocking at

The Greatest Enemy of Rain

the door. A Fatima younger than Radhamma had ever seen her opened the door. She looked dry and stoic, obviously still in shock and not comprehending what was happening or who had knocked at her door. There wasn't even a flicker of recognition on her face as she let Chellappan and Radhamma in and went and sat herself down on the diwan. Her delicate hand clutched the table on which the television set was, as though she couldn't balance herself. Radhamma found herself observing all the unnecessary things, like the fact that Fatima's eyeliner hadn't yet spread to the sides of her eyes and towards her cheeks, because she hadn't cried yet. Or that the young woman still had her anklets on but there had been no tinkle of her footsteps behind the door after Chellappan had knocked on it. She also noticed that the telephone was off its hook on the small table by the biggest chair in the room.

'We just heard,' Chellappan spoke in Fatima's direction, 'and we immediately took a cab. It was Sree…Sreekumar that called us…good he knew where we were. I mean, good we could come over immediately. What I mean is…we can't tell you how sorry….'

All of a sudden, Fatima burst into peals of laughter. Certain that she had gone insane, Radhamma looked up at her in tired surprise. At the same instant a voice spoke from behind the kitchen door: 'That's it, Chellappetta. That's how far my wife will be able to act.'

Radhamma stood stiff as a pole, trying to understand what was going on. Then disbelief in spite of comprehension—or owing to it—turned her face into an unplaceable mask: her husband, who stood smiling and looking at her, couldn't judge if she was relieved or angry, or relieved and angry. Meanwhile, Fatima had come over and was holding Radhamma's hand, which the latter first drew back and then offered to the young woman again. Rihan came into the room and sat down by the television. He was laughing but also looking concernedly at Radhamma's face. In a moment unbound relief and joy came to that face and a smile appeared, as serene as that of a child. But Radhamma's cheeks had turned blue, like someone had slapped her, and it seemed the confusion of emotions would split her forehead in two.

'That telephone hanging was a master touch, Rihan,' said Chellappan, who was laughing the most. He was even clutching his stomach as though watching an intensely funny movie. 'It was just a little drama we put up for you, Radha.'

'I—I can see that,' managed Radhamma.

'You should have seen your face in the car,' Chellappan went on, and the others could see how he was striving to make the whole thing a big joke so his wife wouldn't end up fighting with him. 'Where you even listening to me?'

Radhamma sat down and Fatima sat beside her, still holding her hand. Fatima was trying hard to contain the relief she felt. She was not bothered about any other time that Rihan might visit the city again, no longer hounded by fears of him going away from her, of separation or death or doom. She was just happy that he had returned safe this one time, like it was the only trap life was capable of laying.

Looking at her bright face Radhamma said, even as the tears rolled down her cheeks: 'I'm glad. I'm so, so glad.'

Fatima smiled back at her. 'It was them, Radhechi. It was these men. They cooked up this whole plan. I just…played along.'

'My own husband, such a great actor!' Radhamma said as if to herself. The next instant they saw her looking out the window, biting her own lip as if trying to contain something within her. Rihan immediately suggested that they go over to the dining table

The Greatest Enemy of Rain

for a bite to eat. It was time to celebrate, he claimed. Radhamma turned to her husband and asked: 'So whose plan was it exactly, to fool me?'

'What could we do, Radha?' Chellappan said, giggling. 'Your predictions were causing some real unrest.'

'Radhechi, it was my plan,' Rihan said. 'I'm sorry. Truly, when I saw how much suffering it caused you, I felt bad. But when we discussed what your…your blackspot was doing to Fatima here, I had this idea.'

'What about Prakashan and Malathi?' said Radhamma, still looking at her husband. 'Part of the plan?'

'I told them you needed a change of scene but that you wouldn't agree to it unless we said Malathi wasn't well,' said Chellappan triumphantly.

Radhamma seemed to withdraw into herself. She spoke so low they had to strain to hear her: 'Thanks. Great. Thank you. All of you.'

They gently guided her into the dining room where a mini-reconciliatory feast waited.

Much later, towards evening when Chellappan awoke from his siesta, he did not hear the usual clank of vessels from their kitchen. After a quick search through the house he went out through the backyard to the lakeside. There he found his wife, fast asleep on the mound, leaning on a rock, her feet touching the water. So deep was her sleep that for a moment he feared she had died. It took some effort to wake her up, and even so she was so groggy. He had to support her home the way his friends sometimes helped him home on the rare occasions he got a little drunk.

14

MANI AND THE GHOST

The next stretch of road was what Mani dreaded the most. It ran parallel to the city's biggest cemetery, and at two in the morning it was no fun driving here.

'Providence,' said Mani to himself cynically, immediately shutting his mouth to keep the smell of liquor in. He had had a couple of drinks at the party and the smell hung in the car. His wife would catch it in the morning and then it would be scarier than driving down a pothole-riddled road next to a cemetery at the darkest hour. There were dark patches along the road where the streetlamps no longer worked. On the opposite side of the graveyard was a railway line separated from the road by a thick hedge of sleeping bushes. Directly ahead a huge moon seemed to bob in the sky as if struggling to stay up with its weight. It was the setting of a classic horror movie and Mani was thankful for the alcohol he had consumed. It gave him some confidence even as he could see—where the dilapidated cemetery wall had broken down—a series of gravestones with their long shadows under the moonlight.

Mani was always a little nervous when he passed this stretch in the evenings, returning from office, but at this hour there was an uneasy feeling in the pit of his stomach. That could also be because he had eaten too many clams and now they felt like they

The Greatest Enemy of Rain

were floating around, he reasoned. He tried to hum a tune but it came out a croak. He thought about turning on the radio, but the idea of a voice in the car creeped him out more. So, he decided to think about the office party he had attended for the duration of the one-and-a-half kilometre stretch.

Since Mani had always maintained that he was a rationalist, he strictly did not believe in ghosts. The disadvantage of this was of course that he couldn't pray either because he couldn't acknowledge the existence of gods either. But fear is an irrational feeling, and he gripped the wheel tight until he was squeezing his own bones, trying his best to think about his colleagues and the nice, warm party.

A little way ahead was another big gap in the wall of the cemetery, and Mani focused his eyes on the moon above so he wouldn't have to see the gravestones. But as he approached the gap in the wall there was movement. The car had almost reached it when a man came out of the cemetery through the gap and began walking along the road.

Hot fingers of fear clutched at Mani's heart, even as he told himself that this was just the caretaker going out to find a cigarette shop that might be open at this hour. But the man was unusually tall—indeed, unnaturally so, indeed this couldn't be a man at all, for he was almost as tall as the lamppost! Mani fumbled in his mind with the idea of braking and reversing, all the way to the beginning of this damn road, but his legs were frozen on the pedal. He simply couldn't move as the car continued to bounce over potholes and move senselessly (damned machine that it was) towards the apparition in front. It was walking ahead of him, this apparition, for that's what it was, swinging slightly to the left and right like it was a little drunk too. It had long, dirty hair that hung like coir down to its waist. No, this couldn't be the caretaker, couldn't be anyone at all, and it unnerved him that he could see its hair so well, and its slightly curved back, and everything in such detail.

Mani noticed that its legs were not moving in accordance with the speed at which it was moving; it seemed to be walking some distance and then gliding. It wore a single long robe that revealed only the back of its head and its terribly long fingers with their preternatural, curved nails.

All this Mani saw and took in as he began mumbling prayers he remembered from childhood. His stomach felt as if it might empty itself all over the seat. So tight were his hands on the wheel that he couldn't feel them at all. All he could hear was his own heart throbbing like a trapped bird. The effect of the drinks he had seemed to have quickly evaporated. As the car approached the ghost, his legs seemed to have a mind of their own and pressed down on the accelerator. The car jumped ahead and steered past the figure, crunching blindly into potholes and thudding out of them. A second later Mani looked into the rear-view mirror, very certain that the ghost would have vanished and that he would be laughing at the alcohol-induced hallucination in a moment. But it was there, swaying behind him, walk-gliding in total indifference to him. Such intrusion upon his reality! Why was he seeing it so well, in such specifics? It had an ancient face with brown, rotting skin peeling in places, and dead, yellow eyes. It was grinning from side to side as its great head swayed gently from left to right.

Loudly chanting his prayers now, Mani thanked God that the car had raced past this thing, whatever it was. In a fraction of a second several thoughts passed through his head: here was the memory of him brilliantly observing to a girlfriend once, 'If only dead people become ghosts and if everyone eventually dies, then what's so scary about ghosts? All of us will get our chance to become one.' All kinds of clever thoughts. Another thought was about something he had read some time ago about gigantism, pituitary tumours, etc.; conditions that make human beings grow abnormally big and tall....

That's what he would have told himself and everyone else the next morning. That there was a man by the graveyard who had a pituitary tumour and was therefore abnormally tall, and his mind and the liquor and the darkness of the hour had conjured up the rest: the peeling skin, the gliding walk, the terrible grin. It all might have just been a tale to laugh about if his car hadn't started to mutter and splutter just then.

Mani pumped on the accelerator as fear turned to terror again, but the car gave up. It soon coughed to a halt, and in the rear-view mirror the figure neared. Mani could see the ancient buttons, made out of acacia seeds, on its robe. Again, such details; why wasn't it hazier, wispier, a little more deniable? He was loudly reciting his prayers again, hoping that this thing would just indifferently walk past. With one hand Mani felt the mobile phone in his pocket, with the other he vainly tried to move the gear lever. Realizing that his eyes were shut, he opened them again. The thing had reached his left window and had stopped there!

All his windows were closed, and the air-conditioning was on. Mani must have momentarily fainted, for in a disconnected instant he seemed to have moved into another realm. It was like his brain had stuck a needle into his arm. He was suddenly not so afraid any more. His brain had administered some sort of a drug that nipped away his presence of mind and, thankfully, a lot of his fear. He felt like he was watching a movie as long fingers with dirty, curved nails began to scratch the glass of his left window, making dreadful squeaks in the hush of the night. The nails scratched so vehemently that the window started to roll down...and yet Mani wasn't terrified! Well, not as terrified as he ought to have been, given the situation, but only slightly afraid. There must have been another Mani sitting deep and far inside him performing the function of being actually and fully afraid. It was like something had tripped inside his head, some electrical circuit, due to overload. On the tracks across the bushes a train approached and thudded past, and he felt vaguely sad that it didn't even stop to ask after him. He imagined a sleepless passenger in the train seeing a car parked in the middle of a lonely road next to a graveyard.

Mani actually yawned as the ghost pulled the window completely down. This had to be a ghost. No man with or without a pituitary tumour could bend so low to reach down and roll down a window just by scratching at it. A very strong and unpleasant smell filled the car and Mani realized it was the smell of burning hair. It was old, that smell, old enough to be timeless.

'Come out,' the ghost whispered, and its voice was a grating whisper, drawn out into a drawl. Its yellow eyes darted to and fro, seeming to study the interiors of the car. Then they focused on Mani. 'Come out, I wish to show you something.' It was grinning and its teeth were sharp and serrated, like a steak knife. The words coming out of its mouth were accompanied by the dankest of smells—a combination of squirmy worms and flesh that had been under water for a long time.

'Why?' Mani said, and wondered at himself.

'Come out,' the ghost seemed to request. 'And see what I have to show you.'

'Er... Did you jam my car?'

'Come on out,' the ghost's grin simmered a bit, 'before I come from the other side.'

It seemed that despite not being fully afraid, Mani fainted one more time. The world went dark again, and it seemed time was passing without his knowledge. When he came to, he was even calmer. Sudden understanding erupted inside his head. He realized why these irrational things were happening, and why he was suddenly completely unafraid despite all this.

'All right. I come to get you,' and the apparition glided around from the other side and opened his locked door effortlessly.

'Mmmph. Could you stand back please?' Mani heard himself say. 'You smell of burnt hair.'

'Yeeeeeees,' the ghost drawled. 'They burned me a long time ago.'

Mani noticed that it wasn't as if the ghost was going to drag him out. While it could surrealistically glide-walk or telekinetically stop a car or metaphysically open locked doors, it didn't seem too eager to touch a living human being. That gave him even more courage. 'Stand back, please,' he ventured again, 'My wife doesn't care for bad smells inside the car. And the upholstery absorbs smell, make no mistake.'

'Whaaaaat,' thundered the ghost. 'Who do you think you're talking to?'

'No clue,' Mani said to that one. 'Who or what are you?'

'You wish to see my anger?' And the ghost made a bolt of lightning appear, and droplets of blood fell all over that road from the sky. Then with its long, weed-like arms, it waved at a bush, which burst into flames.

After this performance the ghost folded up like an empty tube of toothpaste and brought its face close to Mani's. Mani indecorously covered his nose with his palm.

'You stupid man,' the ghost drawled. 'Are you too stupid to be afraid? You ought to be afraid. Why aren't you afraid?'

'Because I have understood what is happening,' Mani replied. 'I'm dreaming. I was afraid at first but now I realize, I'm just dreaming. I have dreams like these often. All I need to do is wake up and you'll have to go away.'

'Whaaaaat!' growled the ghost again, and the tips of its long hair sizzled into flames, sending a fresh waft of stink into the car. Mani reached out to shut the door, but he felt a supernatural tickle go up his arm, like mild electricity.

'I don't believe in you,' Mani said with finality. 'I'm a firm disbeliever. I think—I know—that I am asleep, and this is my nightmare. It's you that needs to be afraid. Your existence depends on my sleep.'

'This is no nightmare, idiot,' the ghost growled. 'Come with me and I'll show you the depths of hell.'

The ghost transformed the reality around them. The road ahead was awash in stinking blood and the sound of groans filled the air. A train approached on the track, again, but this time it was no ordinary train. It was larger than a medium-sized mountain, cracking the earth as it passed. Inside it, looking out its big windows, were skulls laughing and holding severed limbs and bits of hair and dribbling guts in their mouths.

When the din of the train had passed, Mani turned to the ghost. 'It's no use. I've had nightmares very similar to this. The more you show me this unreal stuff the more I'm convinced this is only another nightmare. I'm a rationalist, you see.'

'You don't fear me?' the ghost asked, its eyes looking from beyond the grave into Mani's soul.

'That's because you don't exist,' Mani smiled tiredly. 'You must understand, I had too many clams at the party. And I mixed beer with rum, which I rarely do. I always have bad dreams when I have indigestion with too much alcohol.'

There was a rumble from Mani's stomach and the ghost went and sat down on the road next to the car, folding itself down seven times at impossible parts of its frame. It looked thoughtful.

'Look, I'm sorry, okay?' Mani said. 'It's just that I've had too many nightmares in my life to really be afraid of them. In my childhood I really feared them. But not any more.'

'Aaaaaaaarrrrrrrrgh,' reverberated the ghost, snarling so that Mani could see the terrible teeth that dripped blood.

'Let me go now. Make my car start. Or I'll wake up.'

'Noooo!' the ghost yelled, immediately shutting up, for the yell was an acknowledgement of its vulnerability. In quick succession, it showed many more terrible images in one last attempt to scare Mani. The moon turned into a terrible face bleeding from the eyes, the earth throbbed like heartbeats, forlorn cries issued from the cemetery, strange balls of fire landed inches away from the car. But through it all, Mani was talking continuously. The ghost looked at him, a strange expression filling its dead face.

'And I'll tell you something anyway,' Mani was saying, 'about fear and terror and stuff. I mean, if you want all this to be really scary. You see, this is a theory I formed after watching some horror films. Don't bring out the horror too quickly. And DO NOT make the scene too weird. That huge train was in very bad taste, if you don't mind my saying so. I mean, suddenly you have a train filled with thousands of ghosts! For God's sake, that's a dead giveaway that all this is not real.

'And you yourself,' he continued, as the ghost stared at him incredulously. 'Why are you as tall as a lamp post? That itself is unreal, don't you get it? I was afraid at first, but then I realized it had to be a nightmare. Be the size of a normal human, then telekinetically halt a car, look through the window, and ask if the driver needs help. But keep your left eye a little above your right eye. Or have only two small holes where your nose should be. Or something like that. I'm saying, keep it minimal, and that'll freak them out.

'Now, if you'll please let me go. My stomach is upset. I'm sorry to say this but I really need to wake up.'

'N-No.'

Exhausted, the ghost returned the surroundings to normal; a cemetery, a pothole-ridden road, a big moon up in the sky, and a railway track to one side. It was all very peaceful. Then it stood up, undoing its many folds with arthritic clicks. It wordlessly walked and glided back to the cemetery, as Mani yelled, 'My car, please.' Without looking back, the ghost willed it into being and the car hummed to a start.

Mani drove away, struggling to wake up because his tummy felt like molten lava. The potholes threatened to spill its contents.

'Damn clams,' he said.

ACKNOWLEDGEMENTS

A couple of stories in this collection have been published before: 'The Greatest Enemy of Rain' in the *Bombay Literary Magazine* and 'These New-Fangled Ways' in the *Hindu BusinessLine*. I thank both these publications for allowing the respective stories to be included here.

Special thanks to the team at Aleph for doing a wonderful job as always.